Four-Minute Fictions

50 Short-Short Stories
from The North American Review

Edited and With an Introduction by

Robley Wilson, Jr.

Word Beat Press
Flagstaff, Arizona

The publication of this book is supported by a grant from the National Endowment for the Arts.

Library of Congress Catalog Card Number 86-061903
ISBN 0-912527-05-6

Word Beat Press
P.O. Box 22310
Flagstaff, AZ 86002

Table of Contents

Introduction
Robley Wilson, Jr.

Among the many dreams my generation was brought up on, the dream of the four-minute mile loomed large, and the breaking of that temporal barrier by Roger Bannister in 1954 was an event equivalent, probably, to the importance of the walk on the moon to a following generation. In the mid-nineteen-seventies, when the assault on the mile had become an obsession — that is, how far below four minutes could the time be pushed? — *The North American Review* was receiving an inordinate number of fiction manuscripts whose page length hovered between three and seven manuscript pages, and it was a simple concatenation of those two occurrences that led to the first "Four-Minute Fiction" section in the pages of the NAR.

I have nothing profound to say about these so-called four-minute fictions, nor about the "renaissance" of the short story, and even less to say about the popularity of the genre, whatever its length. The short story, and especially "the short-short story complete on these two pages," is an American favorite, to my limited knowledge dating back to the nineteen-thirties and such popular magazines as *Collier's, Liberty,* and *Saturday Evening Post,* and probably going further back than that. In other words, we continue a lengthy tradition.

I will confess — an easy confession — that most of the stories in this book can't really be read in four minutes. A few can. Jayne Anne Phillips' "Solo Dance," surely; Mark Clemens' "Fruit." A few others. For the rest, "Four-Minute Fictions" is merely (merely!) metaphor. What's important is that these are excellent pieces of fiction wrought within a limited frame of space and of time. Each works in its own way, on its own terms. Each is really a "story," and not some sort of Wednesday-afternoon-literary-tea vignette. Each is included here for what it is, in and of itself, without regard for its connection to its fellows and without concern for its integration into some kind of coherency.

In other words, these stories come together here by accident, not by design. Fair enough? I think so. Fiction covers everything, is eclectic, clings to no armature of critical fashion; likewise this anthology. For every Barry Lopez, Raymond Carver, T. Coraghessan Boyle or Stephen Dixon, there is a Henry

Berry or Nicole Cooley or Walter Sanders. For every sad story, a happy one. For every taste, a dish.

"Infinite riches in a small room," Keats once said of poetry. But this is prose, and infinite riches in many small rooms, and the time to enjoy each of them. Or, if one is duty-bound to return to the original metaphor, here are neither sprints nor marathons, but the easy pleasures of the literary middle distance.

R.W.

Four-Minute Fictions

50 Short-Short Stories
from The North American Review

Apples
Henry Berry

"Cox's Orange Pippin, of course."

"Point!" said Clayton ("Clay") Pennyworth, holding up one finger to the scorekeeper.

It would take more than a Cox's Orange Pippin to fool Josh Bradley. Even though it tasted suspiciously like an Orleans Reinette, its nearly perfect blend of acidity and sweetness gave it away. Cox's Orange was not considered the favorite English dessert apple for nothing.

Josh took off his blindfold and smiled delightedly. He had made the finals. Along with Samuel Wright he had guessed in succession the Boston Russet, Lord Grosvenor, Michaelmas Red, Laxton's Reward, Reinette de Canada, D'Arcy Spice, and Merton Charm. The Cornish Gilliflower had stumped him and John sat nervously on the sidelines while Samuel Wright bit softly into a Pitmason Pine Apple and let its succulent juice seep into his tastebuds. Josh was noticeably relieved when Samuel, the only one giving him serious competition, had guessed "American Mother." It was an understandable miscalculation. The flesh of both apples is crisp and the juice bountiful and sweet. Samuel's mistake left Josh in the lead.

"Score?" inquired Josh.

Clay went over to the scorekeeper's table for consultation. "Fifteen-fourteen, you're ahead," he yelled back at Josh.

Josh took his place along the row of chairs set up for the contestants.

Samuel Wright was leaning against the wall, the front feet of his chair off the floor. He had white, bushy sideburns. The hair on the top of his head was thin. He was a large man, not easily identifiable as one versed in the subtleties and refinements of apple-tasting. He looked more like a lumberjack.

Josh, on the other hand, was spindly, and played the violin. It was not surprising that he was able to detect the various proportions of bitterness and sweetness of the different, the multitude of apples. It was not surprising that he was ahead.

Samuel pushed himself away from the wall. The chair came down with a thump and shivered beneath his heavy body. He rose wearily, as if annoyed that he would again have to go through the procedure of sitting down blind-folded and having a bitesize piece of apple brought out and set before him, of having to chew it slowly and discern the type of apple it was.

A Caville Blanche d'Hiver was brought out. The Blanche d'Hiver is often mentioned as being the most delicious of all apples, better even than Ashmead's Kernel. If Samuel guessed wrongly, at least he would be in for a treat. Blanche d'Hivers were like a rare prized wine. They did not appear on the fruit counters of grocery stores or on the shelves of small markets on the sides of roads, but had to be imported from France. This particular Blanche d'Hiver had been ordered from Toulouse months earlier and carefully stored at the freezing point until the day of the contest. Then it had been brought out, just a couple of hours before it was scheduled to begin, and left in the air to regain its normal aroma and texture.

Samuel tapped in front of him until he discovered the small plate. Then he lifted the wedge of apple into his mouth. Biting into the apple was the most important part of the procedure. The quality of the flesh was important. It could be a degree of crisp or soft. Always, unless the apple were over-ripe or had been carelessly left at too high a temperature, it was firm. If Samuel bit down too forcefully, he would slice through the flesh as indiscriminately as a cleaver, thereby damaging one clue to the type of apple. Also, a delicate pressure allowed the juice to ooze out slowly and not become too mixed with saliva. The flavor of the juice was the most important characteristic of the kind of apple. It would be a distinct blend of bitter and sweet. All apples have some tannic acid, but in many — dessert apples mostly — it is almost impossible to detect, outweighed by juice sweet as syrup. Bitterness is prized only in cider apples, and some cooking apples. Otherwise the degree of sweetness determines the apple's value as a handy, desirable, edible fruit.

Samuel brought his jaws together as carefully as calipers. With bits of the piece still in his mouth, he blurted out "Caville Blanche d'Hiver" confidently. His French was poor, but there was no mistaking that he was referring to the proper apple.

It was Josh's turn. He took the seat vacated by Samuel. For him, a Blenheim was brought out. During the nineteenth century, the Blenheim had been the most prized winter apple. Although it was not the most pleasant tasting, relatively acidic, it afforded the burghers and gentry its luxury throughout the year.

As soon as Josh bit into it, his face puckered. He narrowed it down to a Tom Putt, a Gravenstein, or Blenheim. Behind the blindfold, he closed his eyes and let his mind wander, hoping that it would seize upon the correct type. He narrowed it down to either a Tom Putt or Blenheim. It was too acidic for a Gravenstein. Josh was not certain which kind it was, but his chances were fifty-fifty. Luckily he could afford to lose a point and still be in contention against Samuel.

"Five seconds," Clay Pennyworth prompted.

Josh's mind raced. The first thought — *Blenheim*. "Blenheim," he said aloud just as time was running out.

"Point!" shouted Clay.

As early as 1741, apples of New England were being exported to the West

Indies, and by 1759 Albemarle Pippins were sent from Virginia to England. There are instances where apples have been used as the medium of exchange. In 1649, Governor John Endicott of Plymouth traded William Trask five hundred apple trees of three years' growth for two hundred acres of land. The apple, as certainly as horses and molasses, accompanied early settlers and traders from Europe to the southern hemisphere and was carried from Europe or North America to India, China, and Japan, where orchards were planted when conditions, soil, rainfall, and temperature were favorable. No one knows precisely how long the apple has been a part of the human diet, but Cato names seven different varieties. This leads to speculation that the apple was introduced to the British Isles by the Romans. Most apples we eat today are domesticated versions of *Malus pumila,* the wild crab apple. Crab apple trees are still favored for aesthetic reasons. In the springtime cupped pink and white and violet blossoms line their boughs. But the crab apple itself proved too sour and bitter for the palate and today is used only for jellies and preserves. Like the dog, apples were tamed and thus allowed to accompany man through history.

A Stayman Winesap was next. Samuel guessed it easily. Josh guessed a Nonpareil, but missed a Devonshire Quarrenden. After Samuel guessed a Granges Pearmain, the score was tied, seventeen all.

"Time out," called Clay. After two hours of apple-tasting, it was time to give both contestants and spectators a break. "Contest resumes in one hour."

This was the signal for the foodstuffs to be brought out. From the kitchen, hefty men carried jugs of cider and applejack and poured them into crystal bowls. Young girls followed bearing trays of tarts and apple strudel, mounds of applesauce, and dozens of apple pies. There was warm freshly baked bread for spicy apple butter and jams and jellies and preserves made especially for the occasion. There were whole apples, plump and red, shades of yellow and green, Grenadiers, Royal Russets, Autumn Pearmains, London Pippins, and Golden Reinettes among them.

So as not to befuddle their taste buds, Samuel and Josh didn't eat a thing. They sat talking to friends and relatives, watching everyone feast on the spread of apple products. At the end of the hour, Clay stood in the center of the room and announced the resumption of the contest. The men and girls cleared the tables and folded them up out of the way. Samuel and Josh came forward, indicating that they were ready. Clay sat them down and tied on their blindfolds.

"We have one more hour," said Clay, "and then the contest is over. In the event of a tie, you'll share the prize." The prize was a year's supply of apples sent to the home of the winner from all over the world. Each month he would receive one dozen of an exotic and unusual variety, some coming from as far away as Australia and the islands of Japan.

Clay waved his hand for the pieces to be brought out. For the finals, they would each have a bite of the same kind of apple and have to whisper its name to Clay. The first was a Court Pendu Plat, one of the oldest known kinds.

The Court Pendu Plat has been known for over four hundred years. As is the case with most apples, the origin of the name has been lost, but is still exciting and elegant enough to fire the imagination. "Court Pendu Plat" — it is a richly flavored little dessert apple. One imagines instantly that kings of France must have demanded it as a treat for guests at state banquets. Courtiers must have been sent to the orchards of the south, near Bordeaux and Grenoble, with instructions to bid the farmers deliver their harvests to the palace by oxen and cart.

Samuel and Josh each guessed correctly, whispering softly into Clayton Pennyworth's ear so that the other, sitting but a few yards away, could not possibly hear. After the Court Pendu Plat, a Rome Beauty was placed in front of the finalists. With little hesitation, they both named it, Clay having to hurry from one to the other as they raised their hands simultaneously. A Bramley's Seedling was next, followed by a King of the Pippins, then a Beauty of Bath, Lord Suffield, Arthur Turner, King's Acre Pippin, St. Edmund's Pippin, and a Lane's Prince Albert. The score stayed tied all the way; neither Josh nor Samuel missed once. Not a May Queen, a Coe's Golden Drop, not a White Transparent, nor a Christmas Pearmain, nor a Rosemary Russet were able to stump them.

"This is the last apple," Clay told the contestants and the crowd. "If you both guess it correctly, the prize will be mailed to each of you for six months."

White squares of apple flesh were placed in front of each of them. Josh found his first. He passed it under his nostrils and breathed in its delightful, heady fragrance. His face sparkled. He placed the piece in his mouth, closed his lips, and delicately crushed it. He smirked puckishly. A few seconds later he raised his hand. Clay went over and Josh whispered into his ear. Clay shook his head up and down, affirming that Josh had guessed rightly.

Samuel's face was dense with concentration. His brow furrowed and none sensed that, behind the blindfold, his eyes were narrow. His jaw revolved slowly as he let the small chunks of apple tumble over his tongue.

Clay looked over to the judges' bench, at the timekeeper. The timekeeper held up the fingers of both his hands. "Ten seconds," Clay relayed to Samuel.

Samuel's forehead turned glossy and his neck seemed to thicken as he strained to discern the type of apple he was chewing. "Five seconds," said Clay. "Three." "I don't know, I don't know," said Samuel. He removed his blindfold. At the other end of the table, Josh beamed proudly, winningly.

A cheer rose from the crowd as Josh got up, went over and shook hands with Samuel, and was led away toward the judges' table by Clay.

Samuel sat alone, dejected. The crowd passed by him, gathering around Clay and Josh and the judges. He looked disbelievingly at the sign on the table and the small piece of apple left on the plate in front of him. The apple was a Delicious, one of the most common apples, accounting for nearly twenty percent of the U.S. yearly crop. It was an apple any housewife or schoolboy would have known. He had never expected such a trick. It bordered on deceit.

As decorations, apples of all kinds had been hung from the ceiling by ribbons. One red, round, and full, had worked its way loose and now it dropped. It struck Samuel on the head. Samuel looked at it. It was a Flower of Kent. A Flower of Kent, said to be the type Sir Isaac Newton observed falling.

4

The Hit Man

T. Coraghessan Boyle

Early Years

The Hit Man's early years are complicated by the black bag which he wears over his head. Teachers correct his pronunciation, the coach criticizes his attitude, the principal dresses him down for branding preschoolers with a lit cigarette. He is a poor student. At lunch he sits alone, feeding the bell peppers and salami into the dark slot of his mouth. In the hallways, wiry young athletes snatch at the black hood and slap the back of his head. When he is thirteen he is approached by the captain of the football team, who pins him down and attempts to remove the hood. The Hit Man wastes him. Five years, says the judge.

Back on the Street

The Hit Man is back on the street in two months.

First Date

The Girl's name is Cynthia. The Hit Man pulls up in front of her apartment in his father's hearse. (The Hit Man's father, whom he loathes and abominates, is a mortician. At breakfast the Hit Man's father had slapped the cornflakes from his son's bowl. The son threatened to waste his father. He did not, restrained no doubt by considerations of filial loyalty and the deep-seated taboos against patricide which permeate the universal unconscious.)

Cynthia's father has silver sideburns and plays tennis. He responds to the Hit Man's knock, expresses surprise at the Hit Man's appearance. The Hit Man takes Cynthia by the elbow, presses a twenty into her father's palm, and disappears into the night.

5

Father's Death

At breakfast the Hit Man slaps the cornflakes from his father's bowl. Then wastes him.

Mother's Death

The Hit Man is in his early 20s. He shoots pool, lifts weights and drinks milk from the carton. His mother is in the hospital, dying of cancer or heart disease. The priest wears black. So does the Hit Man.

First Job

Porfirio Buñoz, a Cuban financier, invites the Hit Man to lunch. I hear you're looking for work, says Buñoz.
That's right, says the Hit Man.

Peas

The Hit Man does not like peas. They are too difficult to balance on the fork.

Talk Show

The Hit Man waits in the wings, the white slash of a cigarette scarring the midnight black of his head and upper torso. The makeup girl has done his mouth and eyes, brushed the nap of his hood. He has been briefed. The guest who precedes him is a pediatrician. A planetary glow washes the stage where the host and the pediatrician, separated by a potted palm, cross their legs and discuss the little disturbances of infants and toddlers.
After the station break the Hit Man finds himself squeezed into a director's chair, white lights in his eyes. The talk-show host is a baby-faced man in his early forties. He smiles like God and all His Angels. Well, he says. So you're a hit man. Tell me — I've always wanted to know — what does it feel like to hit someone?

Death of Mateo Maria Buñoz

The body of Mateo Maria Buñoz, the cousin and business associate of a prominent financier, is discovered down by the docks on a hot summer morning. Mist rises from the water like steam, there is the smell of fish. A large black bird perches on the dead man's forehead.

Marriage

Cynthia and the Hit Man stand at the altar, side by side. She is wearing a white satin gown and lace veil. The Hit Man has rented a tuxedo, extra-large, and a silk-lined black-velvet hood.
...Till death do you part, says the priest.

Moods

The Hit Man is moody, unpredictable. Once, in a luncheonette, the waitress brought him the meatloaf special but forgot to eliminate the peas. There was a spot of gravy on the Hit Man's hood, about where his chin should be. He looked up at the waitress, his eyes like pins behind the triangular slots, and wasted her.

Another time he went to the track with $25, came back with $1800. He stopped at a cigar shop. As he stepped out of the shop a wino tugged at his sleeve and solicited a quarter. The Hit Man reached into his pocket, extracted the $1800 and handed it to the wino. Then wasted him.

First Child

A boy. The Hit Man is delighted. He leans over the edge of the playpen and molds the tiny fingers around the grip of a nickel-plated derringer. The gun is loaded with blanks — the Hit Man wants the boy to get used to the noise. By the time he is four the boy has mastered the rudiments of Tae Kwon Do, can stick a knife in the wall from a distance of ten feet and shoot a moving target with either hand. The Hit Man rests his broad palm on the boy's head. You're going to make the Big Leagues, Tiger, he says.

Work

He flies to Cincinnati. To L.A. To Boston. To London. The stewardesses get to know him.

Half an Acre and a Garage

The Hit Man is raking leaves, amassing great brittle piles of them. He is wearing a black T-shirt, cut-off at the shoulders, and a cotton work hood, also black. Cynthia is edging the flowerbed, his son playing in the grass. The Hit Man waves to his neighbors as they drive by. The neighbors wave back.

When he has scoured the lawn to his satisfaction, the Hit Man draws the smaller leaf-hummocks together in a single mound the size of a pickup truck. Then he bends to ignite it with his lighter. Immediately, flames leap back from the leaves, cut channels through the pile, engulf it in a ball of fire. The Hit Man stands back, hands folded beneath the great meaty biceps. At his side is the three-headed dog. He bends to pat each of the heads, smoke and sparks raging against the sky.

Stalking the Streets of the City

He is stalking the streets of the city, collar up, brim down. It is late at night. He stalks past department stores, small businesses, parks and gas stations. Past apartments, picket fences, picture windows. Dogs growl in the shadows, then slink away. He could hit any of us.

7

Retirement

A group of businessman-types — sixtyish, seventyish, portly, diamond rings, cigars, liver spots — throws him a party. Porfirio Buñoz, now in his eighties, makes a speech and presents the Hit Man with a gilded scythe. The Hit Man thanks him, then retires to the lake, where he can be seen in his speedboat, skating out over the blue, hood rippling in the breeze.

Death

He is stricken, shrunken, half his former self. He lies propped against the pillows at Mercy Hospital, a bank of gentians drooping round the bed. Tubes run into the hood at the nostril openings, his eyes are clouded and red, sunk deep behind the triangular slots. The priest wears black. So does the Hit Man.

On the other side of town the Hit Man's son is standing before the mirror of a shop which specializes in Hit Man attire. Trying on his first hood.

One More Thing
Raymond Carver

L.D.'s wife Maxine told him to leave one night after she came home from work and found him drunk again and being abusive with Bea, their fifteen year old. L.D. and his daughter were at the kitchen table arguing. Maxine didn't have time to put her purse away or take off her coat.

Bea said, "Tell him, Mom. Tell him what we talked about. It's in his head, isn't it? If he wants to stop drinking, all he has to do is tell himself to stop. It's all in his head. Everything's in the head."

"You think it's that simple, do you?" L.D. said. He turned the glass in his hand but didn't drink from it. Maxine had him in a fierce and disquieting gaze. "That's crap," he said. "Keep your nose out of things you don't know anything about. You don't know what you're saying. It's hard to take anybody seriously who sits around all day reading astrology magazines."

"This has nothing to do with *astrology*, Dad," Bea said. "You don't have to insult me." Bea hadn't attended high school for the past six weeks. She said no one could make her go back. Maxine had said it was another tragedy in a long line of tragedies.

"Why don't you both stop?" Maxine said. "My God, I already have a headache. This is just too much. L.D.?"

"Tell him, Mom," Bea said. "Mom thinks so too. If you tell yourself to stop, you can stop. The brain can do anything. If you worry about going bald and losing your hair — I'm not talking about you, Dad — it'll fall out. It's all in your head. Anybody who knows anything about it will tell you."

"How about sugar diabetes?" he said. "What about epilepsy? Can the brain control that?" He raised the glass right under Maxine's eyes and finished his drink.

"Diabetes, too," Bea said. "Epilepsy. Anything! The brain is the most power-ful organ in the body. It can do anything you ask it to do." She picked up his cigarettes from the table and lit one for herself.

"Cancer. What about cancer?" L.D. said. "Can it stop you from getting cancer? Bea?" He thought he might have her there. He looked at Maxine. "I don't know how we got started on this," he said.

"Cancer," Bea said and shook her head at his simplicity. "Cancer, too.

9

If a person wasn't afraid of getting cancer, he wouldn't get cancer. Cancer starts in the *brain*. Dad."

"That's crazy!" he said and hit the table with the flat of his hand. The ashtray jumped. His glass fell on its side and rolled toward Bea. "You're crazy, Bea, do you know that? Where'd you pick up all this crap? That's what it is too. It's crap, Bea."

"That's enough, L.D.," Maxine said. She unbuttoned her coat and put her purse down on the counter. She looked at him and said, "L.D., I've had it. So has Bea. So has everyone who knows you. I've been thinking it over. I want you out of here. Tonight. This minute. And I'm doing you a favor, L.D. I want you out of the house now before they come and carry you out in a pine box. I want you to leave, L.D. Now," she said. "Someday you'll look back on this. Someday you'll look back and thank me."

L.D. said, "I will, will I? Someday I'll look back," he said. "You think so, do you?" L.D. had no intention of going anywhere, in a pine box or otherwise. His gaze switched from Maxine to a jar of pickles that had been on the table since lunch. He picked up the jar and hurled it past the refrigerator through the kitchen window. Glass shattered onto the floor and windowsill and pickles flew out into the chill night. He gripped the edge of the table.

Bea had jumped away from her chair. "*God*, Dad! *You're* the crazy one," she said. She stood beside her mother and took in little breaths through her mouth.

"Call the police," Maxine said. "He's violent. Get out of the kitchen before he hurts you. Call the police," she said.

They started backing out of the kitchen. For a moment L.D. was insanely reminded of two old people retreating, the one in her nightgown and robe, the other in a black coat that reached to her knees.

"I'm going, Maxine," he said. "I'm going right now. It suits me to a tee. You're nuts here anyway. This is a nuthouse. There's another life out there. Believe me, this is not the only life." He could feel the draft of air from the window on his face. He closed his eyes and opened them. He still had his hands on the edge of the table and was rocking the table back and forth on its legs as he spoke.

"I hope not," Maxine said. She'd stopped in the kitchen doorway. Bea edged around her into the other room. "God knows, every day I pray there's another life."

"I'm going," he said. He kicked his chair and stood up from the table. "You won't see me again, either."

"You've left me plenty to remember you by, L.D.," Maxine said. She was in the living room now. Bea stood next to her. Bea looked disbelieving and scared. She held her mother's coat sleeve in the fingers of one hand, her cigarette in the fingers of her other hand.

"*God*, Dad, we were just talking," she said.

"Go on now, get out, L.D.," Maxine said. "I'm paying the rent here, and I'm saying go. Now."

"I'm going," he said. "Don't push me," he said. "I'm going."

"Don't do anything else violent, L.D.," Maxine said. "We know you're strong when it comes to breaking things."

"Away from here," L.D. said. "I'm leaving this nuthouse."

He made his way into the bedroom and took one of her suitcases from the closet. It was an old brown naugahyde suitcase with a broken clasp. She used to pack it full of Jantzen sweaters and carry it with her to college. He'd gone to college too. That had been years ago and somewhere else. He threw the suitcase onto the bed and began putting in his underwear, trousers and long-sleeved shirts, sweaters, an old leather belt with a brass buckle, all of his socks and handkerchiefs. From the nightstand he took magazines for reading material. He took the ashtray. He put everything he could into the suitcase, everything it would hold. He fastened the one good side of the suitcase, secured the strap, and then remembered his bathroom things. He found the vinyl shaving bag up on the closet shelf behind Maxine's hats. The shaving bag had been a birthday gift from Bea a year or so back. Into it went his razor and shaving cream, his talcum powder and stick deodorant, his toothbrush. He took the toothpaste too. He could hear Maxine and Bea in the living room talking in low voices. After he washed his face and used the towel, he put the bar of soap into the shaving bag. Then he added the soap dish and the glass from over the sink. It occurred to him that if he had some cutlery and a plate, he could keep going for a long time. He couldn't close the shaving bag, but he was ready. He put on his coat and picked up the suitcase. He went into the living room. Maxine and Bea stopped talking. Maxine put her arm around Bea's shoulders.

"This is goodbye, I guess," L.D. said and waited. "I don't know what else to say except I guess I'll never see you again," he said to Maxine. "I don't plan on it anyway. You too," he said to Bea. "You and your crackpot ideas."

"*Dad,*" she said.

"Why do you go out of your way to keep picking on her?" Maxine said. She took Bea's hand. "Haven't you done enough damage in this house already? Go on, L.D. Go and leave us in peace."

"It's in you head. Just remember," Bea said. "Where are you going anyway? Can I write to you?" she asked.

"I'm going, that's all I can say," L.D. said. "Anyplace. Away from this nuthouse," he said. "That's the main thing." He took a last look around the living room and then moved the suitcase from one hand to the other and put the shaving bag under his arm. "I'll be in touch, Bea. Honey, I'm sorry I lost my temper. Forgive me, will you? Will you forgive me?"

"You've made it into a nuthouse," Maxine said. "If it's a nuthouse, L.D., you've made it so. You did it. Remember that, L.D., as you go wherever you're going."

He put the suitcase down and the shaving bag on top of the suitcase. He drew himself up and faced them. Maxine and Bea moved back.

"Don't say anything else, Mom," Bea said. Then she saw the toothpaste sticking out of the shaving bag. She said, "Look, Dad's taking the toothpaste. Dad, come on, don't take the toothpaste."

"He can have it," Maxine said. "Let him have it and anything else he wants just so long as he gets out of here."

L.D. put the shaving bag under his arm again and once more picked up the suitcase. "I just want to say one more thing, Maxine. Listen to me.

Remember this," he said. "I love you. I love you no matter what happens. I love you too, Bea. I love you both." He stood there at the door and felt his lips begin to tingle as he looked at them for what, he believed, might be the last time. "Goodbye," he said.

"You call this love, L.D.?" Maxine said. She let go of Bea's hand. She made a fist. Then she shook her head and jammed her hands into her coat pockets. She stared at him and then dropped her eyes to something on the floor near his shoes.

It came to him with a shock that he would remember this night and her like this. He was terrified to think that in the years ahead she might come to resemble a woman he couldn't place, a mute figure in a long coat, standing in the middle of a lighted room with lowered eyes.

"Maxine!" he cried. "Maxine!"

"Is this what love is, L.D.?" she said, fixing her eyes on him. Her eyes were terrible and deep, and he held them as long as he could.

Fruit

Mark E. Clemens

That night she dreamed she was in the parking lot down by the river. She had just locked the door and started away from the car when she felt the air jump beside her ear and then heard the report of a rifle shot. It was only a dream, but as she put her hand to her ear a white cloud of pigeons erupted from the roof of a nearby hotel.

The next day she drove to the parking lot, to the spot where she had parked in her dream. The space was open and she pulled in. The river, swollen with spring run-off, drowned out the noise of the traffic streaming across the bridge above the lot. A breeze ruffled the grass between the vacant benches along the river bank. She turned in her seat to look at the hotel rising overhead and there were three pigeons perched on top of the dirty gray limestone facade, but no one in sight around the hotel or on the bridge or the stairway down to the lot or among the scattered parked cars or on the grassy bank. Far across the river she saw a man, his raincoated figure dwarfed by the bulk of the old railroad depot, but he was only standing there with his hands in his pockets, no high-powered rifle to be seen.

When she opened the door to get out, there was a spent shell casing lying on the pavement where she would have put her foot. She leaned down and picked the casing up. It was warm and she turned it over and over in her hands, feeling as if she might have just created something, that perhaps her dreams were finally bearing fruit.

Grand Canyon State

Valerie P. Cohen

When Toby Howland asked me on a trip I went because he was so sweet, though I thought he wanted me less than he wanted my credit card. That winter he worked in his mother's insurance office but wasn't much help to her — too vague. Later on somebody said he took up carpentry, which would be more his style. A bit short on personality, that boy...he must have been or I'd remember him better.

As it is I can't recall what we talked about — maybe we didn't talk? — mostly I remember his being there, his voice. He had a soft voice, high as a woman's, a habit of not finishing his sentences. It drove me crazy. He'd say "I was thinking..." or "I figured out..." but by the time I asked him what he'd been going to say he'd forgotten all about it. He used to sing me songs, love songs, the only man I ever knew who could do that and not look silly, only man who sang me songs period, come to think of it. His singing voice was soft too but very clear. He couldn't remember but the first few lines and part of a refrain so he'd hum the rest or make it up.

I do remember how he looked — how could I forget? — all that hair the color of old line Kentucky bourbon, I could fill both fists with it and never hold it all. Skin nearly the same color. Eyes, green they were, pointed at the ends, green with amber spots, bottom of a brook; I'd stare into them looking for trout. Maybe he didn't have to think. Not like other people. Lord knows what he saw in me, reality maybe. He knew I'd put oil in the car and remember to pay the waitress. He made me feel large and ill-tempered. I couldn't stand the way he trailed off like a child.

We never should have left the city but how was I to know? We drove east to the Grand Canyon, Christmas time it was, I was between jobs and he didn't seem to know whether he should be working or not. Off we went inland in his old black Mustang. Its engine knocked and it had no spare but I loved the way that car smelled like a field of wild grass under rain. I don't know where we got the idea to go there, to the Grand Canyon — we felt like traveling and he said this was supposed to be one of the main curiosities of the world. He even got a map.

In a way it was a curiosity. Big, I'll say that. Of course I'd seen pictures

14

but they didn't give any idea. I'd flown over it a time or two — from thirty thousand feet it looked like a gully in a bean field. This time we slid up on it across desert plains, sagebrush, grass, then at the end thick, self-contained juniper and pinyon. I could see indigo forest extending far northward to a long straight horizon, yet all of a sudden, wham! was a big hole right between my feet, I was shocked at how immense. And intricate: uncounted cliffs, ledges, ridges, buttes the color of dried blood.

The only way you could tell how big was when you saw something familiar, trail or building or the Colorado River itself. The place made a noise, a sort of hum like a train so far off you're not sure you hear it at all; when I was little I used to listen to sounds going away till long after they were gone.

Toby was terrified. He said the only way he could stand to look was by keeping one eye on that hotel on the other rim. Said it showed people had the upper hand. I knew what he meant, but still, I thought about walking down in to touch the earth's oldest living rocks. They had big signs all over warning you in three different languages like in an airport: Don't go. Too far. Blisters. Snakes. Heatstroke. I really thought it might be a hundred degrees down at the river even though we stood on snow while junipers wailed in winter wind. No, we just drove down the road, stopping at turn-outs like everybody else till Toby said he was bored and couldn't we drive down to Flagstaff for something to eat. We had to go home next day anyhow for my job, should've gone straight back. Yet I always liked that clear name: Flagstaff.

Driving down, we were happy to be back on solid ground and he sang along with whatever came on the radio. He could follow any tune. It should have been a fine time but I felt sad because I knew there was no real reason to be on this trip together. He'd forget all about it in a month, tell people "Hey, me and this chick went to..." What an idiot. *I* was an idiot, driving all over Arizona when I knew it wouldn't matter when it was over. I think that was the first time I realized nobody was going to stick around me forever and I'd just as soon be alone and not have to bother. It made me feel old. I never expected to turn out this way when I was a kid: never even occurred to me.

Smelling the warm-grass smell of his body from clear across the seat, I watched him. Tried to make myself feel *more* — sorrow, joy, anything — the planes of his face were so delicately balanced it seemed impossible they should not dissolve but could stay that way, day after day. Was there something wrong with me? Twice I had to remind him to get gas. And then too, I felt let-down that the canyon hadn't been more exciting; it did nothing but breathe.

We got into Flagstaff after dark. Lights winked between trees, the whole town scattered through tall pine forest like somebody dropped the pieces out of an airplane. Midair collision. Or maybe it fell off a freight, that's what it is, railroad town. Southern Pacific, Santa Fe? All outskirts. We were somewhere near tracks on a highway that went home one way or the other to Albuquerque, Amarillo, Atlanta. There were bars on the left side of the street among Chinese restaurants, snow piled on the sidewalk in black banks; ice was on the road, pickup trucks.

15

Suddenly one pulled out in front of us. We slammed right into it. Toby didn't have his seatbelt on of course and broke the windshield with his head. People poured out of bars to mill about smelling like sheep-shit and beer, talking: English, Chinese, Spanish, something else, Navajo, I think. The driver of the truck jumped out screaming: he was an indian, we couldn't understand a word. Two men pushed me. Toby didn't know what had happened. Black in the darkness, blood froze on his face in jagged lines. I was afraid somebody would hit him before the police came. I was so mad I nearly left.

Only I couldn't. What they called it was detainment. The cars were bashed in and stuck together like two dogs. Toby asked total strangers in this dreamy voice did they know a good restaurant or were we at the bottom of the Grand Canyon. The other driver kept falling down in gasoline and broken glass, cursing while insanely the crowd cheered. The cops couldn't figure out what happened either. I lost my I.D.

Who did I think I was, anyway? One cop said, "Sister, *you* were in that pickup and we don't give a shit what happens when your old man finds out!" Toby said he thought I was *his* sister but his parents got divorced. They sent him off to the hospital and transported the truck driver and me in handcuffs to their station.

I was glad to be in a warm room away from all those people. They towed in the Mustang; now it smelled like an old oil well instead of wet grass. They did find out I was who I said I was and took my statement. Fifteen dollars for bald tires was our ticket; it turned out the other man was drunk. We were supposed to get called back as witnesses but nothing ever came of it.

Toby showed up at dawn looking like a space-man with a head full of stiches and half his hair shaved off. He smiled but didn't ask me how my night had been. We sold the Mustang to a junk dealer and used the money for bus tickets home.

We sat in back singing songs till a lady asked me was he dangerous and I told him to shut up and try to act normal. Then an old man wanted to know were we married; Toby said we were enaged and I let it go at that. I realized I didn't know a single person in all of Arizona, felt so lonely I had to turn my face to the window so he wouldn't see, looking north to endless cobalt tableland holding inside it, unseen, unknown, a sighing river-canyon.

I didn't see him after that trip. Now and then I think I'll see him again to glimpse trout swimming in his eyes; it's hard to imagine all that hair gone grey but I suppose it must be by now. I don't want to think about it. I don't suppose he'd remember me but he might remember the wreck in Flagstaff. I wonder who he sings songs to now.

Ithaca

Nicole Cooley

On the way, Janice reads a biography of Lucrezia Borgia. A long passage in the first chapter describes the family wine goblets, cleverly designed, with small traps for poison along the rims. The drawing on the opposite page shows the family before they were poisoned, Lucrezia sitting calmly among them, wearing a high-collared red dress and smiling, one of her husbands resting his hand on her shoulder. The book says it is debatable whether she caused all the deaths: no one can be sure. Janice admires Lucrezia's haughtiness.

"I think you're fixated on disaster," Charles tells her. "It isn't normal."

"What do you mean?"

"You draw attention to yourself by associating yourself with catastrophe." He glances back at her through the rearview mirror, waiting for a reaction.

They are driving to Ithaca to visit his sister. Janice reads in the back seat because Charles says she makes him nervous when she sits next to him. Besides the biography, she has brought a copy of *The Canterbury Tales,* which she hasn't read since high school. Charles has been working on a watercolor of the pilgrims on their way to Canterbury, and he checks the accuracy of his details against the book's. Janice likes to read the Middle English aloud to herself; the syllables twist her tongue against her teeth in a pleasant, unfamiliar way.

"I'm glad we're getting out of New York," Charles says. "No one stays in the city for the holidays." His sister, Margaret, lives alone in Ithaca and says marriage would ruin her independence. She wears carefully applied nail polish and wool suits, with matching hats pinned to her hair in the winter. When Charles describes Margaret, he labels her as "competent" and "capable." Her organization makes Janice feel clumsy. Margaret is president of the Junior League in Ithaca and devotes most of her time to what she calls "causes." These include distributing food stamps, restoring parks, and — the one she seems to like best — working at St. Elizabeth's, the orphans' home. Last year, Janice helped Margaret deliver Christmas baskets to the home. Janice knew she should feel sorry for them, but she thought the orphans looked small and evil, like creatures out of a Bosch painting.

Margaret still bakes the family Christmas pudding from a recipe she claims

17

has been handed down from King George III. Inside, dropped in the batter and left to bake, are the traditional symbols — a coin, a bone button, a silver ring. The coin stands for chance, the button for faith, and the ring for a happy marriage.

Another of Margaret's projects is speaking before the Ladies' Hospital Guild and high school assemblies, urging donations of body parts. She herself seems eager to give up her eyes, her lungs, possibly her heart. At her instigation, Janice and Charles filled out forms promising they would donate everything to science when they died. Charles says he hates the whole idea and would rather not think about it. Janice imagines the transfer of an eye, like a tiny plant; she wonders how the doctors would preserve her heart.

"You don't talk anymore. Is it something I've done?" Charles sounds annoyed.

Janice has spread the *Times* over the car seat. "A fire destroyed that cathedral on Lexington Avenue last night," she says to him; "the symphony children's chorus was in the choir loft. They didn't know what was happening until it was too late to jump." She leans forward to show him the blurry photograph. "So elegant — the boys and girls in their long white robes peering out, the flames rising against the stained glass. It's beautiful."

Charles clicks on the radio. More news. A woman in Rochester murdered her husband and hanged herself the next day. "Do you want to play cards?" Charles says. "We could do that now. Shall I pull over to the side of the road for a while?" Janice shakes her head because she can't remember any card games except a certain kind of solitaire where the cards are supposed to be arranged in pairs. She never got the knack of it.

They haven't been away together all year, except for a trip to Mexico last summer when Charles had a magazine assignment to do photographs of Oaxaca. At first Janice was eager to go. She took Spanish lessons but couldn't learn the language properly because she thought it so ugly. The first evening in Mexico City, the prostitutes called to Charles from their balconies, and pedlars shouted from behind tables stacked with cheap blue and silver jewelry. Everything weighed on her; she could hardly breathe, so she spent the rest of the vacation in the hotel room alone, since Charles refused to give up the assignment and go home. Every day after photographing the village in the morning, he brought her bottled water and slices of fruit from the market.

Now the cassette recorder on the dashboard plays Scarlatti. "I hate harpsichords," Charles says, and presses the eject button. Janice thinks the music sounds like steps, each note giving way to the next, rising. He turns the radio back on, this time to a talk show. The guest is a famous psychotherapist.

"What can I do?" a woman is asking, frantic. "My sister and I are identical twins, but everyone thinks we're the same person, that there's only one of us."

"Jesus," Charles says and spins the dial before Janice can hear the reply.

She and Charles met in college in their junior year. They took physics, a required course in which the teacher, an old man who talked very rapidly, stood at the bottom of an amphitheater and rolled red and yellow balls down a slanted tray to show velocity and distance. Several of Charles' photographs were being displayed at an offcampus gallery, and he sent everyone in the physics class a typed card announcing the exhibit. Janice thought this was pretentious, but she went anyway because the theme of the show was the St. Valentine's Day Massacre, and she was curious. Few people were there, and Charles invited her out to dinner.

"Do you still think of yourself as an abandoned wife?" Charles asks.

His question takes her back to the fall night when they separated after they had argued all day. It was Halloween. Children draped in sheets and masks rang the doorbell again and again, and Janice left Charles shouting at her from the back of the apartment so she could greet the trick-or-treaters with candy. She commented to Charles on the absurdity of the situation. He said, "I don't see how you can excuse yourself by trying to make this funny." He told her he was tired of everything.

"You mean you're tired of me," Janice said, pleased by her power, under stress, to use the kind of exact expression Charles would appreciate. She had asked him what she should do; he told her to call his sister, then left the house. Margaret was polite. She invited Janice to come to Ithaca for a while, saying she could help her with a new League project because Janice should keep busy, but Janice declined.

Charles was gone for three weeks, staying at an artists' colony in Vermont. He telephoned every few days to see how she was doing. Janice thought he was giving her openings to ask him to come back. She passed the time by reading. Margaret gave her four cartons of old books, all alphabetized and ordered. Janice piled the vacant half of the bed with them — art books, African folk tales, botany guides. She planned to read everything in the boxes, beginning with "A" and working her way through the alphabet, but Charles returned before she had even finished "B."

He came back at the end of November, bringing a suitcase full of new ink drawings and an art student named Miranda. Charles assured Janice that his feelings for Miranda were paternal, that she shouldn't worry. Miranda was a large, clumsy girl, with red hair that looked to have been ironed straight and flat against her back. She drank liqueurs, and unfinished bottles of creme de cacao and ginger brandy began appearing on tables and behind chairs around the apartment. She seemed always to be carrying a small, sugar-stained glass. Before Miranda returned to school, she did a portrait of Charles, and he asked her to paint Janice in beside him, his hand on her shoulder. Miranda kept the picture for her portfolio. Charles said it was just a student exercise, but Janice had liked the soft arc of shadow around them, and the way their faces seemed to fit, so comfortably, together.

"Abandoned?" Janice says, testing the sound of the word before she applies it to herself. "No, I don't think so."

Pears

Janet Desaulniers

In New Orleans, in the Quarter, there is a crab bar, a tiny sidewalk restaurant tucked between two hotels, call The House of Desire. The first time I saw it, I was twenty-one and somehow jarred to think that such a small cafe would carry a name like that, even in the Quarter with its strip show barkers and narrow doorways that open into a pink wavering light. I asked my waitress if the intended pronunciation was The House of Desirée, imagining a French or Cajun owner. The waitress was a stolid girl, a Southerner, with big feet and hands, and I think she deliberately prolonged her drawl when she answered.

"It's desire," she said. It sounded beautiful when she said it. Her voice seemed heavy with sea smells and low music. At once I thought both she and the little restaurant were very brave.

I am like most people. I don't talk about desire. I think this has something to do with a certain confusion about my body, a lack of control. Once I told a friend: "The only thing that matters is monogamy of the mind. The body is unimportant. It may be ignored, coddled, tossed from bed to bed. Doesn't matter. One does what one must do." A young woman, of course, admires conclusions.

Now I sense that I have underestimated the body's importance: I see that people care about the bodies of others. People are particular, even fastidious. There are rules. For example, I have learned that the body should be held just so. The men who sprawl across sofas at cocktail parties and the women who gesture broadly in restaurants cause others to lean far back into the secret space between their shoulders. Not that the body should be retiring. There is, I think, a general disdain for those who button their shirts to the collar. In short, the body should be sensible. It should be confident enough to take the center of any room, polite enough to hold attention no longer than a moment.

My body is sensible: thin, but not too thin, not fashionably so. My thighs have spread to save me from fanaticism. My legs and arms are very long, almost lithe, but most of the time I keep them pulled close, elbows punching my ribs, knees always together. Sometimes though, for a reason I don't quite understand, my body rebels, and I get into trouble.

20

At seven, I was a dancer. Five days a week, I forced my body through three hours of imposed revelry. All the time, I was afraid for myself. I had to be pulled from the floor where I sat folded up like a wallet, and pushed to the stage. I was terrified my body might break apart. I danced haltingly, waiting always for a sound like the snap of a fresh bean. Later, long after I stopped dancing, I watched myself grow. I was still afraid. At night, with the palms of my hands, I pressed back against the force that pushed from somewhere beneath my breasts. I dressed carefully, using only the tips of my fingers. Then, when my body seemed to have finished growing, when I felt sure that this was the body I would finally have, a change occurred. The wools of my sweaters and skirts suddenly seemed too heavy for my shoulders and hips. My thighs broke out in a rash. Each afternoon, in a tee-shirt and pink shorts, I would run around the duck pond at the park near my house. Women sitting in a garden of pastels watched me and pulled their arms tight around their thin waists as if trying to hold themselves inside their dresses. Later I tied scarfs around my neck and through my hair. I began sleeping nude. I was sixteen and very proud. The curve that started at my hip and shaped my thigh seemed perfect — breathtaking.

Now, ten years later, there are random days when my body, tender with the world, stretches and pulls with yearning, days I want to move through crowds. Once on the bus after a trip to the market my bag split, and four pears rolled clumsily down the aisle. On most days I would have cringed at the prospect of exposing the angles of my legs and hips and shoulders to others. But it was a day when dropping pears was welcome. My body felt magnanimous and kind. Dropping the pears offered a chance to be gentle with my hands and voice, to whisper "excuse me" in just the right tone, to nudge an ankle aside with exact tenderness. My last pear had lodged near the rear exit. The other riders by this time were smiling small kind smiles. We were all enjoying a moment of quiet and warmth. I was pleased by that. I moved gracefully down the aisle. I felt young and happy. As I bent to reach the last pear, a man crouched down beside me. He held his hands in the air just inches from my waist as if in silent assurance that I would not fall. Just before I stood up, he ran his hand along the back of my calf. It was summer and I wore no stockings. His hand was smooth and light as water against my skin. When I turned, we looked warmly into each other's faces the way lovers do after a very long argument. We were grateful and tired. Both of us straightened and lurched as the bus stopped. He got off, the others shifted in their seats, and I sat down with my pears.

So, in a certain mood, I break rules. My body gets away from me, throws off caution, takes charge. This happened when I was twenty-three.

I was in love with a quiet good man. His name was Michael, and he was much older than I, but not so much older as to be extraordinary. Not old enough to break any rules. He was serious, sometimes almost sad, about life. Though he was a musician, a saxophone player, and though the warm smoky music suited him, it did not secure him the solace I always thought musicians found. His was an eerie sound. His power pushed up from somewhere deep inside him though he was a very small, thin man who simply didn't seem to possess mass enough to produce a sound like that. His music was beautiful though, frighteningly so. Listening to him play was like waking up alone from a bad dream to know that it was the tenth bad dream in ten nights alone, and then to hear, as if from the farthest corner of the room, the sound of someone turning and breathing in a deep contented sleep. It was a startling kind of comfort. I'm not sure he knew he offered it because, as I said, he was often sad and quiet.

I, on the other hand, was young. I believed that I gave Michael energy and he gave me calm. I remember once I came home breathless after passing a small gallery near our house. He was sitting near the window, where he always sat, practicing. He stopped when he heard the key in the door. I rushed in, threw my packages on the couch, and said, "The windows are full of winged mules." He was already beginning to smile when he leaned forward to watch my face.

"What?"

"At the gallery. Tiny baroque mules." I began to pace and wave my arms as if trying to stir up the quiet air. "They're on goblets, punchbowls. Some are just hanging from wires, floating. Pink, yellow, green. They're all colors."

"Mules?"

"Yes," I sat down heavily and leaned far back into the chair, grinning. "Mules."

He smiled back at me and then we had dinner. The next evening there was a blue winged mule poised on the brim of my coffee cup. I held it in the palm of my hand and imagined Michael setting his saxophone aside, tearing one check from the packet he kept in the drawer by the bed, and walking down the street. I imagined him hurrying, perhaps even crossing against the light. I still have the mule, and sometimes I try to hold it in my hand in the precise way I held it that evening.

Michael and I were very good together. We shared a house and a bed. This is my way of saying we were lovers though I realize it is a rather vague way of saying it. In old movies, the audience could look at trees or clouds, sometimes even the moon, if the director wanted to imply that two people had become lovers. I have always thought that was a rather gentle notion, but still, it is imprecise. One can never be sure the audience will think of desire. They might think simply of the pink edge around the moon or of how the crown of buds on the trees resembles a new spring hat. There is no sure way of talking about desire. I suppose I could say that we sweated and moaned together even on winter nights, but somehow that sounds either pornographic or very funny. We were neither. In my own mind, I usually think, "In addition to loving me, he gave my body pleasure." But that too is vague and wasn't always true. Some nights my body was almost rigid in its defiance. Michael would try first to soothe me, then leave me alone, then soothe me again. Nothing worked. My body was vacant and invisible. I felt neither his absence nor his touch. There were moments I thought his hands went through me to the tangled bedsheets. For a long time, I didn't understand that, but I accepted it. I live with it even now like a door that never closes completely.

One thing is sure, though — I loved a quiet good man. Then very suddenly, on a day like the pear-dropping day, I walked to another man's house, a man I'd seen movies with, entertained over elaborate dinners, a man who had been my friend for three years. I had one drink. I patted his dog. I talked about sports and good restaurants. Then as he reached across the table to fill my glass, I touched his arm, which was strong and pale. Perhaps I touched him because everything between us had always been so clean, so finely edged, or perhaps I just wanted to comfort him, even congratulate him, for having a pale, strong arm in such harsh morning light. Naturally, breaking a rule like that made a mess of things, but for a moment it was a warm, human kind of mess, like the passion that turns over tables and litters carpets.

When I went home, Michael was there, his saxophone leaned neatly, perfectly, against the sill. He said, "Where have you been?" and I said, "I've been to John's house. I've just slept with him. In the last hour."

He cried for some time, his face turned to the window. Every few seconds, his hands picked at his shirt as though his chest and arms ached. I didn't try to touch him though my mind screamed at me to hurry, to comfort him before he slipped away. My body was blankly defiant.

Twisting in his chair, Michael smoothed his shirt and looked at me. His face was soft and shaken. I thought then that I wanted him to understand, though now I see that such a thing was impossible, and I probably knew it. If I didn't know it, I should have. It's a rule. I could only sit and watch him cry.

Stop

Stephen Dixon

A car stopped. Man got out. "You there," he said. I dropped my package and started running. "Hey wait, where you running to?" He knew. He knew I knew. Car stopping, man getting out, motor still running, driver inside with his hands on the wheel, car door left open so the man outside could jump right back in. And his look. If I could see the driver's face, probably both their looks. But I didn't have the time to explain or speculate on all this. Just continued running.

The car caught up with me a block later. They drove alongside for a few seconds, pointing and talking about how good a runner I was, seeming to enjoy a joke, for they both broke up. Then they parked about 15 feet in front of me. I stopped. Both men got out. Motor still on, doors left open. "You there," same man from before said, approaching me, driver staying behind. "We only want to speak to you about something, so what's the rush?"

Standing in the middle of an intersection I had 4 ways to go. Back, to them, either sidestreet. Back they probably had another car coming by now. Left sidestreet ended in a school ballfield with a chain fence around it with the exits at the other side of it sometimes locked. Right sidestreet I'd never been on before and ran down it. "Oh for godsakes." the driver said, "do you have to? We just ate." They got in the car. Drove slowly behind me. Then accelerated past and made a sharp turn onto the sidewalk right in front of me, cutting me off. I couldn't stop in time and slammed into the car door, went down, got up, legs gave and I fell down again. The man in the right seat seemed shaken too.

"Did you have to stop so fast?" he said to the driver.

"I didn't want to be chasing him all day. Anyway, I immobilized him."

I jumped up. Both doors opened. I was stuck between the right car door and front of the car. Two possible ways out for me were to quickly crawl across the car's front seat, which might fool them, but then the driver shut his door, or run into the building.

"Now please, just a little minute of your precious time," the driver said, climbing over the front fender to get to me. Other man was a couple of steps

24

away from being in arm's reach. I ran down the steps and pushed past the vestibule door. Door to the hallway inside was locked. "Hold up already," the driver said. "My stomach, my feet." I rang all the building's bells. The men started down the steps. I braced one hand against the hallway door and foot against the vestibule door so the men couldn't get in. A woman on the intercom said, "Yes?"

"Let me in."

"Who is it?"

"Just let me in please. It's an emergency."

"Not until I know who it is."

"Police. There's a man we're after who just ran into your building and we want to get in without breaking down your door."

"That's still not saying who it is." The men were trying to push their way in. "I need proof. For this building, in this neighborhood, you have to."

"Look out your window. That's our doubleparked car on your sidewalk. Now would we park like that if we weren't after what I say?"

"I have the back view."

I rang all the bells, kept my hand and foot braced against the doors. The men were caving in my foot. I kept ringing the bells with my free hand. The woman kept saying who is it, she needs proof, will I please stop ringing if I can't give it as she's old, too lame to be walking back and forth like this, till she or someone else let me in. The driver threw open their door and rushed to get to the hallway door with the man behind him practically falling on top of him, but I got it shut. The other man got up and rang the bells. I ran to the back of the first floor looking for a rear entrance. There was none. I ran upstairs. The men were in the vestibule. "Yes, police," the driver yelled into the intercom, "Precinct 17, ma'am. Officer Aimily. Your local patrolman's Grenauer or Pace. Pace then. But we're after a man who just came in your building. That's our car outside." Someone rang them in.

"There a back entrance?" he said to the other man.

"No, all the buildings on this side face the river."

"What do you mean — right on it? I thought we were a block away."

"Flush up against. Absolutely. From some of the back flats here you think you're floating in the sea."

They started upstairs.

"The roof," the driver said.

"Oh damn, I forgot. They're connected."

"You stay on the street, I'll follow him."

"But your stomach. And you said your feet."

"I'll live. Call in for more. He comes out, grab him. Bat him to the ground if he won't stop. I've had enough."

The driver continued upstairs. I knocked on the rear doors as I went up. The roof was out of the question. Unless someone was working up there or sunbathing in this cold. For all the roof doors were locked from the outside in. Once up there you have to keep the door open with something to get back in. Way it was with my own building and all the roofs I'd been on in this neighborhood and by fire law all the roofs in the city. But if some one in one of the rear apartments opened up I could run past him, throw open a back window and jump out and try and swim away. I'd jump 2 stories up at the most. That would be about 3 to 4 stories up because there must be a floor or 2 at least between the ground floor and water. The fourth floor was a little too high to jump from though I might have give it a try if I really felt lucky. But from the fifth floor I don't think I'd be able to survive.

Nobody on the third floor rear opened. The driver was panting as he climbed the stairs. I had youth on him, energy, not as much fat, no recent meal in me if what he'd said was true and no ruse, not that any of that would help me much unless of course I jumped and swam. Nobody on the fourth floor answered my door pounding either and I climbed the last 2 flights and unbolted the door to the roof.

No stick around or anything like that to wedge under the doorknob to keep the door closed. Now the driver was climbing the last flight. "Boy," he said, resting halfway up and seeing me looking down on him. "You're the biggest pain I've had all week. I could throw you off that roof — I'm not kidding. Just throw you off without thinking about it much for what you're putting me through."

I looked around. "Anybody on one of these roofs here? Hey, do you hear me, anybody around?" Nobody answered and I couldn't see anyone. I ran to the next roof. The roofs went on for an entire block. The last roof looked down on the street I'd just run on, avenue I'd first seen those men and run along to get to this street, river on its third side. The man stepped out on the roof, put a brick he found outside between the door and jamb so it wouldn't close all the way. I ran to the last building, hurdling the dozen or so 2-foot high parapets separating each roof.

He followed me, climbing over each parapet very carefully so he wouldn't have to dirty his pants legs and shirt cuffs. "Don't make it so tough for me anymore," he yelled from 5 roofs away. "Meet me at some halfway point from here. Or if you want, I'll go back to that door I came out of and you can meet me there."

"I don't know what you want," I yelled back, "so why you keep coming after me?"

"You don't know, then why were you so quick to run then?" from 3 roofs away.

"I see 2 big men chasing me, I run, wouldn't you?"

"We didn't chase. We walked. We drove. We said where's the rush? We were very polite and showed no harm. You smacked into our car, we didn't to you. But let's talk about it all downstairs. It's filthy up here and the air stinks from the incinerators and exhaust chutes."

He was on the last roof with me. I tried to open the door. Locked. What a fool I was not to have tried the doors on all the roofs I just ran across. They were all probably locked but I shouldn't have been so sure. Though even if I had got in one of them, probably nobody in the fourth or third floor rear apartments in that building would have opened up for me and there was still that other man on the street and by now probably a couple more. I looked over the roof into the street.

"Don't jump. You say you don't know what we're after you for, maybe you're right."

"Who's jumping?" There were plenty of men down there, most looking up, and double- and triple-parked cars. The street had been blocked off.

The man on the roof came up to within 10 feet of me. "How about it know?"

He was getting his wind back but maybe I could run around him. Left or right, where did I have the most room to get by him? When a man came out of the door he'd left open with that brick before and then other men from several more. I ran to the roof side overlooking the river. A liner was out there. *Olympia* it said. Ocean liner. Going for a cruise. All white. People on it outside, probably with drinks in their hands and bundled up in warm coats and furs. It must have just set off. Tugs at both ends of it but now peeling away from the liner so it was probably now starting to get out of the harbor on its own. I waved to it. Took off my sweater and waved that to it. A yellow sweater. Probably could be easily seen. Someone waved back to me. Now people were. Several more. I was sure it was me they were waving at, probably some with binoculars looking at me too. I waved harder at them and yelled, "Hey, hey, have fun, great journey." Even if they knew they couldn't hear me from where I was. Then a whole long railing of them at the bow were waving and then another railingful at the back and it seemed people from the other side of the ship were coming to this side to wave too. They were happy to wave to someone at the start of their trip, even if it was maybe only for a week south to the isles. I know I'd be.

"Your're not going to be rushing me and doing anything silly with that sweater now," the man said. He stayed where he was but the closest of those other men was now only a roof away.

"I wouldn't," I said, still waving. "I don't want to hurt anyone and most of all not myself when I know I didn't do anything wrong."

"Then let me put these on you and you'll come along. Because, really, I'm getting more mad at you all the time."

"Granted." I put out my wrists. He handcuffed them. The closest man was almost right behind him now. I broke away and jumped over the roof on the river side, my hand still holding the sweater which trailed above me.

That should have done it, but they already had a couple of launches below to pick me up. Biggest surprise was popping out of the water alive. All it took for them was a long pole with a hook at the end of it which they got around the chain of my cuffs. They dragged me in, lifted me out of the water gently and rolled me over on my belly on the deck and 2 men sat on opposite ends of me as if I was a very dangerous but prize rare whale.

His Idiots

David James Duncan

It was early spring and misty the day he came to caretake the farm. His gear stowed, he slumped in a rocker at the window and watched the sheep in the distance — gray cloud-puffs grazing the green, transforming rough pasture to lawn. They were his first flock, his introduction to shepherdhood, venerable vocation of nomads and psalmists, of all wise watchers of herds. He left the cabin and strolled toward them, seeking, as with any new acquaintance, the eyes. He expected a pitiable stupidity, a lovable ignorance, an innocence worth the costs of feed and endless care. But as he squatted beside an ancient ewe, as he met for the first time that direct and all-uncomprehending gaze he was astounded: no preconception could foretell such unspeakable non-intelligence. Their yellow eyes were hideous. They understood nothing, never had nor would. Their sight was no perceiving: it was mere radar, a cold, bloodless faculty for determining locations of meaningless objects. The eyes didn't disappoint him: they repulsed him. He rose to escape them and had gone a little distance when for no reason the entire flock started and bolted madly away. Dried balls of dung clattered on their hindlegs and tails and he laughed at the sound. That was the first day. At first it seemed funny.

Weeks passed and he watched them. Sometimes they'd come to him, sometimes flee, but they came only in dumb hope of food and fled only out of habit. They might dash to their deaths but fear did not compel them. They had two supra-anatomical attributes each: hunger and stupidity. These two let nothing else — not even fear — enter their lives. He thought at first he saw some emotion in their movements, some actual alarm and fright. But that was at a distance. Closer he'd see the unchanging eyes — yellow, gawking, mindlessly calm — and remembering those eyes their liveliest body movements became the random eruptions of sub-animal whim, the operations of bleating machines, the deviations of huge woolly insects. And always the adorning excrement clattered out its imbecilic music. His laughter soon ceased.

There were two dozen of them. Then one day a dog came and barked. At this they tore, turds rattling, into the trout pond. Thirteen drowned.

Because a dog barked. A small dog with a small voice. Now he had eleven — the survivors, the best swimmers, products of natural selection. It was weeks before their rattles dried.

An old stone wall protected the garden from the flock. Moss-covered and weather-stained, upright and unfailing, it had sheep-proofed flower, fruit and vegetable for a century. There were endless Achilles' heels on that farm, perennial sources of disorder — the rotting posts in the pasture fences, the diseased trees, the weasels in the chicken house, the tansy in the cattlegraze, the muskrats tunneling in the pond-dike. But the gray stone wall was a given: like a hill, like rain, like seasons, it would serve. He looked once, admired it, and forgot it.

One dusk in late May he returned from town with a pick-up load of chicken scratch. His flock reclined in the garden, too glutted to stand. A mere dozen stones were tumbled from the wall, but through that fissure they poured like a plague of fleecy locusts, devouring the ripening strawberries, tiny stalks of corn, frail heads of lettuce, cabbage, broccoli, bell peppers, twisting tendrils of beans and peas, and no amount of work or money could restore the growing-time lost. The garden was destroyed, yet the sheep showed no guilt, no defiance, not even satiation or satisfaction: they simply drowsed, munching the last of his herb-garden, the same blank idiocy in the ugly yellow eyes. He stood by the wall, frozen with rage, cursing it for a traitor. He ran for a shovel and beat the sheep back to their fold. He fetched barbed wire and strung it in the gap, gouging his hands and thinking as he worked of the vast plains of Spain turned to desert by the grass-killing flocks. He thought of grizzlies and cougars hounded and shot out of existence, of eagles poisoned — vomiting out their entrails in flight, of wolves eating at their own trapped feet, of coyotes nibbling baits that burst, shooting cyanide into their heads, of helpless cubs clubbed to death — all for the sake of these shit-encrusted zombies. He thought of David, of Christ — the impossibly good shepherds with their senseless compassion for these drivelling creatures. What a waste, the love of sheep. He finished the snarl of wire in the dark. It disfigured the wall like a rip in a painting, like a relic of the European War. He was pleased. He hoped the sheep would attempt to cross it.

He had wine for dinner, and mutton — one of the drowned. A one course meal. He gorged himself on it.

Long bitter days of replanting followed. But slow-burning anger lent its crooked inspiration and the work went fast. Before the garden was finished two ewes lambed; both bore twins, but only two survived. The burying of the dead lambs and the toddling dances and cries of the survivors cooled his anger, but he reminded himself that by winter all innocence would give way to the insectile ignorance of the full-grown. Still, he'd catch himself smiling at the lambs and the thought of them caught in the barbed wire began to nag him; so he bent at last to the task of repairing the breach in the wall.

On an early August morning after finishing the chores he decided to fix the breach before breakfast. He began by removing the wire. He then proceeded to drop the largest stone in the gap: to heave it into place took all his strength, and as the boulder thudded down it set an avalanche barking down into his shins. He writhed and snarled out the conventional curses.

He began again by placing the now numerous small rocks in the cracks. When he'd placed eight, thirteen came tumbling. They missed his shins but he cursed the same. Two constructive efforts and the breach was a sheep's length across now. He began again, more carefully, but it only took more time for the same result: avalanche. He swore softly now, confusedly, but crude and clear again as a clatter of dungballs announced his flock come to watch.

He ignored them and began again. And again. And again and again, each time faster and more furious till frustration twisted at his head and empty stomach as the avalanches fell. When the breach was two sheep lengths, he ceased. A creeping desperation put an end to his curses. He pondered instead. The idiot flock remained, patient and watchful — even the lambs. Some stood, some reclined, some slobbered cuds, but all eyes waited upon him; he swore he'd make them his meat in due season.

But this day of this season he stood stymied and gaping like one of the flock, ogling the runestones scattered before him, the wall from whence they'd come but which now refused to readmit them, back at the stones, back at the wall, the stones, the wall, the stones. They were the same stones that had come from the wall, yet he could no more restore them than raindrops to clouds or days to bygone seasons. Even the sheep had done better than he: they'd made a small hole in accord with a gastronomically sensible intention. *He'd* made a huge hole with the intention of plugging a small one.

He stood long and silent among the ruins. At last it occurred to him to wonder that the wall had no mortar, no bracing, no tapering toward the top, nothing to hold it together — yet there it stood, impossibly erect and slender. At last he began to see the beauty of the wall and knew that before he'd seen nothing. He'd seen a wallshaped stack of rocks, a wall like any wall...until it failed him. But its failure now forced him to discover that a century ago a man endowed with nothing but hands and a mind had composed this wall of nothing but rock and gravity. No stone had been placed at random. His barked shins cried out that no stone *could* be placed at random; they'd cracked against a work of art, an art called *drystone masonry*. And he lived in a land of barbed wire fences where the masons worked no more. Were this tumbled wall to stand again his hands must learn what their hands knew. He must find in each stone the center of gravity, for each gap the stone that would not shift as the weight upon it grew. From this rubble of fallen rock must rise a single, solid thing.

He began again. He picked up and contemplated a solitary errant stone. The sun and flock bore witness. From the work of seeing alone the sweat began to pour. Unmoving, he held that first stone long. At last he began to turn, to fondle, to shift it in his stupid hands, pondering moss and weatherstains like an illiterate goggling lines in a book. Slowly, painstakingly, he began to try it in place after place, at last letting it come to rest in the gap it seemed to fill as it filled no other. One by one, stone by stone he sought and fitted, doubted but strove to make from the many a whole. He placed three. He placed seven. As he laid them in he pushed and pulled them, jarred and tested. If they gave too easily he tried another. He placed eleven,

placed fifteen, spending long moments huddled over each stone. At the six-
teenth a piece of wall shifted and five fell out. No avalanche. Just five. His
satisfaction was immense. He placed four, seven, nine more. He began to
place first pairs, then triads, then larger combinations of stones that held
in conglomerates as they couldn't hold alone. He learned to center the balance
of each stone so that gravity pulled it *inward* and down, never outward. He
said later that he began to sense in the most nearly perfect placements a kind
of content, a relief, almost a pleasure in the stones themselves. He said it
entered his hands, his arms, his back, his head, and without thinking he'd
begun to sing. He said the song had no words and he sings poorly. But his
flock listened.

Hours flew past, and birds. Again and again stones would fall, but always
fewer. And always he'd feign detachment, feign an infinite patience, keep
singing. His back grew weary, his hands scuffed but cagey. He lifted, shifted,
pulled, shoved, balanced, tested, sweated, sang. The flock stayed on in the
shade of the closest firs. The sun crossed the sky. The patience and detachment grew less feigned. Glimpsing his audience now and then, he began to
marvel that they remained. He began to talk with them, and with the stones,
to sing to them, to imagine in their eyes an idiotic interest. They watched,
making no comment.

At last, unbreathing, with aching back and bleeding hands he placed the
final stone. He tested it. The wall stood strong. He turned to his flock and
made obeisance. He said both lambs bleated in reply.

He walked slowly to the trout pond. The entire flock followed. He said
he knew they only wanted food. He said he thought he knew. But they
watched as he swam, watched on as he dried and dressed, watched on as
he rested in the shade of the firs and gazed at the green water. They had
no reason for being there. They had no reason for being anywhere. So he
said to himself. But there they were, watching. And as they stayed near he
began to love them. He called them his idiots. They didn't mind.

He looked at the pond and he looked back at them. He said he began to
see that they were like the pond — like water. Neither wise nor stupid, really.
They simply were. That's all. He said he saw then that sheep and water are
old, old things, that they'd been just as they are for a long time. He said
he knew then that almost anything — trees, seasons, hills, walls, sheep, suns,
waters — anything that old could teach him something.

Fall came, and a good harvest from the replanted garden. Winter came,
and the two lambs became sheep without his noticing. He said that taught
him that sheep are innocent as lambs, only uglier and larger. And he didn't
know why, but from the day he restored the wall his idiots never tried to
cross it. Their eyes stayed as blank and yellow. They continued to rattle as
they ran. They remained the dumbest animals he'd ever met. But they were
his idiots. He said that though they could never return the love of shepherds,
there would be no shepherds without them. He said that though they couldn't
quite make him a shepherd they had made him a drystone mason. And he
said they at least let him glimpse the love of shepherds, with their patience

31

like the wind. Like the wind that riffles flame, that flickers water, that caresses, coaxes, embraces — forever and perhaps for naught — even the stolidest of stones.

Death of the Right Fielder
Stuart Dybek

After too many balls went out and never came back we went out to check. It was a long walk — he always played deep. Finally, we saw him, from the distance resembling the towel we sometimes threw down for second base.

It's hard to tell how long he'd been lying there, sprawled on his face. Had he been playing infield his presence, or lack of it, would, of course, have been noticed immediately. The infield demands communication — the constant, reassuring chatter of team play. But he was remote, clearly an outfielder (the temptation is to say outsider). The infield is for wise-crackers, pepper-pots, gum-poppers; the outfield is for loners, onlookers, brooders who would rather study clover and swat gnats than holler. People could pretty much be divided between infielders and outfielders. Not that one always has a choice. He didn't necessarily choose right field so much as accepted it.

There were several theories as to what killed him. From the start the most popular was that he'd been shot. Perhaps from a passing car, possibly by that gang calling themselves the Jokers who played 16 inch softball on the concrete diamond with painted bases in the center of the housing project, or by the Latin Lords who didn't play sports period. Or maybe some pervert with a telescopic sight from a bedroom window, or a mad sniper from a water tower, or a terrorist with a silencer from the expressway overpass, or maybe it was an accident, a stray slug from a robbery, or shoot-out, or assassination attempt miles away.

No matter who pulled the trigger it seemed more plausible to ascribe his death to a bullet than to natural causes like say a heart attack. Young deaths are never natural; they're all violent. Not that kids don't die of heart attacks. But he never seemed the type. Sure, he was quiet, but not the quiet of someone always listening for the heart murmur his family had repeatedly warned him about since he was old enough to play. Nor could it have been leukemia. He wasn't a talented enough athlete to die of that. He'd have been playing center, not right, if leukemia were going to get him.

The shooting theory was better, even though there wasn't a mark on him. Couldn't it have been, as some argued, a high powered bullet traveling with such velocity that its hole fuses behind it? Still, not everyone was satisfied. Other theories were formulated, rumors became legends over the years: he'd

33

had an allergic reaction to a bee sting, been struck by a single bolt of lightning from a freak, instantaneous electrical storm, ingested too strong a dose of insecticide from the grass blades he chewed on, sonic waves, radiation, pollution, etc. And a few of us liked to think it was simply that chasing a sinking liner, diving to make a shoe-string catch, he broke his neck.

There was a ball in the webbing of his mitt when we turned him over. His mitt had been pinned under his body and was coated with an almost luminescent gray film. There was the same gray on his black, hightop gym shoes, as if he'd been running through lime, and along the bill of his baseball cap — the blue felt one with the red C which he always denied stood for the Chicago Cubs. He may have been a loner, but he didn't want to be identified with a loser. He lacked the sense of humor for that, lacked the perverse pride that sticking for losers season after season breeds, and the love. He was just an ordinary guy, .250 at the plate and we stood above him not knowing what to do next. By then the guys from the other outfield positions had trotted over. Someone, the shortstop probably, suggested team prayer. So we all just stood there silently bowing our heads, pretending to pray while the shadows moved darkly across the outfield grass. After awhile the entire diamond was swallowed and the field lights came on.

In the bluish squint of those lights he didn't look like someone we'd once known — nothing looked quite right — and we hurriedly scratched a shallow grave, covered him over, and stamped it down as much as possible so that the next right fielder, whoever he'd be, wouldn't trip. It could be just such a juvenile, seemingly trivial stumble that would ruin a great career before it had begun, or hamper it years later the way Mantle's was hampered by bum knees. One can never be sure the kid beside him isn't another Roberto Clemente; and who can ever know how many potential Great Ones have gone down in the obscurity of their neighborhoods? And so, in the catcher's phrase, we "buried the grave" rather than contribute to any further tragedy. In all likelihood the next right fielder, whoever he'd be, would be clumsy too, and if there was a mound to trip over he'd find it and break his neck, and soon right field would get the reputation as haunted, a kind of sandlot Bermuda Triangle, inhabited by phantoms calling for ghostly fly balls, where no one but the most desperate outcasts, already on the verge of suicide, would be willing to play.

Still, despite our efforts, we couldn't totally disguise it. A fresh grave is stubborn. Its outline remained visible — a scuffed baldspot that might have been confused for an aberrant pitcher's mound except for the bat jammed in the earth with the mitt and blue cap fit over it. Perhaps we didn't want to eradicate it completely — a part of us was resting there. Perhaps we wanted the new right fielder, whoever he'd be, to notice and wonder about who played there before him, realizing he was now the only link between past and future that mattered. A monument, epitaph, flowers wouldn't be necessary.

As for us, we walked back, but by then it was too late — getting on to supper, getting on to the end of summer vacation, time for other things, college, careers, settling down and raising a family. Past thirty-five the talk starts about being over the hill, about a graying Phil Niekro in his forties still fanning them with the knuckler as if it's some kind of miracle, about Pete Rose

34

still going in head-first at forty-two, beating the odds. And maybe the talk is right. One remembers Mays, forty and a Met, dropping that can-of-corn fly in the '71 Series, all that grace stripped away and with it the conviction, leaving a man confused and apologetic about the boy in him. It's sad to admit it ends so soon, but everyone knows those were the lucky ones. Most guys are washed up by seventeen.

The Tom in Particular
Thomas Farber

The cats were pushing for dinner as though they had God on their side, making no allowance for the shift the night before off daylight-saving time. The orange tom, having earlier suffered the ignominy of being shooed out for nagging, dropped off the garage roof (from which he could survey most of the human movement in the cottage) onto the redwood fence, sailed to the ground when he reached the gate, and sprinted through the cat door into the kitchen. Arriving at the threshold of the living room with heartfelt urgency, convinced at the very least by his own velocity; surely it was time to eat.

Though the two other cats — the huge tortoise-shell female and her much smaller black-haired mother — spatted obligingly as the tom made his entrance (their strategy being to demonstrate that only hunger pains could drive them to such uncharacteristic squabbling), their mistress was too preoccupied to pay them any mind. She was unpacking, finally, the trunks, bags, and suitcases she'd brought back from her parents' home, the welter of childhood baubles, inherited valuables, and flea-market finds she'd left there the nearly ten years she'd been on her own.

She'd always insisted that nothing of hers be thrown out, arguing long distance more than once against her mother's resolve to "clean up the children's rooms once and for all." It was not until her parents announced their decision to give up the house for an apartment, however, that she'd gone to fetch what was hers.

Of course she had always kept with her some few treasures. A black cashmere overcoat, once her mother's. Two Mesopotamian spun-gold earrings that tinkled like bells when she wore them. A necklace of black seed pearls given to her grandfather by fishermen on the river Don. And several silver buckles, from a belt of her grandmother's, each engraved with a maiden in profile (right hand cradling a crescent moon, left bearing a garland of lilies).

But at last, now twenty-seven, she finally had all her things again. "Market value four hundred dollars, tops," her husband said from the soft chair in the corner. Newspaper in his lap, shaking himself awake to survey the unpacking.

"Oh stop it, will you," she said, thinking she'd just as soon be alone. "You don't even know what these things are."

"Artifacts from a previous incarnation? Salvage from Pompeii?"

"Is that supposed to be funny?" she responded sharply. "I don't need to hear it." Just looking at the work ahead made her want quiet and space; she found her husband's voice particulary intrusive. It would help considerably if he — and the cats — just disappeared for a while.

"Sorry. No offense," he said.

Unable to tell from the tone of her husband's voice if he meant it, or if his grin was really apologetic, wondering why she even had to try to figure him out, she glared in his direction. Even this took her far from her thoughts.

"I said I'm sorry. I meant it."

"O.K., O.K. Forget it. I'm busy."

Shaking her head, finding none of her husband's tricks amusing, her mind teased by the rush of associations each object summoned up, she walked over to the stereo. Putting on her father's favorite. Stravinsky's *Firebird,* which she'd heard so many times as a child, Pachelbel's *Canon in D* ready to follow, wearing white tights, a black leotard, and black tooled cowboy boots, she began to cull the jumble into three categories.

CLOTHING

A grey linen schoolgirl's jumper, at least fifteen years old, which still fit her. A sleeveless cotton tennis shirt. A poor-boy sweater with jewel neckline knitted by her sister. Two pairs of straight-leg corduroy pants. "Way too short for my father. Mother got them in a thrift shop."

"What?" her husband said, busy in the sports page, unable to tell if she was talking to him or to herself.

"Nothing."

Jodhpurs with leather kneepads. A visored riding helmet covered in black velvet. Leather pants. "Ruined," she thought, remembering how, years before, she'd waded into a saltwater pond when the family's German shepherd had fallen through the ice. And then stood shivering in the cold, watching the dog, memory so short, chasing a cormorant down the beach, while she'd wondered if the pants could be saved. Now holding them up, inspecting them carefully, she was sure they were finished.

She pressed on. A sky blue velvet dressing gown with an Elizabethan collar. Two mutton-sleeved bodices: one red silk, the other forest green taffeta with ivory cuffs and dickey. Anderson tartan Bermuda shorts. A silk Anderson dress tartan scarf, with bits cut from it. Rosettes for her grandmother's grave.

A skirt of French ribbon grosgrain. A mustard seersucker peasant skirt and blouse. Pleated cream crepe evening pants. An English wool houndstooth jacket. A pair of turn-of-the-century silk ladies' drawers. Her mother's old bathing suit: flowered pleated rayon with full skirt and fitted bodice. Bright pink.

A pinafore with whale spouting. A brick-red Ferragamo knit suit, never worn. A white terrycloth beach jacket. A pencil-cut purple raincoat. A natural raw silk overcoat, also her mother's.

37

Chartreuse linen shorts. A Georgian flannel dress with lace collar. An A-line unbleached muslin wraparound skirt, with buttonholes in the shape of dolphins. A velour hat, cabbage green. "I'd never wear something like this, would I?" Her husband, dozing off again, was slow to respond. "Would I?"

"Would you what?"

MATERIAL

Black crepe with embroidered silver clouds. Strawberries, lots of them, on a circular flowered patchwork. Organdy and piqué patchwork, all in different whites. Swaths of voile and poplin. French silk organdy, cloud blue with salmon polka dots. "The color of St. Joseph's Aspirin for Children," she thought. Blue cloth flowers. Satin ribbons. Sequins. A lace butterfly.

Several yards of Chinese linen, small golden horses crossing at full gallop. "It hung over my bed when my room was yellow. I was a horse maiden."

"How old are horse maidens?"

"Are you awake now?"

"More or less."

"I was eleven or twelve. That's horse-maiden age. I had to ride an enormous pinto. Cherokee. He was almost impossible to control. He gave me nightmares. He had a hard mouth."

"What's that?"

"You could rein in hard, but he'd keep on going, biting the horse in front of you. Then that horse would wheel or kick. Cherokee was more like a pony."

"What's wrong with ponies?"

"They're vicious and ornery, cunning, they don't respond easily. Cherokee was full of tricks. He'd rear when you put a foot in the stirrup. Or try to nip the person who was giving you a leg up. When he got too far out of control, my teacher would come over and poke at him with a pointed stick."

"Why did you ride him, then?"

"I had to. It was my teacher's way of making me learn not to give in to a horse. I was always scared of Cherokee, but even so he was a beautiful animal. I loved him."

"Pre-pubescent maidens turned on by their noble steeds?"

"Very funny."

USABLES (AND SOME OTHER THINGS)

Damask curtains. Moss green linen sheets, soft and worn like flannel. A wicker laundry hamper. "I'm going to paint it white. It should be white." Several silk lamp shades. Red tumbleweed from the Mojave Desert.

Bags of metal shavings (curls of copper and brass). Scissors from Finland. All sorts of biscuit tins, tall and cylindrical, from Fortnum and Mason's or Jackson's of Picadilly. Three Dundee marmalade jars. A picture frame of plaster — painted to look like wood — set on wood, with ailanthus leaves engraved. A pair of finger cymbals for belly dancing. An ornate silver pomegranate.

"What can you do with that?" her husband asked.

"With what?"

"The artificial fruit."

"The pomegranate?"

"If that's what it is. Why does it go with the usables?"

"It's good for storing things in. Like hairpins."

"Oh."

A needlepoint pincushion, filled with sand. Eaton's cards, embossed with her name, for thank-you cards her mother had to force her to write. A box of perfumed dusting powder, with puff.

Ernest Thompson Seton's *Rascal. The Peregrine,* by J.A. Baker. A guide to ferns. *The Art of the Japanese Kite.* Four books on coyotes. And an enormous index, with watercolor illustrations, of North American wildflowers.

Cans of oatmeal, a gift from her mother. Not to be eaten, but to be used instead of soap (packed with a bottle of vinegar for restoring the pH balance to the skin). And from her father, a recording of Donizetti's opera *Betly.*

"Betly's a beautiful girl who spurns her lover."

"Sounds depressingly familiar."

"But she accepts him, finally."

"Then there's hope?"

She paused in her sifting, exhausted. Too much of the past had been opened up, and, with her husband in the room, the present was too well represented. She'd have to take it much slower. In the morning, when he was out of the house. As it was, she'd made it through less than half her things.

Still in the corner in the soft chair, newspaper at his feet, her husband was staring at the disorder as if trying to find something — negative, she thought — to say.

"What's the matter?" she asked.

"Nothing. I was just wondering when you're going to have this mess cleaned up."

"Is that really what's on your mind?"

"No."

"Then what?"

"I've given you lots of things too."

"I know that," she answered, startled to find tears welling in her eyes. "I remember."

"Well I forgot. Particularly looking at all your stuff."

"But I didn't."

"Then let's pile everthing I've given you in the living room too."

"What? Now?"

"Come on, come on, give me a hand."

HER HUSBAND'S GIFTS (A PARTIAL LIST)

Three authentic Indian baskets. A treadle sewing machine. One pair of Red Wing Irish Setter work boots. A book of plates of Georgia O'Keeffe's paintings. One down parka, one down sleeping bag. A set of foul-weather gear, including Captains Courageous rain hat. An electric juicer. One rigging knife, one Swiss army knife. An oriole's nest. A wasp's nest. A duck's wing. A set of salmon's teeth. The sound track from *Saturday Night Fever.* A recording of Bach's suites for cello. "And there's lots more," he said as the pile grew, "not counting the roses for your last birthday. Let me think."

Still not fed, the cats practiced the feline equivalent of Zen meditation: tortoise-shell haunched on the wicker hamper; her black-haired mother curled on the damask; orange tom camped on the chartreuse shorts. The tom in particular despaired that the inventory would ever end.

Pink, Blue and Gold
Patrick Foy

The girls played well, but it was not an obsession with them. They were French, beautiful, childlike and sophisticated, lived in the countryside, and had their own tennis court in their backyard and plenty of free time in which to play.

In the afternoons during the summer he would ride his bicycle over to their château, on the banks of the Saône, and they would play tennis. Afterwards they would follow an arbored footpath which led to the Saône, and they would go for a swim. The river was murky close to shore and cool. If the girls did not feel like a swim, then he would untie the old rowboat and row them out to a medieval stone bridge not far away, where they could observe the fish under the arcs, resting in the shade.

There were in all six girls and they were bright blondes. The eldest was nineteen and the youngest, five months. The château they lived in was on the outskirts of a small village near Mâcon. This was a region of vineyards and wine cellars which was formerly part of the Duchy of Burgundy.

Architecturally, the château was undistinguished. It was scarred and weather-beaten. It was perhaps two hundred years old. But it was a thing of beauty and made you daydream about the past.

One day while waiting for the girls to come out to play, he sat down under a tree in the backyard. He closed his eyes and listened to the leaves against the wind and to the sounds of an occasional car passing through the village.

Gabriel was standing in front of him a few minutes later when he opened his eyes. She was smiling. She put her hands on her knees and said. "*Bonjour, Jêrome!*"

He had been wine-drunk when he stepped off the train from Paris at the beginning of the summer, and on a whim he had introduced himself as Jêrome. He liked the sound, but it was not his name. It sounded especially good in French.

He lifted himself from the ground and shook Gabriel's hand and then gave her a kiss on the cheek. Gabriel pouted her lips in a playful fashion. She told Jêrome to follow her.

He followed Gabriel to the house, then through the kitchen, across the pantry with all those dishes in all those cabinets, and between antique furniture

41

to the staircase. They climbed two flights of stairs, and arrived at a hallway on the uppermost floor, a kind of attic. The ceiling was low and slanted up there. Jêrome walked quietly behind Gabriel as she went down this hall and through a door which led into yet another passageway. She had not spoken a word since first greeting him.

Then Gabriel stopped in front of an unusually wide door and said "*Regarde*" softly. She placed a finger across her lips. She opened the door. They walked inside.

Across a small and irregularly shaped room Jêrome observed a round window, wide open. It framed the summer countryside below. A gentle breeze came from the window, and he could see the stone bridge downstream, a dark blue sky, and the Saône. The rolling countryside, interspersed with poplars and vineyards, led to the horizon. An old fisherman sat on the opposite bank of the river. Overhead, shafts of sunlight cut through the sky, turning the clouds pink in anticipation of sunset.

In the center of the room was a very small antique bed. An empty space of wooden floor separated it from the five walls. Down within the cozy interior of this bed rested the youngest member of the family, who was wide-awake. She was staring out the window at the clouds.

When Jêrome placed his two hands on the rim of her crib, the child reached up at once to grasp a hand. Cheerful and excited, she held onto it as tightly as she could. Then her sister took his free hand and held it for a much longer time.

Sable's Mother
Pat Therese Francis

The first time he came into me I felt it again — the sweetness that takes hold of you so deep it brings tears to your eyes, the sweetness you know you can never quite hold. Somehow things just never go right between me and the men people. As for this one, I knew he was half-crazy, in and out of the place polite folks call "the retreat", and married to that fat woman who sits out waiting for the mailman every day like she's expecting something. Lots of times I've wanted to go out and ask her what the *hell* she thought that mailman had in his truck for her. Lots of times I've been tempted to go out there and shake her heavy shoulders and say, "Don't you know ain't nothing coming for you? Nothing!" But instead, there I was in bed with her crazy man.

After Billy Snow, I really thought all of that was over for me. I had come to Billy with one baby, and when all the sweet was used up, I'd left with four. Now what did I want with more of that?

And you know, all I really wanted from that married crazy man was a ride. I was walking home from the grocery store with Scottie, my youngest, riding one arm, and a bagful of fruit and milk in the other when he stopped his beated-up car. It was hot; Scottie was tired and whiny; and my paper bag was about to give out. I guess you could say he came along at just the right time. If the bus to hell had pulled up when that crazy man did, I would have surely got on it, as long as it was air conditioned on the way.

I'd seen him before. I'd seen that he was built long and lean, that he'd let his wife get fat having his babies, while he just got leaner and crazier. I'd seen him, but not close enough to look at the flecks of gold in his eyes like I did when I found myself in his car. That's when I saw there was something still strong in him, something still hungry, something the woman who sat by the mailbox couldn't touch. But what surprised me most was that I found out there was something strong in me that answered him, something that wanted to lay down in his craziness and fuck until I had no tears left, until my back ached, and my arms were sore from trying to hold what I never could.

I didn't come. I never do anymore except when I touch myself in the gentle, easy way the men sometimes forget. I used to come and come, but now all the sadness gets in the way, and the only way I know to give in to the sweetness of men is to cry and ache.

I stopped taking from the men two years ago, a short time before Billy Snow left. If I could have faked, like they say a lot of women do, maybe me and Billy could have made it right again. It sure didn't help things any when he saw me lying under him with my eyes wide open, just staring as if to look clear through to his skull, as if to look right past everything alive in him and into the black hole behind it. One night when I lay there like that, not moving, not feeling, he just let loose and surprised my jaw with his fist. Once he started, he couldn't stop. He beat me till he came, till all the house was awake and full of lights, till I learned to cry and ache whenever a man touched me.

That was right around the time my oldest girl, the one I got before Billy Snow, started to grow breasts under her cotton shirt. She was only nine, like I'd been when I started to learn about the womanhood thing. "So fast!" I said to her, slapping her face, not because she was starting to become a woman, but becase she *liked* the idea, because she started looking in the mirror a lot, tilting her face this way and that, and asking me if I thought she was pretty.

When she was born, I was fifteen. I called her Sabra, because I'd never known anyone named that, and because it sounded like sabre-toothed, or a sabre sword — something you better look out for. The first and only time her daddy ever came to look at her, he picked her up and rubbed her soft baby skin against his cheek. Then he unbuttoned his shirt and held her inside it against that close hair I used to love. "What you say my girl's name was — Sable? Is this my little Sable?" — he said. He knew damn well that wasn't her name, but after he left, I never called her anything but Sable. I kept remembering the way he held her against him like he couldn't get enough of the feel of her skin, and the way he stroked her like a fine fur coat.

Now she's eleven, and the way the boys look at her could make me cry. Even Billy Snow, the last time he came by to see the kids, gave her that look I haven't seen rush to his eyes in a long time. "Come here, Sable girl," he said. "If you aren't getting prettier every time I look at you." Course, I just about went wild, slapping him right across his face, and reminding him he'd never been her daddy and would never be her man, so he could keep his thoughts to himself.

Billy just looked at me real calm and said "You know your trouble, Maggie Snow? You're jealous of that little girl of yours. You're jealous because she's got it all ahead of her."

"What would you know about what's ahead of her?" I said, lashing out like I was the one named after a sabre. "I'm her Mama. I know what's ahead of her — that's what's got me worried."

After he left, I held Sable and stroked her like her daddy did the day he give her her name. "So fast, girl," I said, but this time I didn't say it like I was mad, but just because I was her Mama and I *knew*. And somewhere inside her, she knew what I was crying about because her black eyes were wet too, and she kept saying, "Don't worry, Mama," and petting my hair like she was about a hundred years old.

That's how she acted that hot day I come out of my room with the married crazy man following behind me. I had put Scottie in for a nap, and hadn't expected Sable and the other kids back till supper, so I was a little thrown off when I walked out into the kitchen and saw Sable rocking Lonnie on the hind legs of a dinette chair, rocking and humming. She just looked at me standing there in the white silk slip Billy Snow used to love to take off, as if it weren't nothing unusual for me to walk around half-dressed in the middle of the day.

Of course, when he saw all my kids looking into his face, that lean crazy man wanted to be on his way as soon as he could. "I'll be back," he said, but even Sable looked at him like she didn't believe it.

After I took out the hamburger meat and canned corn I was going to fix for supper, I went to my room to change back into my jeans. When I come out, where was Sable but sitting in front of the mirror, trying on the cinnamon colored lipstick I'd put on for the crazy man. "Sable!" I said, already feeling how bad I needed to slap her face. But when she looked up at me, her lips dark, and her eyes still full of me in that white silk slip, there was nothing I could say. Nothing I could say at all.

Notes from the Bloodwell
Thaisa Frank

Our journey to the rockbed began fifty yards due south where softly-lit tunnel winds underground to the deepest point. As we burrowed along, we felt people inching along in back of us — and in front of my face were two large shoes. Up close, the thin, endolithious membrane was warm, palpable, deceptively opaque — an illusion created by the uneven thickness of the blood. As my eyes got used to the dark, I saw shifting layers of indigo, lavender and vermillion blood, floating like glass beneath the surface. My colleague and I lay on our backs and saw people at ground-level taking samples from the well: Aware that the well is a one-way mirror, they paused and waved — like tinted icons.

Yesterday, our committee was shown slides of a man going quietly to the well at night when other campers in the forest were sleeping. We saw him lower a wooden bucket into the well and allow blood to pour over the laminated sides. He brought the bucket to his car, poured it on the ground, then sat near a cluster of laurel. Blood seeped into the furrows of his corduroy pants, small half-moon crusts formed on his shoes. And we liked imagining the smell of pine, how quiet it must have been.

"The grandmother sitting on her blue-and-white kitchen floor, blood hardening in the cracks, the young father at home alone with the blood...All Americans developing their own approaches to the bloodwell..." (source unknown)

Found a scant half-hour in which I could experience the bloodwell alone. In the course of its cycle, noises rose and fell like waves, and the frail biconcave discs floating on the blue diffusing membranes seemed to make a soft,

46

moaning noise. There was something lonely about this experience — like lying in the dark, listening to another body.

The diurnal rhythm of this gelatinous, 24-foot ellipsoidal sphere remains a mystery as it sways over its hollow 16 feet below the earth. It heaves, sighs, sucks air into its permeable membrane, then reverses its undulation, leaving threads of dying tissue on the soil. The bloodwell is always changing: When we touch its streamers, it becomes an event. When we lean against its soft surface, it's a pillow. And, when we assemble to discuss it, it's a subject of anxiety — so at night, in the tents, there is restless joking. We tell the jokes in the dark and remember them, reluctantly, in the morning.

Activity is constant in the damp tunnel beneath the well: Blueprints. Arguments. Debates. Then sudden departures. Silence.

I find the activity exhausting.

More slides — this time of children, lowering small plastic pails into the well. There were five children, and the delight on their faces was obvious. Each took a small amount of blood in the bucket and ran to the forest to deposit it on the ground. There was no sound-track, but we imagined their voices.

Reports show that everybody who draws the blood feels a 'pervasive sense of peace', forcing our committee to reconsider proposed restrictions.

Every day, we struggle to explain it. There are those who think that the bloodwell is congealed bison blood from a glacial age, those who think that it's a stagnant pond. We have loud, bellowing explanations for the insane, unrevealed explanations for the dead. Today, a Canadian bio-physicist said flatly: "I suppose you're hoping that a confluence will be found — flowing beneath states, connecting Kansas and New York, Georgia and Oregon, Louisiana and Ohio. But what is an explanation but a cat's-cradle of selected facts? You people can't explain. You don't know *how* to explain..."

Today, the head of the committee brought me to his tent and showed me a collection of porous rocks: I think that I'm in love with him.

47

Nov. 1

Met the Canadian scientist while taking samples at the surface. "You Americans meet your parents nervously," he said " — just like weevils in the soil: and *that's* why you're hoping for a confluence."

Nov. 3

Can we pin down the elusive colors of the bloodwell? The forms behind them? Patches of blue fade before my eyes, only to surface in a tenuous response to light. Is the low-keyed blue on the left a reappearance of the deep purple clot I say yesterday? or a new colloid?

Nov. 6

The head of the committee has traveled to North Dakota to retrieve the remainder of his rocks. Sometimes I think I'm fond of him: Then I call him in North Dakota, sharing my hopes, my doubts, my confusions. At these times my thoughts of him are large.

But at other times, my thoughts of him are small — like last night, when I intuited him by his bed, in Mrs. Muteberner's rooming house, looking out a window (at a dog), lying down (it was time to sleep), and dreaming (about a town) — my thoughts going into his dream of the North Dakota night.

Nov. 13

Five days of research on the clotting properties show that platelets increase at ground level — new evidence of differentiated activity. Some feel this makes a stronger case for the existence of a source, while others say it's simply a reaction to increased oxygen at the surface.

Nov. 15

The director of the committee has returned from Fork Falls, North Dakota, with fifteen orange-crates of rocks. Today in the tunnel, he grasped my hand and I pulled him towards me. As we embraced, he murmured: *"Was ist die Blutquelle?"*

Nov. 18

Yesterday, we saw slides of a young couple visiting the well at dusk. They walked cautiously to the well, and the woman lowered a bucket while the man looked on. As she raised the bucket and poured the blood to the ground, he sat near a cluster of laurel, demonstrating the width of something with his hands — as though she'd asked him "how deep is the earth?" and he had answered "this deep!" But as the blood seeped into his clothes, he became quiet, and soon both were leaning against the tree, holding hands.

Nov. 19

The head of the committee left again for a brief lecture tour. I remember his warm hands, his cool face, the rancid smell of the bus terminal. . . And I hurried back to the state forest, not bothering to stop in town.

Nov. 21

Today, when we were shown pictures of a group of people at the bottom of the well, raising paper cups in a kind of toast, we found to our surprise it was ourselves. Although nobody could remember the occasion, close-ups revealed fatigue, a day in mid-fall. Work characterizes the life here: There is talk of remodelling the well into a windmill, and the issue of rationing will come up in the near future. But all of us agree that a close relationship to the blood remains central. To use the well, many of us still struggle to overcome an aversion to the pungent smell, and the sight of our faces reflected in the dark liquid — like the moon on a bright night.

Quills
C. P. Fullington

Gold, yellow from the color of old newspaper clippings to that of overripe corn, orange and all the divisions of red: crimson, scarlet, burgundy, garnet and ruby, russet and cherry, blood and fire. Down below all this color, walking through the leaves — scuffle, scuffle — goes a middle aged woman. By herself. Dangerous business, wandering these woods alone. Especially, the way the small town neighbors would put it, especially for a woman. Who, after all, has no reason to be there. She's not looking up at all that roaring autumnal extravagance overhead, not hunting mushrooms, not collecting bark for some weird crafts project or leaves for the open house at the new junior high. Anything could happen. A convict from the prison. A runaway bulldozer from the county dump. A late, sleepy and irritable water moccasin in a drift of leaves. Concealed holes in which to break an ankle, falling branches, abandoned twists of rusty barbed wire. Better to stay home where the unpredictable was not so available.

Two kids, a husband, a dog and a pair of ricebirds: that's home. The husband is a chemist, the dog's a yellow Lab, and the kids — right now — are a football player and an artist. And the woman, crunching and rustling along, has just turned forty-three, at 6:15 this very morning, has had to suffer through breakfast in bed, one romantic and two cute birthday cards, and a mostly unintelligible telephone call from her aunt Greta. The birthday presents are waiting to be opened after dinner, after they all come home from dinner 'out', dinner at some overpriced family restaurant which she will have to appreciate, in twenty words or more, several times during its course and at least twice afterwards. She knows that routine, just as she knows pretty well what she can expect to find in the presents.

She snorts disgustedly, thinking about the presents, and looks around to see if there's anyone who might have heard. A reflex, that caution, and of course there isn't anyone. That's why she's out in the woods, because nobody goes down the hill from town into the trees except hunters in bird season, and children, and the old guy who owns the hundred acre wood (which is really eighty-seven since the highway went in, according to the old guy himself). Hunting season doesn't start for a week, and all the kids, hers and everybody else's, are in school, so she has the trees and the leaves all to herself. She thinks,

50

slightly amused, that maybe it's the other way around, that maybe the wood has her all to itself for awhile. So she says, out loud and rather slyly, "Show me something. I dare you, old forest."

The forest doesn't produce on command, so she turns off the old cart road she's been following and heads down a gully toward the stream. There at the place where the path branches off the overgrown road, there's not even the faintest suggestion of water talk in the air. But a little way down, ten or fifteen steps, no more, the sound begins, almost indistinguishable from the sound of bees high up in some rotten-crowned maple. She likes to stop when she first hears the stream and back up a few steps until she can't hear it, then step forward again, trying to find the exact point where it begins. Sometimes she stays there for so long, rocking back and forth those two or three steps, that she gets dizzy and has to sit down on one of the logs and shake the faint, insistent humming out of her head.

Today she doesn't try it. The wind is blowing toward the stream anyway, carrying noises away from her. This is not good, she reflects, thinking about why she has come today. The noise she makes, clumping down the slope, is probably audible a quarter of a mile away, to anything other than a human being.

Coming out onto the ledge above the stream, she stops, checking for company again. Several kinds of ferns at her feet, growing out of cracks in the rock; a small fluffy looking woodpecker on the trunk of a maple below the ledge; lots more trees, but the stream bottom is empty of people, or animals for that matter. Sometimes there are deer. She likes finding the animals down there. They're a kind of company she understands, quiet, not too close. Not like her family, who never seem to shut up.

She sits down, after piling up a cushion of leaves with her foot, and leans back against a beech, waiting, looking up and down the black and silver shimmer and riffle of the moving water.

It is those birthday presents which have sent her off today. She would like to know how she ever got such a predictably American family. She picks up a chunk of rock out of the leaves and leaf mold and chucks it at the water. It falls a foot or so short, without even a decent thud. A can of almond roca, she thinks, an engagement book, or address book covered in blue imitation leather, and a record and bathrobe or nightgown from Sam. She can't remember if it was a bathrobe for Christmas, last winter, or if last year was the time he got her those awful after-ski style bedroom slippers with the imitation fur.

"I want," she says, looking up into the branches over her head, "a tin of barley sugar drops, a pair of cashmere and kidskin driving gloves, a two week vacation in Rio with my sister Elizabeth, a new piano, and a llama."

The leaves and branches move, telegraphing a reply down the trunk into her shoulders. She smiles. Leans forward to get a better view of the open space along the stream.

All right, she thinks, not a llama. A porcupine. Make it a slow, prickly, not very intelligent silent porcupine.

"You'd better hurry up with it," she tells the woods, "or I'll be finding my way back through the dark." Then reaching into her pocket for the chocolate bar she's been carrying all week, she settles back into a more comfortable position to wait for her porcupine, or the dark, whichever comes first.

Simpson Among the Angels

John Gerlach

Simpson, a guest at a cocktail party honoring a friend's retirement, finds himself among angels. The one by a window faces a young woman whose dress reveals virtually all of her back, and a fine back it is. Red pendants on her ears bobble as she chats. Another angel, scooping almonds from a dish by the sofa, smiles in response to Simpson's stare. The lady with the fine back and pendants laughs seductively. Simpson wonders if angels flirt.

For the next three days Simpson remains indoors. Aspirin, Rolaids, and herb tea have not dispelled his malaise, and he feels foolish for having taken anything at all. The sky has been overcast and there are stipples on the puddle in the driveway. He knows it's raining even though he hasn't seen the rain fall. Why can't he bring his feelings to words? Lately language has seemed parched and inadequate. He has become as inarticulate as the cat, which has been motivated as long as he's had it only to try to reach the ceiling, and lately it has given up even that. It sits unmoving and simply regards. Simpson is grateful: he has had enough of its scaling the drapes and clawing its way up the front of the fireplace to rest on the mantle.

That evening in a restaurant of high repute, Simpson dawdles over dinner. Before him sits Pompano en Papillote, tiny potatoes, and zucchini sprinkled with parmesan cheese. He is unable to identify any of it, though all of it seems familiar. A lady to his left, recently come from Spain, turns and haltingly confesses that she is in love with the English language. Simpson, touched, shares with her several adverbs and adjectives, a few prepositions, and a possessive pronoun. Perhaps English is after all an adequate vehicle. For the next two days the sky is a brilliant blue, and the cat sits on the porch in its porcelain pose, blinking at the first buds of spring.

A week later Simpson makes his annual visit to the Buick showroom. The air is thick with the clunk of closing doors resonating over the freshly waxed linoleum. He is at the brink of a purchase, an Electra sedan, when he starts — those figures by the blue Skylark coupe — are they angels? Surely he imagines. As the salesman approaches him he slips through the side door. For the next few days instead of retreating he forces himself to public places — the zoo, museums, the parks. Within the week he is overtaken on the golf course by the angels, wishing to play through. They act as if they had been drinking since the first hole. As Simpson opens his mouth to speak, the words stick in his throat. He bogies the next two holes and loses count on the last.

The next few months he spends largely indoors. He drifts, reflects. Sometimes it seems as if each day has been the Fourth of July, and small children wearing fireman's hats and waving tiny flags have ridden bicycles decorated with streamers up the street, screaming with delight; other times it seems as if none of this happens at all. In an effort to settle himself he moves in with his sister Louisa. Still there are questions: will the cat, left at home, rub against the leg of Mrs. Caliguire, come to feed her, or attack, as it did the Feeney girl? And his new situation: Louisa, nearly deaf the last ten years, insists that she doesn't remember inviting him. Nevertheless, she and her husband have been gracious to a fault. They do all they can at Scrabble, accepting his words without question, and do not gloat as they trounce him.

At twilight one evening, Simpson sits with a French grammar in an orchard at the back of Louisa's yard. He reads until the light fails the page, discovering phrases forgotten since school days. French unfolds before him as never before, an arid field surprised by rain. As crickets begin to chirp he eases himself with the recollection of a day as blue as a little girl's dress. When Louisa calls, he is the one who plays deaf. Moments later there is a murmur in the trees. The angels appear, bright as apples, several with wicker baskets and one with a white tablecloth. The one with the tablecloth recognizes Simpson and lifts his hand.

"*Voudriez-vous donc nous accompagner?*"

Simpson rises, elated. The breeze swirling about him, he spreads his arms to greet the visitors and his hands detach, float free. He has begun to liquefy. Silently, invisibly, he and the angels depart. Should Louisa remember to search for him as the night deepens, she will find only the moon and the crickets' chirp.

The Black Daffodil
Ruth Goldsmith

Phone lines went where power lines hadn't yet reached. One can imagine her standing not quite chin-high to the table in those days, eyeing the phone. It would have been the kind that looked like a black daffodil, rising from a solid base on a straight stem to flower-shaped mouthpiece. You lifted the receiver from its holder and the Operator said, "Number, please." The telephone was a weapon against isolation. Somewhere in that little skull, even then — it doesn't seem possible that *all* its uses as a weapon were being realized.

She had a nice bust and ankles, the two most important parts of the American female sex symbol. Also, she photographed and moved best in a framework of chrome or steel, glass, plastic, almost like a maze. The place where her career was born can be traced, too, to the point where she was picked, from the tiniest TV appearance: others never passed beyond that point and most never reached it.

Even when she was at the peak of at least two professions — television and marriage — there was about her what's tagged as the little-girl quality, and if there's a better way of saying it, it must be: she didn't know what was in store for her. Indications are that she realized the real power of the phone at one particular moment, in the manner that some religious awakenings take place.

She said, "If you talk without mechanical assistance, you talk to not very many at a time, and they have to get to the place and you have to get to the place. If you use the phone, you can talk to a number of people in succession, from the location of your choice, moving around if you wish, and finding them wherever they are. And you can keep it secret. It saves the other people something. In fifty minutes, allowing a minute for each completed call, you could talk on the phone to fifty people. Even if they lived fairly close to where you want them to be, it would take most of them more than fifty minutes to meet you there and get back again to where they were. Therefore you are saving, say, fifty people forty-nine minutes each, a total of two thousand four hundred and fifty minutes, or forty hours and fifty minutes. Translate that into dollars at twenty-five dollars an hour and it's one thousand and twenty dollars and eighty-three cents."

"Isn't she a doll," he said. She was in the process of losing her second husband and he was on his way to being the third. They were a match. At that point he could have snapped her in two. He was a powerful American male figure, but not in the public-public eye, only in the small, powerful-public eye. He was as crafty as a dog that doesn't growl because it relishes winning.

She started from a small point on the map and rose to world mention. She progressed from the soaps to shows, to larger parts, and finally to personality, talk and games. The twenty-four inch diagonal of blackmail.

Where does blackmail begin? There may be a correlation between the telephone and liquor. Many a drunk reaches for the phone. Many can't resist long distance. It is not shyness, surely, that makes a person say "Hello". Nor summons another to say it first. An imperative. The habitual caller doesn't mind amplification of own-self in any way, likes publicity, prominence. Someone had to stop her.

There follows a correlation between the telephone, intoxication and violence. One can get intoxicated with the reach of words, the power to strike, and another, someone close, can be forced to strike to stop it. Whoever's at the other end of the line can't. In a telephone, a sounding body is always vibrating and the more rapid the vibrations the higher the note produced. The telephone and alcohol involve the lips and power, hold in thrall. She'd crawl to the phone if she had to, and crawl back if he knocked her away. Ultimately.

Before that, she devised the most magnificent game show of all time, called TELL-A-PHONE. In it — she was hostess, and it worked — the contestants sat in a row of tulip-shaped phone booths, plastic, colorful, and she sat up above them in a suspended sun-shaped booth with switchboard, monitoring their calls. She was the Operator. In advance, contestants told why they'd like to call a particular person, and the calls were made simultaneously. As the conversation in a particular booth became most interesting and revealing, she plugged into it. Switches were frequent, the revelations daring.

Potential contestants were interviewed by the talent coordinator first, then by her, before they were placed in the studio audience to be selected from it by applause of the studio audience. They had interesting stories to tell, associations, links, nuances, innuendoes.

She said, "I can manipulate the whole thing well enough so that I can get what I want from anybody. National or international, a touch of a button and they become ridiculous or scabrous. Men's pants and it's an alcoholic, sex deviate, Communist, bribee and/or wearer of lace drawers. Women's pants and it's silicone from the neck down, pill-popper, lesbian, courtesan and/or lover of blacks. I have control."

She said once, "It takes some of us three tries before we find the right marriage partner. Did you know that it takes three figures repeated to make a design — because the spaces in between have to be established?"

He said, "You're a doll." In his way, he loved her. Finance was his partner, with its handmaidens, politics and arts.

Tele as a word means psychic affinity between two people, no wires. He warned her. He urged her to fly on a certain plane and then urged her not to, and it ended in flames. It was only a warning, because too many too close to too high had crashed in planes to use that as a means.

She never told *all* she knew, whether from warning or from a kind of loyalty or from a backwoods common sense. It was death finally by telephone, a device, tool or weapon strung by electricity. That was part of the mystery.

He put wooden crosses on her grave, poles with crossarms strung with wires and bejewelled with blue glass petticoat insulators. That was back where she started and in time the insulators were stolen because they've become collector's items and there are collectors even out in the sticks, or just passing through.

Childhood

Peter Gordon

Dance grabbed us that year. Dance and exposure and noise. The crowds were easy, the adulation, the envies. You didn't get pegged on conspiracies then, you accepted the anonymous kiss. We developed skills, we wouldn't founder. This was 1954 and we were early in our lives, coming to bloom. America asked for us by name: Mary, Marie, Otto (what the country would have given for Otto's yellow hair), Harry, Bonnie, and me.

Mary was 12, our baby dancer. Harry, Bonnie, and Otto were 13, while Marie beat me to 14 by three days, three lousy days. Really, we were only ballroom dancers at heart. We didn't break much new ground that year. We waltzed, we foxtrotted, we rearranged syncopated feet of the cha-cha with something our manager, Mister Z, called the Pop. The Pop featured the male dancer (Otto, especially, was so adept) kicking his feet at the shins of the female dancer, who backstepped in counterpoint. Done by children, it was fast and lovely. Sometimes Mister Z dressed us in blue tights and we did flips and backflips on rubber matting. We flopped. Mostly, we waltzed, we fox-trotted, we Popped.

We danced in chiffon and tuxedo, under Mister Z's delicate invention. Mary appeared onstage first, curtsied, began to spin. Otto emerged from the wings, beautiful Otto, to take Mary's small hand. They waltzed. They giggled. They stopped. They watched Harry and Bonnie come dancing down from the north end of the stage, maybe waltzing, maybe not. Harry was skinny and Bonnie was thick and slow. But Bonnie dominated the dance, holding Harry at bay, smiling at his feet. Otto and Mary began dancing and smiling with them until something else happened: Marie tiptoed onstage. Dark hair, dair eyes, the beginnings of breasts under chiffon. The four dancers froze. The boys took heart. Otto approached Marie, begged for a dance. Marie refused. Harry approached and Harry was refused. Marie stood waiting, waiting. Who would come to dance with Marie? Onstage, that year, it was me. I danced my way across the floor, towards Marie. Marie noticed me. Marie noticed what a hand-some boy I was. Not as handsome as Otto, but a handsome boy. She put out her hand and I took her hand. Otto took Mary's hand, satisfied with Mary's hand. Bonnie took Harry. We began to Pop pop pop.

Marie and Bonnie were miniature women (there was nothing girlish about the way they danced with a boy), aloof before performances, body-conscious, pretty. I guess you could say I was in love with Marie, who was in love with Otto. Marie was my dancing partner, my height, my weight, my age, but she was in love with Otto.

Then there was Mister Z, who only loved us, only understood us, as dancers. He loved to see children dancing. In 1954 we danced from the Atlantic to the Pacific, performing in casinos and old river ballrooms and glitter dancehalls, transported by Mister Z and his white Cadillac. Onstage, we were celebrated for our lightness. Offstage, we were adored for our reality. I guess that meant our bodies. Being superior, we wore white suits (handpicked by Mister Z) and bunched centerstage at lawn parties like pelicans. It was easy to feign poses for the photographers, getting wild, grabbing headlines out of the blue or out of the toilet (famous photograph of Mary yanking up her underwear in a Newport stall). We were the ones to mention. Mail flooded in from tiny outposts of American life, positively begging for our scribbled initials or locks of our hair (how the country coveted Otto's hair).

We stood for dreams discussed and not dreams deferred, that must have been it.

In 1955 we tried to go back across America, west to east this time, against the grain. It was okay. The photographers took less notice of everyone's prettiness (excepting Otto's). We were a rocket on a downward arch but still a rocket. The dance was rewritten and Marie was dancing with Otto now. Marie danced with Otto and she could have been dancing with me, it didn't matter to Otto. Marie mooned. Mary seemed less fragile. Harry filled out. We played shorter performances, highlighting Otto. Only Otto was extra-magnificent in 1955. Otto was worth everything.

But in September, in the hotel across the street from the Philadelphia Star Theatre, we lost Otto. Everyone lost Otto.

We were about to go on stage.

"Otto is afraid," Harry reported. "Mister Z is holding Otto's head over the toilet."

We wouldn't dance without Otto. Mister Z came to say Otto wouldn't come. Otto was exhausted, Otto was sleepy.

"I won't dance," Mary declared.

We knew what the photographers knew: Otto's beauty made the dance possible in 1955. Mister Z knew. Mary, our baby dancer, knew.

Mister Z was shaking. "Please go dance."

So we tried. After spinning alone, Mary vanished. Bonnie and Harry, even Bonnie, danced hopelessly. Marie and I danced together again, it was very disappointing for Marie.

There was no Pop.

We saw Otto after the performance. He was lying on the bed in Mister Z's suite, wrapped in Mister Z's bathrobe. The radio was playing at his feet. Otto, smiling, said something nice to every one of us. We didn't know what to say to him.

"Fred," he said to me, "I got sick and I can't dance anymore."

I started to cry, and Otto hushed me, and pulled me towards him so Marie wouldn't see.

The next morning, Otto was lifted into the white Cadillac by hotel bellboys. Mister Z tried to keep the curious away but there were flashes of light everywhere. In his last photographs, Otto was wearing a white sweatshirt and sky-blue yacht pants. There were groans because Otto's hair was underneath a baseball cap. The newspapers were speculating right there in the street that Otto was bald from disease.

Without Otto, we returned to earth. By the wintertime, no one was watching. Mister Z cried and cried and cried. When he closed his eyes in bright light, we knew what he saw.

We were obsolete by 1956.

Alan and Arnold

Mark Halliday

June 1963

In a few days Alan and Arnold will graduate from junior high school. During their ninth-grade year they have developed a loquacious friendship. Both boys are shy with girls and smaller than the school's athletes, hesitant and awkward at dances and sports. In the cafeteria and walking home from school they discuss the biggest things, life and death, time and fate, love and ethics. Their conversations are fueled chiefly by Arnold's knowledge and Alan's imagination. Both boys are conscious of this division of gifts and both are willing to make the difference between them seem more absolute than it is. Arnold has already read at least a hundred books whose titles Alan has noted anxiously in libraries and bookstores. Alan has won some notoriety at the junior high for his satirical vignettes about teachers and students. Arnold enjoys Alan's flights of fancy and counts on them to animate each conversation. Alan, proud of his flair for whimsy, is content to bask in Arnold's admiration, while expressing awe and envy of Arnold's precocious erudition. So they play their parts: the dreamer and the philosopher, the writer and the reader.

Tonight they arrive at Anita Schiffler's party together, driven by Alan's father. Anita's parents are wealthy. Their house stretches along the top of a small hill surrounded by rolling lawns and a screen of forest encircling the lawns.

There are more than forty guests at the party when Alan and Arnold arrive, and more are expected. The two friends are quickly alarmed. They only know a third of the guests. Many are older, some are even so awesomely mature as to be within a few days of graduation from Sipples High School. Remarks made by several of the older boys indicate that they *drove* to the party *in their own cars.* This is frightening — if there is one thing guaranteed to win a girl's approval, Alan knows, it is the ability to drive to a party in one's own car. Arnold probably knows this too but is less conscious of such matters, being more resigned than Alan to the fact that love and sex will not transform their lives for a few more years, at least.

Alan and Arnold help themselves to cheese and crackers. Their alarm does

61

not fade as they observe that white wine is available. Wine! Anita is only in ninth grade yet her parents allow wine to be served at her party. Alcohol in any form is a token of adulthood, or pretended adulthood. Alan and Arnold, sensing inevitable defeat, have made it a policy to refrain from competition in the games of pretending adulthood. Their response to this pretense (which they detect in almost all activities of their peers) has matured from timid withdrawal to sullen abstention to defiance — though their defiance seldom manages to become publicly noticeable.

They see Anita chatting with Jack Kempley, who wears an expensive blue sportcoat and a scarlet tie and who has been described as "one of the fastest playboys at Sipples." Kempley is lighting Anita's cigarette. Cigarettes: another token.

"Why are we here?" Arnold mutters. He wants a serious answer.

Alan prefers to joke, gaining time in which to figure out his own attitude. "We want to get married, and the room is filled with eligible divorcées."

"I'm a confirmed bachelor, myself," says Arnold without smiling.

Alan rapidly eats three pieces of cheddar and drinks half a glass of ginger ale. He says, "I feel about as welcome as Mickey Mantle in a hockey rink."

Arnold doesn't reply, but Alan sees he is listening. "I feel about as well-located as George Washington crossing the Danube," Alan offers.

"Or John Howard Griffin crossing the color line." responds Arnold

"Who?"

"I'll tell you later," says Arnold.

"I feel about as local as Huck Finn on Wall Street."

"All right, that's enough," Arnold says flatly. "Let's get out of here."

They pass through sliding screen doors onto a patio. Terry spots them and calls out, "You guys aren't leaving already are you?"

Alan turns and notes that Terry has one arm curled as-if-casually around Joyce's waist. "We're going to play a few holes of golf," Alan says. "Then maybe we'll buy a Jaguar and drive back here."

"Okay, Alan," Terry laughs. Alan and Arnold move down across the dark grass of the back lawn toward a group of maple trees. They can both feel Terry smiling at their backs; he will make some remark to Joyce or Suzie about how weird "the straight A's" are — eggheads.

Leaning against the maples Alan and Arnold ease into a discussion. Both are wondering how candid they want to be about their dislike for the party, their resentment of Jack Kempley and similar Social Successes. They gaze up across the lawn at the bright lights of the long house. Seeing that no lights are on in several upstairs rooms, Alan imagines that boys only a year or two older than he are at this moment exploring untold realms of delight with the loveliest girls of the ninth grade.

"Have you read any James Baldwin?" Arnold asks.

Alan is startled to find that Arnold is even now thinking about books. "Who is James Baldwin?"

Arnold waits a minute before answering, as if to indicate that there are several complicated ways of answering the question. "A writer. He's black."

"I don't think I've heard the name."

"Every single one of these people at this party has white skin," says Arnold.

"I guess that's right. But some of them have managed to acquire fabulous tans." Alan thinks of the most impressive girls, who spend a lot of time at the beach.

"James Baldwin is a man who makes you wonder why there are fifty people here, all of the same race, when more than ten percent of the American population is black."

"A smart Negro wouldn't come to this party if he was invited," says Alan, intending a joke. He realizes this is not a good time for humor because Arnold turns away and falls silent. For five minutes Alan respects the silence. Then he says, "Let's explore the estate."

Arnold shrugs. Alan starts to move, and Arnold slowly follows. They begin to walk silently along the outer edge of the moonlit lawn, in the shadows of the trees. Seven minutes later they have completely circled the house and they pause at the group of maples.

"That's one lap," says Alan. He wonders if they will go back into the house for more snacks, maybe some rum-flavored cake.

"Let's do twenty," says Arnold. His tone is almost grim.

By the time they are finishing their fifteenth circumnavigation of the Schiffler estate they have attracted considerable attention among the partygoers, particularly those most bored and those most anxious for something to talk about. A group of eight or ten gathers on the patio and hails them each time they pass. Alan and Arnold, by unspoken agreement, refuse to acknowledge the boisterous audience in any way. But they do increase their pace so that they circle the house every four minutes, and their acceleration makes their mysterious travel appear strangely purposeful to the loud onlookers up at the house. Those who feel most unpurposeful in their revelry (or simulated revelry) are the most intrigued by these two silent walkers out there at the edge of darkness.

Alan grins at Arnold. This is starting to be fun. Arnold allows himself a tight smile. Discipline, he seems to be saying, discipline — the success of their mission will depend on the steadfastness of their dedication to this silent repetitive journey. After the twentieth lap Alan whispers: "What is our goal now, Captain? Thirty? Forty?"

"Just to *be* here," says Arnold. "Out here in the dark."

Some of the partygoers decide that the walkers' challenge — if it is a challenge — must be met. They move out to the edge of the lawn below the patio and form what is either a greeting party or a roadblock. When Alan and Arnold come into view they are hit with a barrage of mocking salutations. Alan is excited and scared. Some of those boys are big and powerful — they might try to interrupt the walking by force. Arnold remains utterly silent and does not slow down. Alan stays in step.

When they are within twenty feet of the assemblage and it is clear they don't intend to stop or even pause, several angry voices rise: "What are you guys, zombies?" "How can they be the straight A's if they walk in circles?" "You'll never make the Olympics at that speed!" "Some people really know how to waste time!" Other voices (including Terry's) are just curious: "Why don't you guys take a rest?" "Are you trying to make some kind of a statement?"

Jack Kempley, or someone like him, grabs Arnold's shoulder. Arnold twists free and says in the sudden silence: "No more water, the fire next time." Then before the assemblage reacts he leads Alan through it and they go on walking, ignoring the cascade of derision thrown after them. When they reach the other side of the house Alan asks Arnold what he meant about the fire next time.

"I don't know. It was just a quote," Arnold says.

They smile at each other in the dark. This, they know, is a triumph they will remember. They have made themselves more interesting than the party. They do a few more tours around the house, then Alan phones his father for a ride home.

Love in the Library John

Carolyn Hardesty

Listen. I was just standing in the library's third floor bathroom, and I was drying my hands under the dryer — you know, the ones I love that talk about the danger of diseases transmitted by towels. Ick. Towels. The very word. Anyway, I'm standing there and the only other woman in the place has already dried her hands, in fact pushed the dryer button for me on her way to the mirror to primp. Do people still say "primp" and mean it? She's pulling her fingers through her hair anyway, and I'm standing there rubbing my hands under the air like it says to do and suddenly she leans toward me, puts her hands on my cheeks and kisses me on the mouth. I'm stunned. In the safety of my own bathroom. I mean no way. So I don't know what's next. Do I go to the information desk and report a — what? An attack in the can? That'd get a big hoot in the staff lounge. And look at me. A mid-decade hair slashing — not one of those rainbow dyejobs, but let's say it makes my dad uncomfortable. They'd probably think it was a lovers' spat.

She leaves, by the way, right after the — well I suppose I have to call it a kiss though I'd rather not. She smiles a little but hardly looks at me. I'm just using peripherals, of course.

After she's had plenty of time to disappear, I grab my book bag and go back to the study lounge. But I can hardly work. The thing's driving me crazy.

The next morning I run into Morgan at the union. Do you know him? We both figured it out. And now we just swap tapes and he asks me who's my barber and sometimes we have lunch. So I decide that Morgan can be trusted. That's how I feel about him. And I tell him about this weirdness in the library.

You know what he does? He bursts out laughing. I mean hysterically and people are looking and I'm dying and I could kill him. But since I can't, I just yell. "Morgan, get the hell out of my life." And he leaves, but on his way says I made it all up. "A great story," he says. What an ass. I'm sure he believed me. He just wanted a laugh. I mean, *me*. How could I make up such a thing? Who would want to?

Well O.K., laughing's all right once in a while. In fact listen to this. I don't think I ever told you. Remember Harvey? The guy from the sailing club? Well, Harvey had his faults but omigod, what a lover. He put me on a tightwire — terrific. But I always hyperventilated — not terrific. I called the women's clinic, right? I mean it's not something you write home about. The receptionist thought it was a scream but she wouldn't let on at first. She just said it was a new problem and maybe I wanted a doctor to call me back. Ha, no thanks. We talked some more and came up with the obvious. Yes, a paper bag. And we started rattling off all the jokes we knew about having sex with someone who's wearing a paper bag. She probably got fired. The hyperventilating? Harvey fell for some blond who wore pink and green all the time. As it should have been.

So my concentration tumbles some. I study and I go to the library, but I find myself thinking about this woman and about the bathroom and I go way out of my way to find a john that's hardly used. Not easy but some on the upper floors are sparse. Every time I go in, even if it sounds empty, I look everywhere just to check. Empty is always empty, but it's exhausting. I get terrified when I jerk open a stall door, think I'm going to see somebody dead or working on it. You know? It's all the movies we see. Depressing.

Once I thought I saw her going in the doors of the mall, and you know what I did? I headed straight for her. Weird enough? But it was noon and crowded and I lost her right away. If I ever had her.

Another time I was in the bookstore, the one in the union and I was hunting for my i.d. so I could charge a bunch of stuff — they had some great sweats on sale — and it wasn't in my wallet and I eventually found it in my French book. Of course there's a line behind me. Where on this campus isn't there a line? And the guy's ringing up my stuff and there she is about four people back, looking at me like I'm a marble. Like she thinks she knows me but she can't remember why. Boy, did I remember.

You must think my whole freshman year was a fixate on this one thing, this woman. Not true. I had a life. I went to class and had coffee with friends, met a lot of guys, hardly slept, and hit some terrific parties. And I studied, too. I've got to survive this thing. I'm not going to be left out in the cold.

But the inevitable. One morning during finals week in January, I was in the undergrad reading room — my T.A. (a real drip — remember drip?) calls it the undergrad breeding room, thinks he's so funny. No comment. Anyway, for that hour, the place was fairly full, and quiet too. That end-of-term squeeze. I was doing anthro notes and feeling pretty confident about it all. And she's there — three tables away, full face at me. I couldn't believe it. I don't know where she came from. You know when it's all still everywhere how a moving streak of color could just as well be a siren, like a swish in a mud bottom pond. So, a miracle? I doubt it. Just some comment on concentration, I suppose. I'm doing my term paper in psych on it — it's something to be so sucked into your brain that you miss part of the world. Like a private black hole there on demand. Dazzling paper. Well, so there she is. And not just sitting there, but looking at me. Would you die or what? We just keep looking at each other and these little smiles start twisting our lip edges and I for one think I'll burst out laughing. Wonderful. Self-defense, I guess.

She stands up and bounces her head toward the door. I follow, needless to say, right? I mean, it's not the end of the world. We book straight into the john. Yes, *the* john and if I try to tell you my stomach wasn't doing hurricanes...Well. But, believe me, it was O.K., the start of a good thing. It's true. You'd be surprised.

The Emissary
Shulamith Hareven

He came through the back door, weary and angry, even though I had opened the door before he rang. The truth is I had somehow expected him while drinking my coffee, in the vague knowledge that today it would happen again.

He came in like smoke, grey, somewhat stifling, with an unpleasant smell. His remaining hair was yellowish, like parched, abandoned stalks. He sat down on the kitchen chair without leaving hold of his open briefcase, into which he directed his anger.

"Well?" he said impatiently.

"For whom is it today?" I asked, defending myself by making conversation.

He made a disparaging gesture with his hand. A piece of cigarette paper clung to his mouth.

"Orphans from the Sahara. Well, give, come on — give."

I turned slowly to the wardrobe and with submissive hands took out several pairs of shoes. I held them out to him with bowed head, though I had no idea what orphans from the Sahara could do with my high-heeled shoes, which were no longer mine and perhaps never had been, having been lent me for that one evening, for that walk hand-in-hand in the street, for those slightly intoxicated hours, when I was not responsible either for my words, which became impertinent, or my hands, which came to life in a kind of movement of their own, while the heels drummed and soared.

He spat on the floor.

I went back to the wardrobe and selected a dress which had a stain. He fingered the cloth and found the stain at once.

"You, too," he rebuked me. "Just like the rest."

"Perhaps the stain can be removed," I said. Unsmilingly he bared two rows of grey teeth. A profound weariness was reflected in his eyes, a sorrow intermittently replenished; he was like a boxer's old punching bag, still suffering blow after blow, still returning to the hand which struck it.

"A dress," he said bitterly, "a rag with a few threads, while *there* — do you want to me to tell you about it?"

I felt the tears brimming in my eyes even before he began. A curse has afflicted me since birth — call it empathy; for that reason there are some dreadful expressions I pretend not to hear: words like orphans, poverty, accident, bombs, or murder. But that morning he was merciless. He wiped his forehead with open, dirty palm, and said:
"Nuclear tests last year. They were born without . . ."

I blocked my ears so as not to hear, not with my hands but by a kind of faculty I have developed to make myself completely deaf, and knelt down beside the wardrobe drawer, choking back my tears. Time and again when he returned — from Asia, the North Pole, Honolulu, Timbuktu, and the jungles of Brazil — he would threaten me with his stories. And the terrible thing was that I guessed all of them, as if they came out of me. As if they *were* me.

I took out all my coats, and then added my stockings. He pushed me aside, went to the wardrobe and took out a striped, red-and-white skirt, which I used to wear only on mornings when I got up absolutely certain of triumph. I shared a secret with that skirt: it belonged entirely to me and I belonged entirely to it, in days of roaring light.

And now it was being pawed by the ugly, nail-bitten hands of the emissary.

"It's mine," I protested weakly, though I knew what his answer would be.

"Yours," he sneered and spat on the floor, "yours, you—rs."

I asked forgiveness from all my gods for committing the sin of self-adornment, the sin of arrogance. For hadn't I known all the time, all the time, even when wearing it, that it was not mine? — because nothing belongs to you in this world, not even your own body; and the exhilaration it used to arouse in me was but the sweetness of stolen waters, the joy of transgression, the pride of transient sin.

I wanted to give him the skirt myself, but before I could do so he had deposited it, crumpled, in his brief case, leaving me choking on chagrin and pride.
The emissary paid no more attention to me. He brusquely removed everything from the shelves: lingerie, cosmetics, all the contrivances of woman lurking in hiding, beckoning from the shelves, all the delusions of the great hope, all the little acts of creation compounding fantasy.

The wardrobe was now completely empty. He began pacing about the room, as though concluding a repulsive task, removed the roses from the vase and put them in his brief case, stripped off the sheets, leafed quickly through the books and took the best ones.

"What's that?" he suddenly asked, his said, heartrending eyes contemplating the housecoat I was wearing.

"A housecoat," I answered, "there's nothing else left."

He sank into the chair and didn't even get angry, just covered his eyes with his hand.

"In other words," he said slowly, "you're just as rotten as the rest."

I wasn't rotten. I didn't want to be rotten, to dole out pittances, to give in exact measure, like half an oath, half a fast, a divided city, like a broker forever multiplying and dividing. I didn't know how to be rotten, a kind of latent truth is always lurking in the air around me. And only terrifying expressions like orphans or nuclear tests can make it materialize and illuminate it around me. They were born without . . . and I was quibbling over a housecoat.

I undressed. I took a large plastic bag, in which I had once bought all the fruits of the season, and put it on. The red drawstring dangled slackly down, like a wound from my throat to the lower part of my stomach, but the wound did not hurt. The summer sun warmed my arms through the thin plastic. The roses, which were once mine, emitted perfume from the emissary's shabby brief case. I was glad they had left me their memory.

He suddenly turned his head to the wall, leaned his forehead on both clenched fists, and began to cry.
"If you knew," he said, "if you had seen what I saw there. It's incredible, it's incredible that man can do that to man — and to little children too."

I wanted to console him from the depths of my plastic, but I knew there was no consolation for him; that he carried all those things in his heart, bitter and alien.

He went out weeping into the street, and I stood beside the window warming myself in the transparent bag. It occurred to me that it resembled the bag of waters enclosing the fetus; and perhaps that was how it should be — it is always possible to be born.

The smell of monstrous pity remained in the empty room.

(Translated, from the Hebrew, by David Weber.)

Zebras

Edward Hirsch

Think of the sky as a barren desert with a sparse wind rustling through dead grass and the last clouds beaten down into colorless vapors and then hoisted back up as flags, or as the pock-marked fowls of desolate hunters. It's a Sunday afternoon in late August, 1957, and, despite the fact that the day has progressed like a series of long blasts from the furnace, you're still at the zoo with your parents. You've been here since early morning. In fact, the day has gone on for so long that the last cactus has already wilted, the wolves have given up howling, and the wind has lain down in the grass like a broken king, although the sun, the belligerent summer sun, keeps flaming and flaming and flaming up in the sky like a toothache or a heart attack, like something interminable going on inside of you. It won't stop and finally, out of some final boredom, you begin to attend to things. By now you've noticed that the sidewalks aren't white as you'd first thought, but a deep calloused yellow, and the immaculate stone buildings are blemished and stained with colors. For some reason this makes you, well, almost happy, so happy that soon you've discoved all the cages with faded iron bars and doors which haven't been painted. The vendor's umbrella is hardly a rainbow and the walls in the washroom are scarred with strange writing. Perhaps you can't understand all the words yet, but you know they don't belong there. You'd like to memorize the sayings. And later when you run up to ask your father for a dime you decide not to blurt one out, you notice that his hands are bloated and sweating. The sleeves of his shirt are frayed. His collar is dirty. He digs deep down into the cave of his pocket and somehow you already know that the coin he'll find will be thin as paper, yes, and it will be blurred and worn down from traveling.

Once, to test them, you put your hands inside a vicious cage, but all day your parents have been quarreling and quarreling and by now they've given up any pretense of watching you. Not that it matters much since the animals are all too listless to move anyway. The lions no longer even bother to swat away flies, and the last squirrels have stopped chasing each other in the feeder. The monkeys have actually given up mocking you and gone back to sleep, and the giraffes have finally taken their heads out of the treetops. And still the dull rancor of your parent's voices keeps intertwining like rope, driving you away and then, like an undertow, pulling you backwards; snapping your backside and then, after you've moved back into the sun, circling like buzzards and snaring you.

You keep gravitating back to the zebras. What intrigues you about them is that they don't seem to do anything. They simply stand there and remain striped. Like ribs of light. Like a rainbow without colors. Like convicts standing in barred windows, and waiting. The zebras don't have the agility of tigers and they can't fall with the gracefulness of gorillas. They refuse to quarrel in small feeders, or to tumble out of swings like acrobats, or even to grow tall enough to vanish in treetops. They don't mimic or ignore us, and they don't seem to be waiting for us to feed them. But somehow, locked in their exotic skins, they must know we can't help but notice them. And you keep wondering what they're thinking about, what they're waiting for, what's going on inside them. But no matter what you do, even when you shout and throw peanuts, you can't rile or rouse them. You can't get them to reveal themselves. And no matter how many times you go back, you can't separate or name them, you can't pick out individuals. You can't decide which are the males and which are the females, and finally you decide not to return to their cages. But even when you leave the zoo at suppertime, even when your parents have finally stopped quarreling, even when the sun has softened into a soft mist, you know that the zebras are still standing there, vigilant, visible, waiting for something which may not ever happen, patient as early morning, and anonymous as daylight.

On the way home your father says something to hurt your mother and you tell him to shut up. Suddenly he leans over into the back seat and slaps you in the face, just once but hard, though you press down even harder on the floor and refuse to weep. That is itself an achievement, but you've been on your own all day, you're tired, and now you want to punish him.

"Why can't you just leave her alone for once? Why can't you stop picking on her?"

Your father's voice sounds very dull and distant, as if it's coming from far away, from inside someone else. And perhaps it is. "That's not your business, son. I'm afraid that your mother and I have some things to straighten out and I think it would be better if you stayed out of it."

"Do zebras ever eat cactus?" you blurt out suddenly.

Both of your parents look back at you, surprised. You can tell they're gauging the question, gauging you. And you notice that the sky above the car is tinged with color. The highway ribbons out into a long blankness. And the wind bristles on the windshield.

Your father says, "No, they don't."

Thoughtfully, your mother says, "They do, yes, I think they do."

But you can tell her answer is defiant. She doesn't really believe it. And you don't either. Because the question doesn't mean anything. It doesn't make sense.

And now you're lying in bed looking at the ceiling. The lights are out. In the next room your parents have begun quarreling again, an interminable muffle of voices, and though you strain forward to hear them, you can't make out the words. You wonder if they're talking about you, you wonder how they

72

can go on talking to each other for so long, and later you wonder if you're already sleeping. Occasionally headlights slide slowly down the wall. There's a slight lowing of wind at the window. A door slams. Someone starts a motor in the distance, stops, starts it again, and then drives off. The lights are streaked on the ceiling, and all night the moon is revolving in and out of the treetops like an empty carousel; sometimes you can see it, sometimes you can't but always the wind is turning and turning it. There's a sudden creaking of the wheel. A man is standing in the doorway in a dark shirt smoking a cigarette. There are a few ribs notched on the wall. Someone is pulling you up by the back of the neck, someone is reaching for your throat, and suddenly you can see the zebras marching into the room, stretching out like a caravan of mules or a long string of lights, riderless, dazzling you with their eyes, dazzling you with their shuddering striped manes, rolling their heads and then moving past you, ignoring you, moving off into the wind, moving past the cactus, climbing up through the desert toward the stars.

Animals

A. C. Hoffman

The contractor building the house slashes a long gash into the hill — his workers bring their cars, parking them against the foundation. Trees torn from the valley by the bulldozer lie scattered at the edge of the new lane, uprooted boulders line the edges of the highway. Cars and vans bouncing toward the new house in second gear soon wear the soil down to clay. When the rains begin that autumn they are mired up to the hubcaps. An enterprising garage owner ten miles away is called to the site at least once a week and charges them portal to portal for using his wrecker.

The animals who had been living in burrows and hollow trees close to the excavation leave the area. The hibernators make new escape routes to their burrows, digging tunnels above the bedrock but well under the house. The foundation now sprouts fingers toward the sky as the men work overtime to close in the house before the first snow. Each night flocks of geese land in the pond, landfall until the next dawn when they rise, wings quivering to meet the light, massing for another day's flight.

At first he lives both inside and outside the house — creating new paths in the woods, finding the ravine where a stream runs clear in spring only to dry in summer, where patches of ice form in autumn and disappear under the blankets of heavy January snow. He walks freely, never doubting that the paths and the woods belong to him. He sees no one, hears nothing — he looks down at the stream gliding passively, small boulders marking the path of water. There are snakes in the water, he sees them curling sluggishly. Birds dart among the briars seeking berries. Occasionally he hears bird song, but he is ravished by the silence. It is as if he has suddenly grown deaf, living in a land of trees and lost stone walls.

There is shooting in the woods — the quickening winter brings the animals closer to water, to shelter and forage in the higher hills. Sounds carry long distances. He can not guess where the hunter is stalking. Sometimes there is crashing in the thickets, he sees a deer once in full flight, bucking and rocking through the landscape, miraculously sure of foot on hillsides spread with sharp and treacherous boulders.

Dogs bark all night from the other side of the valley. Their baying echoes through the rooms of the house, the fog distorting the sound. Restless, he walks through the rooms, afraid to venture outdoors, cautious not to let them know he is here. In this wilderness it will be a long time before they catch his scent.

The trees grow back — saplings obliterate the contractor's gash, falling leaves disguise the broken terrain. The woods march back. Little by little, the paths to the stream close, pencil thin markings to the water. He knows the way. He wants no one else here. He is at peace. He drives the car into a gully near the house, covers it with tarpaulin and soon forgets that he has ever driven down the lane, into the web of secondary roads that lead inexorably to the interstate.

Deliveries of food are left at the end of the lane once a month. Soon he notices that he can manage two months before walking down to thumb a ride to the nearest village. With better planning he can now exist for three months at a time. No one is curious. Like the land which has begun to recover from his arrival, the village has accepted that he lives somewhere in the hills and his arrivals and departures are unpredictable. He does not subscribe to newspapers or need a mailbox. He has no past to follow him there.

In the winter storms trees fall. He cuts the wood and hauls it to the house. He notices how the house no longer dominates the hill. It has begun to disappear now into the trees. He knows there are animals in the woods. He hears steps on the roof and recognizes that these are squirrels racing from side to side, playing games from house to tree, chasing each other up and down the trunks, sometimes taking flight and swooping from branch to branch like birds. He realizes that there are other animals, yet unseen. One evening as he peers out the door he notices an opposum drinking the cat's milk.

Unbelievably, after all this time, the cat disappears, walking away one evening into the woods and never returning. He whistles and calls and bangs the cat's dish for over a week. Now field mice move into the retaining wall and later he watches chipmunks racing to store seed against the coming winter. Some animal digs a burrow beside the lower level of the house; overnight a mound of earth appears as if a careless child has tipped a bucket of sand. Coming down the stairs one twilight he confronts a raccoon peering into the windows. He does not move. The animal stands for a long time taking inventory of the room, the rows of bookcases, the shabby overstuffed chairs — considering whether these quarters would do, now that it is vacating the old ones.

Soon he hears soft mewing and movement in one of the chimney flues. His ears refuse to provide him with the necessary clues — mice, squirrels — who is it now living in the flue of the downstairs chimney, the one he never uses, preferring to spend his days on the upper level of the house, looking out into the middle of the trees?

Shots again in the woods. Unable to sleep, he staggers to the kitchen. Outside frost shimmers in the grass. He heats the water, makes coffee. He does not turn on the light, saving the generator. A large animal steps quickly from the edge of the clearing — fur hanging from the belly, heavy claws already firmly digging into the side of the house, as it climbs toward the nest in the chimney flue.

He fears that the animals will find a way into the house. He inspects the chimney flue — the damper is tightly closed, the weight of the animals keeps it secure. There is always a fire now in the upstairs fireplace. Before he goes to sleep, he closes the damper even though the fire still smokes and crackles. He carefully locks and bolts all the doors. Despite his precautions, he believes that animals have penetrated the foundations. On his hands and knees he inspects each corner and the length of every wall. He has never made such a thorough inspection. He finds lost postcards, a catnip mouse discarded by the cat. He should be reassured, but he hears a crackling in the walls as if something is working itself inexorably into the house.

With the coming of spring, dead carpenter ants begin to drop from the ceilings — the walls are riddled. Each new generation pushes out the old, rolling them out through the cracks. The ants are everywhere. From the windows he watches the nests grow larger, swarming with armies of workers. Again some animal hides its young in the chimney flue, clawing up the side of the house, padding restlessly to and fro across the roof.

Another year. At night the animals press their faces against the windows. He is a prisoner inside the house. He no longer walks in the woods. The radio batteries expire, the generator falters, the pile of wood sinks dangerously low. There are still cans of food in the pantry. When they are finished, he will try to escape.

He hopes it will snow again. Then the dogs will stop hunting on the ridges above the house. He hears them now night after night. Lying in bed, his heart pounding, he knows they are hunting him.

He heats the last can in the fireplace, scorching his hand while retrieving it from the flames. He spoons the beans into his ravenous mouth, scraping the sides of the tin long after it is clean. No more. Tomorrow he must walk to the village. Tonight, he will sleep inside the sleeping bag, only body heat can sustain him. He is already zipped into the bag when he remembers that he has not pulled the damper. Fear sends him frantic to close it. Down, down. The metal is hot, the fire still active. No worry, it will die soon. The smoke curls up the sides of the granite fireplace, but he is already back inside a warm cocoon.

As he sleeps, an animal presses against him, seeking warmth. He wakes, the pressure is there against his back. He shakes it loose. He falls asleep again. Smoke swirls through the house, covered in vines, cloaked in trees, lost to view. Only the animals know it is there. Now they push against the swollen door. It opens. Crowding into the house, pressing into every room, they wait for him.

Comments the Fireman

Eric Johnson

Up, polishing the big engines, that takes much of the time, every day, and the long hoses have to be coiled, too, like so many canvas sausages verging on the infinite, or rotund thin men. At dawn, or what suffices for it, we start, if not before, some of us sliding down the brass pole, but most preferring to clump down the stairs in their rubber boots saving the pole for fun later. Then rags are taken in hand and the red enamel of the engines is lovingly caressed and shined to a sheen rivaling that of the fires which they will attend. Grime, soot, smoke, abuse will dull the sheen by day's end, but at the dawn no sun is brighter than a newly readied fire engine.

When the alarm comes in we are up and out in under thirty seconds, perhaps thirty-five, but there is no excitement shrieking through the streets, no, we wait for that until we see the fire, there are too many false alarms. A false alarm during a blackout once resulted in the death of a child wandering unnoticed in the street. There is no excitement. Fires are transient things. If we waited long enough the fire would go away, but it is our duty to extinguish its brief life sooner even than normal, like exorcising the ghost of someone in a coma, or washing a pair of pants with the person wearing them. In time there are two nows that encompass a fire in which we try to perform our task, no one cares about before or after. We are not unlike musicians.

At one time I kept track of each fire attended. Now I take note of the times I get to sleep. There is some evolutionary tendency towards nonexistence of the latter. I am sure that biologists will be quite interested when they learn that some firemen have not slept for three or four years.

We live in cities. I am told that somewhere there are places with volunteer firemen that go out only occasionally. I myself have never seen one of these places but it is nice to think that they may exist. I do know that the Milky Way exists. This does not affect my perception of reality. Sometimes you think about it but it really doesn't matter.

Now, today, or yesterday, we have been called to a fire. We are at the fire. A great burning building. Long streams of water root in the smoke like snakes looking for holes.

At first, the heat and smoke are frightening. But what really gets you is the noise. You never expect what toasts marshmallows and illumined Abe

Lincoln's reading to roar with such stupendous fury and vengeance. It sucks in air like a huge fan and blows bits of ash and pieces of things out the top. When I was in school, fire fighting school, we used to wonder what it would take to blow out a big fire, How big a mouth, a hurricane. I know now nothing could. The voice is too loud, speaks with too much insistent authority. We resort to slow poison. It takes time to get accustomed to approaching a big fire. You must learn to ignore sensory impressions, just concentrate on seeing. After a while one learns to step assuredly forward. Like fighting battles, I suppose, you must ignore and then forget whatever it is that affects you in the first place — fear, some say. In my case it is the audacity involved in pitting a body, equipment and mind arrived at after five days of exhaustive training against six stories of burning wood that made me hesitate at first. All of that goes away, eventually, and you realize that no matter what you do, fire burns at a mean temperature of 2000° C.

Since today or perhaps the day before yesterday or yesterday one man has been killed at the fire when a roof collapsed on him. There are no living inhabitants in this building. We have had to hook up to the auxiliary mains, so much water has been used. The mains are under the streets, naturally, like subconsious knowledge. In the summer kids open the hydrants, reducing the pressure to zero. They dance like spirits, evil desires. In the winter things freeze and we use foam. At least the adversary remains constant, like death, like orbiting suns. Should the air vanish from the Earth there would be no fires; often I have thought of this. This would require some kind of miracle. It would require another miracle for people to remain alive.

This fire resembles a wall, it is a sheeting effect which means we have lost. The coruscation flails like ants, birds of prey, we writhe at its base, hooking up hoses that have have water in them so they're not too hot to handle. Reds and bright colors, everything is bright, must be bright, for infiltration. We are the usurpers here. Chrome, fire trucks running like blood, or eyes with tears from heat. We must take on new aspects. This environment demands adjustments which can't be made. Or else you lose or forget something which was there before, might be necessary again, but not at present.

Taking chances, you approach the burning, arm upraised, white suit livid against the glare. Someone said there might be someone in there, a kid, a mother. It is always thus. Never a drunkard. Never a rapist. A kid. A mother. You have to go. It is impossible. Nothing could survive this. You walk on melted plates of metal, pipes, sprigs of cement fall, you look, wilting; these suits can only take so much. A window which emits clotted smoke, has been for days. You look. No one can be there. This organic process, growth, it is too much for you. You are a bacterium witnessing a rooting, destruction, you can only hope to move. Back out through the smoke. You mustn't run, a fireman never runs from a burning building. All strata have their rules, not necessarily intelligent.

Water is curiously ineffective against a fire gone out of control. You can increase it and increase it until the very ocean starts to fall but it is gone as if it too feeds the flames. It is vaporized, changed by the situation into which it is thrust; reform is impossible. Water will not rehabilitate rubble.

We are like the kings seeking answers in a well of oblivion, a maelstrom which crushes aspirations only after they are embarked upon. On some days we move the trucks, seeking new angles. Others ask what is going on. I have collapsed, awakened, collapsed. I question my motives. Surely this is not what I would do normally? Does the immediacy of a situation preclude logical analysis, rational cognition, conclusion? Yes. Situations possess the characteristics upon which logic is based. Such as falling over a precipice. At the time you do not consider things in a coherent manner. Or if you do, you have already mastered the situation.

Some days ago, or days hence, a truck breaks down. Like entropy, fatigue gets in the engine. Technology can keep up with the problems as long as they do not persist, then it breaks. We lost fifty thousand gallons an hour of pumping capacity. Another unit is promised.

The flames have induced a curious effect. Everything jumps, even the not burning. Everything moves as though reflected in waved mirrors, insubstantial; even perusal of the feet does not help, one stands in swirling tide-bound sands. They have dispatched a great crane above the building to rain water down upon it. Men go up with breathing devices, mountain climbers, like Zeus without the power of lightning and precious little storm. It does not help.

It is easier to stand mothlike before the monolith of shaking combustion than to turn one's back on it. To turn at all, to walk requires immense amounts of will. Living like this, eating at great intervals, staying in suits that chafe the skin, or heavy coats that weigh you down much more than the heat, one becomes aware that, physically, rest is the most necessary thing, to rest is to forget, to renew, reality is so harsh that some kind of escape is needed, therefore the state of rest is the highest evolutionary goal, otherwise we are not perfectly suited for the environment.

Like angels, or independents not union men, helicopters have come, flitting about the towering corona like minnows, dumping chemicals, water on the blaze. It is not to be explained why they were not here weeks ago. Or why the building was built in the first place. Existence induces our poetic obligation. So says the fire chief.

A number of days ago other firemen arrived. They say more will come. We are running short of everything. The flames have consumed all but the skeleton of the building. It will last a long time, in obscurity, smoke drawing wordless pages before true events. I work at prying ways through the rubble to plant explosive charges to destroy the fire's cohesion, to alter it. It is too hot. When my oxygen runs short I retreat in confusion.

They say we will continue to fight this fire, though containment must be impossible. A month ago I had wondered why we had shined the engines so well beforehand, what purpose it served. It all glints in certain lights, especially at night, or during the day, when flame and smoke make the sun incorrect, or hide it altogether. I will consider the fire. Someone must.

A Little Death in the Venice of the Orient

Alice Jurow

Habib Boktou, fat and inert, sits under a tree in a square of meadow enclosed by laundry lines and furnished with his pillows and water-pipe.

"You will want to stay here in Srinigar at least a week," he is saying. "You must see the Mughal gardens, the glaciers at Phalgam, you must relax, you must swim — besides, you cannot go to Ladakh without making your arrangements. We will see about a hotel for you, and the food there — not good. Better to buy your provisions here."

"Here, yes," says the deep voice of the fat wealthy newspaper editor from Delhi, "this place is Paradise; even the ducks go by saying 'quack quack quack."

"Above all," Boktou adds, "You must not take the bus. If you can't get the plane or hire a jeep, you must stay here and become a Kashmiri."

"Ha-ha, not such a bad fate," booms the editor.

Gliding past waterlilies, close enough to see the trembling dewdrop on each one, Thalia drowses against the chintz pillows in the moist morning heat. The curtained shikara rocks like a cradle; she can hardly open her eyes long enough to nod at the mosques and islands and gardens as the shikara-man points them out. Back at the houseboat they are angry with her; she didn't ask Boktou's nephew to arrange the ride.

"Don't tell Mr. Habib," the shikara-man winks, as he prepares spiced tea for her outside the Shalimar gardens. The thick mug has a lassoing cowboy on it; has he rinsed it out with lake water? The tea is good and soothes her stomach.

There is a power failure, and the clerks at the Indian Airlines office, working by candlelight, are even slower than usual. After an hour and a half Thalia reaches the counter, holding her place firm though a pair of Kashmiri men keep trying to insinuate themselves from the side.

"Yes, your ticket to Ladakh is confirmed for Friday," the clerk says at last.

"But the plane may not go?"

81

"Oh, the plane will certainly go. Twice a week, it always goes."

"But it may not land?"

"True, he admits. "Sometimes, the weather is bad, the plane must turn back. But don't worry. Your plane will certainly go."

In the afternoon, in her houseboat room, Thalia naps uneasily, inhaling the pervasive odor of sandelwood and shit. A paddle laps outside the window; she lifts the curtain, hoping it's a fruit-wallah with more cherries. But instead, it is a shikara full of bundled shawls.

"Good afternoon, Madam. My name is Butterfly. May I show you some of these beautiful things? Things truly worth having."

"Not right now, please. I'm not feeling very well."

"Just for a few minutes, Madam. These are the finest quality. Do you know why I am called Butterfly? An American lady — you are American? — gave the name to my grandfather...I will tell you the story: may I come in?"

"Not now, I'm sick. And I don't have any clothes on."

"All right," Butterfly says quickly. "I will come back tomorrow."

"No, not tomorrow; come Friday."

Mutton in a rich dark sauce, peas and potatoes, dal, rice, a plate of cherries. The Friday plane to Ladakh turned around in mid-flight, drifting clouds over the airfield in the magic Himalayas. Back to Srinigar and the flower-lined road from airfield to terminal. The Indian Airlines office mobbed. Boktou's nephew waiting, with a knowing smile, to take her back to the houseboat. Shit and sandalwood. The toilet has a tank and a porcelain bowl but it empties into the lake as directly as a hole in the floor. Runny yellow dal, an efficient food, goes straight through her body and into Dal Lake. Thalia kills a mosquito on the bathroom mirror, wondering if she should bring its corpse to Boktou, who has said,"If you find one mosquito, you stay here free. This place is Paradise." Rocking gently, boxed in carved sandelwood, she sleeps through the hot afternoon.

"Madam, good afternoon, Madam. It's Butterfly."

Complex and interminable dreams.

"Butterfly, you remember. Look, what a beautiful shawl for you, Madam. Reversible embroidery. This side, summer," a flourish, "this side, winter..."

Invisible Malls
Ken Kalfus

*Kublai Khan does not necessarily believe everything Marco Polo says when
he describes the indoor shopping malls visited in his travels around the empire,
but he listens to the young Venetian with greater attention than he has shown
any other messenger or explorer. He has already heard Marco's tales of invisible cities, of Diomira and Despina, of Zirma and Isaura, calvinoed metropolises
built from memory and desire, and he waits for further intelligence. The aged
emperor has reached the melancholy moment in his life in which he needs to
comprehend his conquests, when he is only frustrated by the illuminated maps
hand-drawn in rare inks and paints by Tartary's greatest cartographers. As
beautiful as these maps are, they are unable to show the borders of his vast
territory, and they are also very difficult to fold. The Khan has no use for the
blunt, irrelevant reports of functionaries, emissaries, generals and spies. Only
in Marco Polo's account is the Khan able to understand what his will has
accomplished.*

INDOOR SHOPPING MALLS AND MEMORY 1

Leaving there and proceeding for three days toward the east, you reach Sheila,
an indoor shopping mall entirely occupied by the past. Crowding one bou-
tique after another are Mickey Mouse watches and souvenir ash trays from
the World's Fair, stretched Coke bottles, incense candles and Day-Glo posters
and Smile decals and fake gas lamps. Sheila's merchants have already placed
orders for merchandise destined for obsolescence but not yet in fashion. The
mall has structural defects, and a short lease on the land, but the merchants
know they will stay in business forever. They envy their customers, who believe
they were happy when they owned what the merchants own now.

INDOOR SHOPPING MALLS AND DESIRE 1

In the shops of Alicia, you can buy philosopher's stones, golden fleeces, holy
grails, concubines of absolute beauty and passion, books that answer the questions posed by wise men and children, and elixirs that deliver eternal life. Each
of these items, however, is priced at slightly more than you think its worth,

especially if you include the sales tax. After you've left without making a purchase, you feel the difference between what you want to pay and what the goods cost as a little hole burning into the lining of your stomach. You realize that the item is worth more than you thought. You return to the store, but find the price has been raised to a new figure that is really unreasonable. Annoyed, you again leave empty-handed, reconsider and return, find the price has been raised again, leave once more and so on forever.

INDOOR SHOPPING MALLS AND MEMORY 2

Shoppers promenading down Shirley's marbled avenues are entertained by the music of Bach, Mozart, Gershwin, Ellington, the Beatles and the Temptations, all of it performed by the Percy Faith Orchestra. We identify the music as soothing, and our slight unease, an ineffable frustration, is laid to some other cause.

INDOOR SHOPPING MALLS AND DESIRE 2

There is no parking lot at Danielle. Would-be shoppers drive around it for hours, looking for a place to park their cars. Bewitched by the illusion of a parking space glimpsed in a rear-view mirror, or through the windows of intervening vehicles, or in some parallel universe visible only from the corner of the eye, some drivers abruptly back up, turn, accelerate without warning or attempt to squeeze between other cars. There are numerous collisions. Most of the drivers, however, allow themselves to be entertained by their car radios, snack on whatever provisions they have brought with them, and then return home. If they voice any complaint, it is only with the amount of traffic they have encountered.

INDOOR SHOPPING MALLS AND THE SKY 1

Like other indoor shopping malls, Edna is roofed, its internal climate regulated by hidden machinery. Daylight is allowed into the building only through its doors. Yet before the shopper can focus his eyes on the racks and display windows ahead of him, they are directed upwards to a fantastic apparition. Where in other malls are nondescript ceilings, Edna's master engineers have installed an intricate mechanism of lamps, gears, pulleys, cams, flywheels, springs and weights that approximate the silent churnings of the universe. Clockwork drives a mammoth lamp, the mall's sun, across a painted sky, and then raises a lesser lamp, a manic face etched in glass, the mall's moon. The mechanism's motion is accelerated to encompass a full day from sunrise to sunrise, during the mall's business hours. Planets dance one way and then the other, and hundreds of thousands of lights suspended by wires wheel above our heads. As a service to their customers, Edna's merchants have also arranged to make visible to the unaided eye what God could not: galaxies, nebulae, clusters, quasars, dwarfs, pulsars, novae, planetary dics, meteoroid swarms and interstellar dust clouds. The shopper need not emulate the astronomer's patient attendance to the heavens. Rare and spectacular celestial events, such as eclipses, occultations, conjunctions and transits, are scheduled to appear at least once every day.

INDOOR SHOPPING MALLS AND DESIRE 3

From the moment you step into Felicia, you are besieged by aromas sweet, pungent, sour and meaty. The only merchandise for sale in Felicia is fast food: ice cream, pizza, popcorn and tacos, but also amrita, manna, loquats and ambrosia, all of it deep-fried. Strolling down the concourse with a Coke in one hand and a hot dog in the other, you pass strangers who are drinking kvass or goat's milk, or nibbling at some couscous or a satay, and, enveloped by the flavorful steam wafting over the formica counters, you wonder what you will eat next. But food is the least of what you need. Like every other indoor shopping mall, Felicia does not have a single public washroom.

INDOOR SHOPPING MALLS AND THE DEAD 1

In malls from Zanzibar to Paramus, adolescents wash down every promenade, crowd every aisle, besiege every register and monopolize every video game. A population in pained transition, its records, jeans, toys and bedroom decor are also in transition, coveted one day and discarded the next. The exception to this state of affairs is Gloria, an indoor shopping mall located in a subterranean fissure. It is patronized exclusively by the dead, who shop without hurrying, who can wait for closeout sales, and who buy goods to last forever.

Marco Polo does not know if the Great Khan is sleeping or awake: his eyes are closed and his breathing is slowed, but the long lines of his face are drawn into a contemplative frown. The emperor is, in fact, awake, contemplating indoor shopping malls so far unmentioned in Manhasset and Shaker Heights, in Boca Raton and Bel Air. He is thinking of the Galleried legions, and of big old GUM staring down at the stars. "So this is my empire," Kublai Khan murmurs. "These are the subjects who send me their tributes and raise my armies, who follow my laws and who whisper my name to either threaten or calm their children. These are the people whose poets address their songs to me." "No, sire," Marco Polo replies. "The malls are only home to goods. The promenades are emptied, the shutters are drawn, the fountains are stilled, and the coin purses are fastened shut with the fall of dusk, except on Wednesdays, when they are open to nine. The shoppers return to their residences, where they are alone as if in death, subject to nothing, part of nothing. Your empire is quiet halls and shelves, locked display cases and bare cash drawers." As night rushes into his palace's luxuriant gardens, the emperor cannot tell if the traveler smiles or weeps. But he knows now, at least, why Marco Polo needs so many charge cards.

Small Fishes
Pat Kaluza

She found the little gold-speckled fish dead that morning. Floating on top of the miniature tank, the other three fish carefully pretending they knew nothing. She had known that the aquarium was too small, knew it when her brother gave it to her. And now Susan B. Anthony was dead. Strangely pale, her bright red faded, like blood mingling in water. Dead, floating on top of the tank, the one spike of seaweed tickling it as it drifted so absurdly on its side. An omen, she thought. How can you flush an omen down the toilet?

She wrapped it carefully in waxed paper, then white tissue paper, and placed it in an envelope, addressing it over the hump of the small body. To her brother, to show him she was right: the aquarium was too small. She watched the other three fish. Many Rivers, the tiny blue striped one who always ate last, crouched behind a shell, quiet, afraid of death. Ginger Rogers, the prettiest of the four with her spangled fins and black hooded eyes, swam near the top looking for food now that the body had been removed. And Annie Oakley, zebra-striped and always looking for a fight, she simply waited and watched.

Her eyes moved from the small aquarium to the phone, which hadn't rung in two days. Once again she checked to make sure it was still working. And once again she heard the dial tone. She set the receiver down carefully, then adjusted it to make sure it fit securely, picked it up again, listened, replaced it, and began to cry. Soft, hopeless tears, why wouldn't he let her call him?

She would have to tell him soon. He won't be happy, she thought. He'll think it's on purpose. I'll tell him when he comes tonight. After we make love. I'll say, "Listen, I think I'm pregnant." Then his head will swing around, slowest thing on earth, and his eyes will finally lam onto me, and I'll get all whimpery. And have to sit down. And he'll say, "How late are you?" And it will only be 10 days now, and he'll say "Big deal!" And I'll say, "But I can feel it; it's different this time." And he'll say, "Shit!" And he'll stomp out of this room, those engineer boots, bigger than life. Snorting.

Then he'll get used to the idea, she thought. Men have that soft side. Squishy inside, about mothers and all.

She walked pigeon-toed toward the full-length mirror, stomach pushed out, fair wispy head leaning back. She turned sideways and puffed out her skirt.

Don't gain any weight, she thought. End up with piano legs. I could borrow Ma's Singer, make some tops. Ma. I'm going to be a Ma.

Standing still, waves of wonder, rounded and gray, rolling over her, suffocating her. She shook herself, found she had been staring at the aquarium again. Too small, she thought. Well, this baby's going to be a big one. Roy will know it's his.

She moved her rocking chair next to the aquarium and waited there, waited for the phone to ring. With each rock forward, her whole body strained toward the phone, then, rocking back, she relaxed. A reprieve from the waiting. Then forward again, tense, willing the phone to ring. The rocking chair slowly inched toward the table leg till finally with each rocking motion, she jarred the table and the aquarium. The three fish huddled together in one corner, water splashed, scum swirled, and she continued to rock there, waiting, not waiting, for hours. Till the phone rang.

"Yes, hello. Roy, is that you?"

"Listen, baby, about tonight..."

"I have a secret message for you."

"Secret message. Christ. I got business."

"Come over after?"

"I can't do business thinking about you sitting around with one dinky light on, eyes hanging down to your knees."

"I don't just sit around. I'm thinking, listening. I sing to myself, I think about things. In the quiet."

"You're weird, baby, too weird for me."

"But it's nice to sit here and wait for you. And sometimes it's like hell. Sometimes you're so late I just start to cry."

"This whole thing is getting too fucking intense for me. I'll see you around sometime." And he hung up.

She stood holding the receiver in her hand, dumb, depleted, till an electronic voice blared out at her from it telling her to hang up. She placed it gently on the phone, then picked it up again and waited for the electronic voice to begin again. She moved the phone to the aquarium and sat down. Each time the electronic voice ended its demands, she would replace the receiver and then pick it up again, hanging it on the top edge of the aquarium. The voice would send reverberations through the water, stirring up soft eddies of scum on top, gently rocking the fish.

I should change the water, she thought. Or they'll all die. I should feed them; I don't remember feeding them. But she only sat and rocked, listening to the voice, watching the fish trying to escape the voice.

In the morning she found Ginger Rogers floating on top of the water, her fins limp, her eyes white and putrid in their black mask. She wouldn't cry for a fish so pretty. The beautiful are always ill-fated. But then she spotted Annie Oakley's tiny body caught in the spike of seaweed. It didn't move, that tiny fighter fish. And so Annie Oakley was dead too, her black stripes already looking spotty and her belly swollen. She would not cry, the aquarium was too small and she would not cry.

She took the bodies and laid them out on the tablecloth. Each had a thin black strand tailing from them. She would not be disgusted; that is how it is in life. She would send Ginger Rogers' body to her mother, to tell her. About the baby. But it was harder with Annie Oakley. She had been her favorite. She found a small, clear plastic box and lined it with a piece of white bread, mashing it down to a soft gray dough. She put Annie Oakley's body on it, straightening out the thin black strand of excrement, and then closed the cover. She placed the small casket on the phone where the receiver should have been.

The phone killed her, she thought.

She remembered about Many Rivers and then turned to the aquarium. The tiniest and shyest of the fish, she couldn't be found. Had she just disappeared, some sea god riding in on a charging white sea horse, whisking her away, saving her from this house of death? No, she's in the shell. Hiding from death. "You silly, you're all I have left of my fishes, I wouldn't dare let death get you. You'll be my baby's godmother. I'll name her Little Rivers, after you."

She covered the top of the aquarium water with flour, to keep out death. "Death won't go through white," she told the fish. Believing her, Many Rivers inched out of the shell, her blue stripe trembling in the luminescent body. She would dart out of the way of the small grains of flour which floated down from the top, but she seemed to like the shadowed water.

"The others have gone on a long trip," she told Many Rivers. "They're happier now. They have a really big aquarium where they are. Ginger Rogers has a million lovers, and she just preens and preens. And Annie Oakley is captain of a whole army, and she's taken to polishing her stripes, and she growls now, too. She always wanted to growl."

She spent the whole day rocking in front of the aquarium. Someone knocked on the door, but she only stilled her rocking and motioned to Many Rivers to be quiet till the knocking stopped.

"Maybe it was death, maybe it wasn't," she told the fish. "I'll keep you safe. And the baby. After she comes, we'll find the others in that big aquarium, all shiny and clean and lots of food, and we'll teach Little Rivers to swim right off."

In the evening, she thought that the tiny fish seemed sluggish. Yes, it seemed like she was slower and slower and her blue stripe was fading. She poured more flour on the top of the aquarium; she could smell the dank, dark odor of death. She promised the fish that she would stay up all night to ward off death, He could not have her, the last of her fishes.

But she fell asleep in the night, rocking. And dreamed of a cat, a big black jungle cat, straining inside of her to be free of this body. Straining against the fluid walls. And she knew in her dream that her period had come, her blood was flowing, and the baby was dead, had never been. She felt the slow dark ache pulling her body down, pulling at the earth, at all the sadness of the earth. The big black cat screamed to be free, and she cried in her sleep for the blood that flowed back into the earth, in exchange for all the sadness.

In the quiet light of the morning, she grieved for her lost baby, her tears spilling onto the paste that covered the top of the aquarium. She found Many Rivers after much searching, her dead body almost transparent in her favorite shell, the pale blue stripe still faintly glowing. She left her there in the aquarium and rocked and rocked, watching the small body fade more and more till only the thin silver backbone could be seen through the murky water.

Mommy Dear
Eduardo Gudiño Kieffer

In which Blanquita (18) speaks with her dear mommy (41) in a dialogue which reveals the intense communication between generations.

Perfumed and learned Blanca, language
is a collective institution
whose laws impose themselves
on individuals and it transmits itself
in a coercive way from generation to generation.
Social signs, Blanca, little sounds,
little burps.
And once there was someone who wished to reduce
mathematics and logic to linguistics
and all mental life to speech.

—Fernando de Giovanni, "Keno"

Mommy dear was stretched out on the purple shag rug of her dressing-room, leafing through *Votre Beauté*, stark naked under the ultraviolet lamp which was focused on her legs, so smooth so firm so pretty much prettier than mine.

I told her lend me the Fiat 600 mommy dear mommy darling mommy dear-darling she said maaarvelous really spleeendid and I said or rather I asked what's so maaarvelous so really spleeendid about the Fiat 600 it's a mess since I wrecked it the other night when I wrapped it around the light pole on Libertador you remember: dear dear mommy raised the magazine and said again this is maaarvelous really spleeendid look Blanquita and she showed me the page the photo the title decouvréz ce sein and then mommy read me la mode est aux robes transparentes et aux décolletés vertigineux and she stood up and her breasts were really very nice, perfect, you don't need treatments mommy I said I swear you're fine will you lend me the Fiat or not. Do you think so Blanquita dear mommy darling said looking at herself in the mirror with her hands on her hips observing herself critically and I said I think you should tell me if you're going to lend me the car or not and mommy dear answered I'm still pretty good.

Then I sat down on the floor I unplugged the ultraviolet lamp and I said well I'm going to get it out of the garage anyhow at least tell me where the keys are and mommy dear asked what love what keys.

The keys to the Fiat 600 mommy sweetest, I'm asking you for the car I don't know if you understood me I have to go out, ay Blanquita did you notice all the new things now it's the maxiskirt by the way I haven't seen your maxiskirt why didn't you put on your maxiskirt and while she asked me she leafed through the magazine again and said maaarvelous it's Simone Laube's column it's fantastic doesn't miss a thing about beauty tips next month when I go to Paris I'm going to Jeanne Piaubert's or Pier Augé's by the way Blanquita you should think it over and come with me I don't understand why you don't want to go to Europe there are even the museums you like.

Yes but now I need the car mother I said dear mother said I think I went to L'Orangerie once and I thought how tremendous it would be to have that Van Gogh in the livingroom just imagine Viñas Arrigue's wife's face I said Viñas Arrigue's wife's face doesn't have to be imagined it's one of those things that just exists and please listen to me tell me where are the keys to the Fiat 600.

Six hundred thousand pesos mother dear said six hundred thousand pesos it cost Madgalena for the clasp to her pearl necklace that's awful I think that's too much I don't know why people spend so much on frivolous things but it's a diamond clasp and tell me if that isn't too much.

Shit I said and dear mommy said ay dear how lovely for you to say shit how modern of course it's better in French merde and they even have a verb enmerder and I said here they say screw and it's the same thing and shit tell me where the keys are to the car because I'm in a hurry I have a date and it's getting late; ah afternoon is the best time to go shopping said mommy dear and you'd better go the Promenade Alvear because Florida is impossible and no one goes to Santa Fe with those terrible people everywhere. Mommy dear was still facing the mirror looking at her profile and experimenting with how her hair looked piled to one side and half pulled up and she said to me what do you think shall I go to Christian's or do my hair myself tonight I'm going to the theater at the Colón I said do what you like or do whatever you please because anger made me super correct and I added listen carefully I need the car now tell me where the keys are I have to see somebody it's important mommy dear said I like that Blanquita you must keep in mind that you are important and do important things I began to laugh and I said it's super-unimportant look I'm going to go to bed with Juan Antonio and mommy dear stood still and looked straight at me all of a sudden and said how horrible child how horrible what you've just said to you own mother who gave you life.

And I asked her if it seemed so horrible to her for me to go to bed with Juan Antonio and she said horrible I hope young lady you won't have anything to do with Jorge Antonio I said mother you're confused about his last name it doesn't matter what does matter is what I told you I was going to do with him did you hear or didn't you hear what I was going to do with him, what I am going to do with him in a little while.

Mommy dear looked at me a little upset and said I didn't hear the only thing I heard is that horrible last name Antonio just imagine if I were to be a relative of that horrible Peronista Jorge Antonio child what a terrible role I said mommy Antonio isn't his last name it's Juan's second name his name is Juan Antonio Pierino mommy dear sighed and said well Pierino isn't too bad it's all right I guess one can say that he has noble relatives in Italy at any rate people may believe it the terrible thing is for someone to associate him with Jorge Antonio; mommy dear said all that and put on her bra and panties and I said by the way I took some of your underwear because mine wasn't right for the occasion, what occasion mommy dear asked. I just told you mommy I'm going to bed with Juan Antonio and it won't be the first time and I think he's great I swear I think he's great I think he's great listen to me I think he's great because he's crude and he looks down on me and because he thinks I'm a spoiled kid then he even hits me think of that mommy he hits me he insults me he says filthy things to me and makes me do things that would blow your mind but what I'm telling you is that I like to do them I like to humiliate myself crawl in front of him ask him on my knees please love me because I'm proud that a guy like him loves me and he does love me even though he says I'm a sad case and an idiot and a fool with no sense of reality I think he's great because I wish you knew what he looks like he's very tall with his fingernails all bitten off with enormous hands and when he puts them on me I feel like dying and besides that he works in a packing house, he's twenty-eight and every time I go to bed with him he gets at least five thousand pesos from me.

Mommy dear was finishing putting on her stockings, biting her tongue because putting on stockings is so difficult, when she finished putting her stockings on she looked at me and asked what were you saying dear weren't you talking to me.

Then I said mommy go straight to hell and she said ay Blanquita I don't know why you're so aggressive at times toward you mother I stood up and said ciao and please shut up, mommy dear said but why are you in such a hurry wait a second I'll finish getting dressed and if you're going to mass at the Socorro as you were saying to me I'll go with you, look for the keys to the Fiat 600 they're in the second drawer of my dressing-table.

(Translated, from the Spanish, by John G. Copeland)

Gabon
W. P. Kinsella

I have lived in this massive, old frame house for four years. Only Gabon has been here longer. The house leans at odd, erotic angles. I'm still not sure that I've been in all the rooms and apartments. Multiple additions have been built on over the many years since the house was new. Some owner, desperate for money, rented a sunporch or pantry, and built on a new sunporch or pantry, which was later rented out by a subsequent owner. Years ago, the doubled garage was converted into an apartment. Later, a room was added on top of the garage, then still another room was piled on top of that.

A Mrs. Kryzanowski owns the property now, inherited from her husband, a hollow-cheeked, cancerous-looking man who cashed in his pale soul soon after I arrived. He had purchased the house from the estate of an elderly Chinese, who had died in one of the sun porches amid stacks of Chinese newspapers and three bamboo cages filled with thimble-sized canaries.

Before the Chinese, history blurs.

Gabon lives in the attic above the third floor. He occupies a tiny loft with one dark, triangular window that overlooks the back alley. The attic is reached by pulling down a metal ladder, which hugs the ceiling like a long, wrought-iron spider, and climbing through a trap door.

I'm sure Gabon's presence in the attic must violate thousands of fire and building code regulations, but none of us are about to call in outsiders, who, in order to protect us, would evict us. The rent is cheap; the house is warm; and each of us lives with our own secrets, which may be as frayed as a favorite blanket or as vicious as a Tasmanian devil.

Gabon is small and brown with bird-like ankles and wrist; his nose is hooked, and black tufts of hair bristle from his head at odd angles. I knew someone from Sumatra who looked like him; tiny, starved-looking, cinnamon-skinned. There is a sour, bachelor smell about Gabon, of emptied ashtrays and soiled clothing.

Whenever I meet him on the sidewalk or in the halls, he nods shyly. "I pay my rent," he informs me, speaking in a sibilant whisper, his accent unidentifiable; Spanish? Greek? Arabic of some ilk? I suspect he knows only two English phrases: "Nice day," offered even when it is raining torrentially, and "I pay my rent." The latter is delivered as if he is asking a question like, "How are you?"

The phrase must have impressed Mrs. Kryzanowski, for when I say, after counting twenty-dollar bills into her bluish hand, "Tell me about Gabon?" she replies, "He pays his rent." The expression on her pink, naugahyde face lets me know unequivocally that Gabon is a good tenant, and that she would be happier if I paid my rent on time more often and asked fewer questions.

"I pay my rent too," I say, trying to smile disarmingly.

"Sometimes," says Mrs. Kryzanowski.

But I refuse to be dismissed so easily, I stand leaning on the doorjamb, waiting. Mrs. Kryzanowski is wearing a ghastly, flowered housecoat; her white hair has incongruous lemon streaks in it and is wound around candy-apple-blue rollers. Her face is paved with makeup that may well have been applied with a palette knife.

"Noisy, noisy," she finally says. "A jockey. Broked his neck once," and she makes a cracking motion with her large hands, like snapping invisible kindling.

"Noisy?" I say.

"Walk, walk, walk, Ax-ercise maybe? Who knows. Everybody's crazy over there."

"He has a doght," she volunteers, smiling conspiratorily. "He thinks I don't know."

Mrs. Kryzanowski obviously has a spy at the Castle. It is probably Grabarkewitcz, who lives in a room below me in the company of a magical cat. Mrs. Kryzanowski had Grabarkewicz's room painted last month, the only maintenance she has authorized since she's owned the Castle.

A dog. Interesting.

Night and day I haunt the halls of the Castle, inhaling the odors of varnish, cooked cabbage, mothballs, and dust. Mrs. Kryzanowski harbors quite a genteel collection of loners and losers. Tenants who disturb the status quo are dealt with swiftly. Last summer, a stringy-haired thug rented a first-floor room and soon had it swarming with beer-swilling friends who argued, fought, played a tinny radio at full volume, and urinated out the window into Mrs. Kryzanowski's caragana hedge.

One afternoon, a lithe Oriental with steel-colored hair and bitter eyes called on the thug and his friends. The caller was verbally abused and threatened. The young Oriental bowed curtly as the door was slammed in his face.

The next time the thug exited by the side door, there was one sharp bleat of pain, brief scuffling in the caragana, then silence. Late that evening, the thug moved out, his thug friends carrying his few possessions. The thug carried only a few soiled clothes crushed to his body with his left arm. His right arm bore a blazing white cast resting like an angel in a clean, white sling.

I knew how Gabon reached his living quarters, but had never seen the deed accomplished. Like most of us here, Gabon had no employment and kept irregular hours. I lurked behind my curtains for two days before I spied Gabon approaching the house. I huffed up two flights of stairs and down a long corridor. I was loitering beneath the black ladder when Gabon arrived.

"Evening," I said.

"Nice day," said Gabon. He was clutching an apple in his right hand.

"It is," I said. It was.

93

"I pay my rent," said Gabon, again treating the statement as a question. Perhaps he had been misled by a deceitful English-as-a-second-language instructor.

Gabon nervously forced the apple into a side pocket, then, flexing his knees, sprang straight into the air and grabbed the bottom rung of the ladder with both hands. There was barely enough of Gabon — ninety pounds would be my guess — to pull the ladder down until the bottom rung was a foot from the floor. When the ladder was in position, he quickly scampered up the eight or so rungs, like a native scaling a palm tree, and pushed open the trap door to the attic. He disappeared like a burglar and the ladder swung eerily back into place, emitting a few soft, metal groans.

I remained in the dim hall for a long time. Gabon did pace about a great deal, sometimes seeming to break into a run. He also seemed to be talking to someone, though the words were indistinguishable, and could have come from a radio.

He must have been uneasy about his encounter with me, for, after about twenty minutes, the trap door creaked open and Gabon hung his head down and peered furtively around. I was pressed against the wall at the head of the stairs out of view.

Back in my room, I opened the window and climbed out onto the porch roof below me. I crawled about twenty feet, where, when I carefully stood up, at shoulder height there was another addition to the Castle. By pulling myself up and over two more portions of the building, and risking great embarrassment and multiple fractures, I was able to climb onto the roof of Gabon's loft. I slithered forward to the very peak of the roof and, by hanging precariously over the edge, was able to peer into Gabon's triangular window. It was a crisp October night and I was silvered by the moon as I hung grotesquely, like a broken TV antenna.

In the loft, which was lit by the yellowish light from one sixty-watt bulb, sat Gabon not on a chair or bed, but on the back of a small shaggy, brown-and-white pony.

Gabon, no larger than a ten-year-old, was dressed in jockey silks of parrot-green and ivory, a white-and-green jockey's cap on his head, goggles resting on the crown of the cap.

The pony was a bit over three feet tall. Gabon sat on a scaled-down racing saddle, it and his tall boots polished to the color of gleaming liver.

In one corner of the loft was Gabon's pallet. In the other, cordoned off by small packing crates, was straw for bedding and grass for eating. Gabon rode the pony in a slow circle; the middle of the room was covered with brown indoor-outdoor carpet. The pony pranced. Gabon waved to the crowd.

I tried to imagine Gabon smuggling the pony into the loft. It was too big to remove now, but I suppose as a colt it would have been no larger that a full-grown spaniel.

Now, on this brilliant October night, in one of the loneliest places on earth, Gabon parades around the winner's circle under the blazing sun of Hialeah, Pimlico, or Churchill Downs, accepting the accolades, remembering the clash of the starting gate, the yelp of the crowd as his horse lunged forward — sleek, powerful, pliant as butter between his thighs.

El Amor No Tiene Orgullo

Sandra J. Kolankiewicz

My husband wants to make love with you, the Algerian woman told her in Spanish. You will not, will you?

They were standing in knee-deep water in front of the Algerian woman's hotel. The woman held a chubby son, Marco, on her boney hip, and he pulled the ends of her long, tight curls.

Patricia tried to read the eyes behind the woman's smoked sunglasses. They seemed calm and assured.

But I've never met your husband, she said. In all of the days I have talked with you here, I've never seen him.

The woman bent, splashed a handful of water onto her son's shoulder, and rubbed it in. Some of it slithered down her forearm to her elbow and trickled into the salt water around them. She shifted her weight and her son at the same time to her other hip, then wet his back, caressing it.

He has seen you running, she said. She laughed quietly. It is enough for him.

It was late afternoon and the sun was less aggressive. The bare-breasted women were gone; the season was over. Still it seemed a perpetual summer. Change was the coming and going of regular rain and the ebb and flow of foreign visitors on their vacation.

Patricia had taken to visiting the woman on the beach while she waited for the Cuban to return from fishing. After talking with the Algerian woman for awhile, she would take off running toward her cabana a half mile away, pumping and pumping through ankle-deep water until her stride was a fluid movement and she found her rhythm, fixed her breathing. She would gallop through the water, splashing it up her legs, the blue channel stretching tranquilly beside her, and watch her white cabana at the end of the beach by the lighthouse float closer and closer.

I do not know if he will approach you, the woman was saying. But I wanted that you know.

When Patricia looked at her again, she was smiling.

Did he tell you this? she asked the woman. She turned and surveyed the nearly-deserted beach. Calypso music floated from the open-air restaurant tucked into the shade under a giant palapa.

The woman smiled again and tried to lift her son from her hip to dunk him lightly into the cool water, but he squealed and clung to her neck, his eyes popping tears, saliva drooling over his bottom lip.

Chhh, Chhh, Chhh, she said and jiggled him up and down until he stuck his fingers in his mouth. She turned to Patricia.

He painted a picture of you, she told her, still rocking the baby.

Patricia planted her hands on her hips and stared down at her thighs, where they met the water. The day had been hot and terribly humid. She could smell the brine of her own sweat.

Would you like to see the painting? asked the woman. Without waiting for an answer, she started to move back to shore, her strides rippling the water around them. Her son reached back over his shoulder at Patricia and pawed the air.

I think what he did with your hair is perfect, said the woman. She closed the hotel-room door behind her and set the baby down in the middle of the tile floor. She turned the knob for the overhead fan and it started slowly, then whipped itself round and round. The room was bright, clean but cluttered, and she crossed it back and forth, shuffling newspapers, making piles of rumpled clothes. There was a shiny silver flute on a rusting music stand in the corner. The baby began to whine and pull himself along the floor.

Patricia stood by the door, her body oiled and glistening, and stared at the painting. The water-color was taped to a large pressed-board square, and set on the kitchen table. It leaned back against a creme-colored wall.

In the painting, the figure of Patricia wearing her green and white bathing suit ran down the beach at sunset, holding the fiery weight of the sun out before her in her palm as she ran. There were flaming streaks in her hair, and her body was a puzzle of spheres. The water that stretched out behind her was striped blues, meeting the clouds at a horizon that glowed yellow and red.

But the most compelling element in the painting was the face. The eyes were lightly closed to the ball of power in the hand, and the mouth was smiling.

Immediately Patricia felt attracted to the man. She turned from his image of her to his wife.

It is something, is it not? asked the woman. I think it is very powerful.

Patricia crossed the room to sit on a plastic covered chair. Her sticky thighs clung to the seat. She looked at the woman, then back at the painting.

I'm sorry, she said.

The Algerian woman laughed and made a hopeless gesture with her hand. She scooted into the kitchen after the baby, and set him in the middle of the floor with a pile of crackers.

Patricia looked at the painting again, and then away, out the window. Three floors down there were people mixing on the beach. The windows were polarized and their light was cool.

This is not the first time, the woman was saying, sitting down on the floor beside her son, playing with his black curls. He has had many women since his work became famous. In Paris he was an alley cat.

Where is he now? asked Patricia. She had been watching the woman's lips move around a language that was native to neither of them. The woman was in her mid-thirties and was still beautiful, with a fine nose and high forehead. When she braided her thick black hair, the braids held together at the ends by themselves.

He is with Beto, said the woman. This is the son of his first marriage.

That is the boy you were with yesterday? asked Patricia, looking again at the painting.

No, that was Tito, she said. He is the son from the second marriage. She placed her hands on Marco's head and slipped her fingers between the shiny curls. We are the third that he has married.

Why do you stay with him? asked Patricia, looking at the woman's hands. The fingers were long and thin. It was her silver flute on the stand in the corner.

The woman laughed and hugged her son to her thigh. She picked a piece of cracker up off the floor and handed it to him, placed it in his wet hands.

I stay with him because I love him. She smiled at Patricia. *El Amor no tiene orgullo.* There are some men who can never be satisfied by one woman. He needs to believe in the kind of love that does not exist. If he suspected how practical love really is, he would despair.

Love is not a decision, Patricia said lamely.

For me, said the woman, it is more important to love than to be loved. I need to love.

Patricia looked again at the painting.

He has slept with her, said the painter's wife. She nodded with her eyes at a table they were passing.

A woman sat alone, blonde kinky hair and a low-cut man's T-shirt, smoking a filterless cigarette. She watched them pass from the corner of her eye, her profile perfect in the light from the restaurant.

They passed her without saying anything more.

He only likes beautiful women, said the painter's wife at the corner. And they never know what to do with me. She smiled at Patricia; I am so nice.

They continued up the sand street, past the long distance telephone office, a cantina, the panaderia, until they reached the Zocalo. It was nearly deserted. They plopped themselves down on a bench in front of an alamendra tree. Patricia wiped at her face with the end of her skirt.

And what of your Cuban? asked the Algerian woman.

Patricia stretched her legs out in front of her and pulled down on the hem, where the material was fraying.

I don't understand it, she said. He comes to see me twice a day, spends every night with me, but he does not give me what I need. He is a body, no more. He holds something from me.

The painter's wife reached, picked up a corner of Patricia's skirt and began to play with the frayed hem, folding it as if she were going to repair it.

And you? she asked Patricia. Are you waiting for him to give you everything first. She folded the hem further along where it was just beginning to unravel.

Patricia watched her slender fingers.

We are waiting for each other, she said. It is ridiculous. But I know he feels proud to be with me.

The woman laughed and dropped the material.

Are you proud to be with the Cuban? she asked. She was not looking at Patricia. Instead, she watched a Mayan woman pedal a cart topped with peeled oranges out of the square. The woman had long greying braids hanging in a pair down her back.

Yes, said Patricia.

Wait for me, said the Algerian woman. She stood up, fished in the pocket of her skirt for some coins, then chased after the Mayan woman. Patricia saw her catch the woman at the edge of the Zocalo, drop a handful of coins into her palm, and choose six oranges. She held them in her skirt and trotted back across the center.

Here, she said, and handed one to Patricia. She sat down again, the oranges piled in her lap, and picked out one for herself.

The others are for my family, she said.

Patricia separated the sections and made flower designs on both of her thighs, then began to eat their petals, spitting out the seeds in front of her.

If you feel pride in the one you love, then you are in love with a reflection of yourself, how this person makes you look, she was told. *El orgullo te engaña,* pride tricks you. She sucked the seeds out of an orange slice and spit them delicately into her palm.

Patricia sighed.

The first time I made love with the Cuban, he left me saying he would come right back, she said. I did not see him for three days and then he did not apologize. He just presented himself one night and expected me to let him in.

Did you?

Patricia laughed grudgingly. I let him in and he left at dawn to fish for lobster. When he came back to my cabana, he had an extra pair of pants and some shirts. He did not ask me if he could move, he just did it.

It is difficult for some men to ask, said the woman. She played with the oranges in her lap, lifting her skirt and rolling them back and forth across her thighs.

Patricia looked at her impatiently.

You make excuses for selfishness, she said. There is something wrong with me. I am in love with an egotist.

The woman looked up at her in surprise.

You have to tell him what it is you need, she said. If he cannot give it to you, you must go. It is that simple.

But you! said Patricia. How can you say that when your husband has so many lovers and leaves you alone?

The woman folded her oranges into her lap.

I have made my needs very small, she said.

Patricia was dancing alone in the sand to a scratchy reggae, a plastic cup filled with Kahlúa in her hand. She swirled her skirt with the frayed hem around her with the other hand and moved her hips softly to the even beat. Couples danced beside her.

I'm tired of it, she had told the Algerian woman when they parted. I'm going to drink and dance by myself.

But now she felt foolish dancing alone. She knew that the Cuban was canvassing the sand streets on his motorcycle, looking for her.

She spun, twisting her skirt, and when she faced again the direction where she had started, she was surprised to find that she had a partner. The man was wearing white pants that tied at the ankles and at the waist, and a white baggy shirt with wide sleeves, stitched with red X's around the collar. He smiled at Patricia and nodded.

You dance well! he called loudly over the music.

Her rhythm was affected. She stepped to the side and bumped into someone. The drink she was holding spilled out, onto her skirt, into the cool sand. The man in the white pants pulled her by the arm from the dance floor. He steered her to a table outside in the sand, and reached for a handful of napkins.

I can do it, she said in Spanish. She took the napkins from him and began to blot the brown stain from her white skirt.

It will come out with bleach, said the man, in English. You should watch where you are dancing.

She kept scrubbing. He waited until she laid the wet napkins on the table, then gestured toward a seat. She remained standing. He held out his hand.

My name is Uvat, he said.

She shook his hand loosely and looked at his dark, thin face. His bottom lip was wet, shiny, and full.

I have seen you running, he said.

The Photographer

Barry Lopez

There came a point in his life, a point common to us all, when he decided to strip away his ties. Although he had left home some years before, he perceived there was still a bond, so he put that in order. He took care of it. He took possession of an independence which all men strive for and few attain. Because they are detained (he realized) by the details of lives fashioned haphazardly, or too casually. He had known from the beginning what he would do. He would photograph endangered and possibly extinct animals. He would go to the places where the last of a species had been reported and he would systematically set about capturing the animals on film. Not quick, sharp photographs, which would have been satisfactory, surely, but portraits. He wished to make a gallery of such portraits of animals on the verge of extinction. To this end he spent some years, then, not in the study of photography, but living on the reservations of the northern plains, among Crow and Blackfeet primarily but also on the Turtle Mountain Reservation with Chippewa hunters in North Dakota. From these men he learned enough of movement in the wild, of concealment and patience, to have some reasonable chance of success.

The first animal he chose was one of the hardest, the ivory-billed woodpecker. He thought privately that if he did well with this one, he would go back up on the plains and photograph the black-footed ferret. It had been clear to him from the beginning that his teachers did not think much of his hunting with a camera. It was like walking a long way to someplace just to get on a bus and come back. He harbored an uneasiness over the thought, but he knew his teachers were not white men and what he was doing, he explained, was for white men. One day, when he was finished, he would stop in some small town in Nebraska — Chadron would be nice — and go into a cafe (it would be a summer day, he could almost feel the thick heat, hear the screen door stretch and slam back in its frame) and he would give all the camera equipment to a family of tourists eating lunch. He would set the things down with them and go out the door and drive away.

But for now he was headed south, to the Big Thicket on the far side of the Trinity River in Texas to photograph the ivorybill. He rented a canoe in Lufkin and bought groceries and maps and with a confidence like granite (which he had also learned from the Indian hunters but which he could not recognize in himself) he penetrated the swamp. On the nineteenth day he saw an ivorybill. On the twenty-seventh he saw another and photographed it for half an hour before the bird became aware of his presence and flew off. On the fifty-first day, toward dusk, he located two birds in the branches of a sweet gum tree and began to shoot. The birds (he could sense they were gradually becoming aware of him, for he allowed himself to be seen: it was the part he found most exciting, his own gradual exposure) became used to him. As the sun settled on the western horizon and the long red-gold rays hit the birds they seemed to stand away from the branches, like supernatural creatures. The stout white bills looked like weathered chalk against the blue-black feathers and the red pompadour seemed irradiated with light as if about to burst into flame. The yellow eyes with their enormous dark pupils had a depth the man found startling, almost terrifying. It was exactly what he wanted. A portrait of an endangered species that would terrify. The sun went down. The birds receded into the darkness. He was sure of what he was doing. He left the swamp that evening.

He drove north and, as he had intended, photographed the black-footed ferret on the flat, dry plains of Wyoming. The weasel was swift and crepuscular and presented him with some difficulty, working in open country. He concentrated on making himself each day more invisible. Eventually he was able to photograph from a distance of less than twenty feet. One evening during a thunderstorm he caught a ferret looking over his shoulder exactly at the moment the prairie dimness disappeared under a stroke of lightning. This took almost three months, and he thought to himself that it would take three months to photograph each of the animals he wanted. It would take that long to find them, to get close enough, to create a photograph in which the look was unsettling. He thought the look he was after might seem to be anger, but he was not sure. It was just an expression, peculiar to each animal, which seemed truthful, as if in seeing his own stare returned he was stripped naked.

From Wyoming he went to the deserts of California to photograph pupfish. This was a lark. The fish were the prisoners of shallow pools. But it took three months anyway, waiting for the expression.

In the months that followed he photographed the small Everglade kite, the red wolf in the coastal swamps of Louisiana, the Labrador duck (listed as extinct by the Department of Interior since 1875), the Mexican grizzly (photographed at dawn in the Sierra Madre Occidental at 10,000 feet among yellow poppies), Cooper's sandpiper (listed as extinct), the California condor, the heath hen (listed as extinct), and the Eskimo curlew. He photographed the curlew last, on its nesting grounds in the arctic and then in Argentina where the bird summers. Curious about the quality of light in the southern hemisphere, he eventually went to the winter grounds of each of the birds he photographed, but there was nothing outside North America that held his interest.

In eight years he made thirty-one portraits. He was thirty-seven years old, and he thought privately that he had done what he set out to do and that in an odd way he was now free to go. He had a series of prints made in the finest photographic studio in New York and took the portraits to the Audubon Society. He also delivered to them his extensive field notes, although he was careful to delete references to precise locations. He would not reveal his name, insisting that whenever the photographs were used they were to be credited "Anonymous." He accepted no payment, refused to make speeches or to accept assignments to photograph other animals.

At first the excitement over the photographs was incredible. Everyone who saw them was stunned by the lighting in the faces, by the positioning of the heads. But there was something unsettling about the portraits and initial enthusiasm gradually changed to a sort of fear. The portraits, which had been hung on the walls of a long, wide hallway, were taken down after a week and stored, very carefully, in the Society's library.

A meeting was held at which it was decided that the curious reaction people had had — first general astonishment, going almost numb at the looks, then uneasiness and finally, they agreed, a primitive fear — was no reason not to produce a special issue of the Society's magazine. It would be an extraordinary publication. No expense would be spared. In addition to the photographer's notes reproduced facsimile, they would commission the greatest bird and mammal writers in the country — Teal, Peterson, Brooks — to do pieces. They would include for contrast the faded, torn, fuzzy black and whites, the odd blurred snapshots taken by lucky tourists that up until now had been the best available. There would be introductory essays by the president of the International Union for the Conservation of Nature and Natural Resources and by the Secretary of the Interior. Reproductions of the thirty-one photographs would be offered in gift sets at $2500, the money to be set aside to provide sanctuaries and to cover legal expenses in lobbying for new protective laws.

The day following the meeting the photographs were removed from storage and work was begun. A room was cleared, the photographs were hung around the walls and work tables were set up in the middle. The photographs had only been up for a day when they began to fade. In spite of desperate measures taken by the most gifted technicians the photographs faded beyond recognition in a matter of hours and it was not, incredibly, until they were all gone that anyone thought to photograph the photographs. The man who had been director of the project for the special publication wished to take what was left of the photographs home with him as mementos, but it was finally decided that they should remain at the Society's headquarters. They were inventoried for tax purposes and the loss, an enormous one, was written off the following year.

The man who had taken the photographs stopped at a small town in Nebraska where, as he intended, he gave away his cameras. He proceeded northwest to the Crow Indian Reservation where he stayed for some months before moving to Alaska where each day he rowed about Norton Sound in a small boat, miles from the coast. He thus began to study the behavior of humpback whales.

In Hock
Lissa McLaughlin

This particular woman, Sally, decided to drive off the road and buy a pig. There was the sign PIGS in crooked letters on the Maine roadside shoulder. She had a hankering for a pig, to be her lover hadn't occurred to her yet, on the way up the walk she thought it would make a funny story, how the pig turned up at the tail end of her vacation. She went up the walk to the pig store, a farm actually where farmers were handling the pig's hind quarters with sticks, poking at high flesh lizarded with mean hair, listening hard to all the whining and coughing like doctors overseeing their patients, the same anxious strokings of hooves Sally now saw inside the pen the farmers bid across. A business woman herself, she was impressed, awed, and held her brief-case up against her stomach. A sow dotted with piglets gave her a shot look out of the corner of her eye, lying there squashed under her size, breathing. Sally didn't know the difference between a dream and all this and felt something rise inside her. Hello there! she called to the mother, with the little gimlets of the piglet boys and girls gnawing into her side. Sally felt hungry, and this made her dizzy. The pigs' smell impeded the air. Give me that one, she said. I'll treat it just like a little dog. The farmer had a beard. You will, will you? he said. Don't you know that's a pig? Confound you, don't you take no action against my pig when you find out he ain't no dog, you hear? His Maine accent somehow made him blend in with the shrill distinctiveness of his property. I won't, said Sally dreamily. I'll be responsible, and pushing her arm up against the car window and the farmer aside, she let the piglet swing back and forth in her grasp with short hops and little strainings, like a tiny half moon trying to break free. All Sally could see was the top of his head. Then he swung his face sideways and nosed her hard in the breast, Sally stood still, her car key in her hand. Don't worry, she said, We're going right home. And she kept her eyes on him.

They drove along the big Maine pines. That's where I got him, Maine, she'd tell people. Isn't he a sight? From Maine you came, and to Connecticut you shall go, she sang. She didn't know yet what she'd do with a pig. Would you like to listen to the radio? With one finger she scratched his back. She knew she'd hold his face out to her guests, too happy and heedless to look at him. The pig's eyes glanced intensely sideways. They were like little sewn-on blue beads. He arched his back and butted the seat. Then he came swarming into her side. Be quiet there! she cried, honking the horn by accident. The pig wobbled away as if drunkenly reconsidering, then slid down and fell asleep. Sally held tightly to the wheel.

Sally was a small, strong-bodied, full-willed woman used to dealing in images. She was in advertising. She could make anything look good. But this cast no reflection on her own personal ability to discern. I am a hard woman with good eyes, she used to say. This is what points me, she said, striking herself in the forehead. Let's drink to that, Boys! The startled ad men in a row would rise with their glasses. They believed her, the way she flopped down on a sofa during meetings, or pushed her hand over desk tops until the wood seemed to stand up under her fingers, grow shiny from her persuasiveness. You just have to be suspicious, Sally laughed, striding along beside the men with her jacket lapels wallowing in the breeze. In fact, Sally's lack of faith meant the men could have fun with her. She distrusted everything, so she always loved a con. You're too much, she'd beam, when someone put a fake sign up saying the john was out of order, or got an ad man to run off to lunch with a nonexistent account.

Now Sally hesitated to put her hand down on her own car seat. But she wanted to very much. One of her dark eyes gave her a shocked look in the mirror. What's gotten into you? it said. The other darted down at the little form curled against the seat. She could pick the piglet up and sit him in one palm. But look how he breathed, what a monster face he had. She wanted to get right down there and look at it. She wanted to lie down beside him on the seat. The pig snoozed. He had more skull than most people, pointing resolutely, yet plaintively toward the dashboard. Imagining the blood beating there made her even more giddy. She thought of lifting him under the narrow chest, showing him the weather. But when she reached out, she felt scared to touch him. She pulled her purse closer to her. She felt guilty he couldn't see out. Her palm floated in middair, scratchy. She had no idea yet about her intentions, but instead played the wheel just like any responsible woman, fixing her eyes on the asphalt road, hazed with the dust of Maine heat. She only knew, sitting there, that the sound of his hooves on the seat rattled her. After a long time he woke up. She was still wondering, was he wanting to find his mother, was he embarrassed? She thought and thought. Or worse, was he indifferent? Then she almost lost the wheel. Oh it's you! He'd plunged his head into her side then run blindly against the far door. She sat back up very straight. Then he turned and rocking forward ran right against her again. The whole car almost tipped over. Sally was shouting and laughing, and the car drove in and out of its lane.

Finally they crossed the Connecticut border. Sally was still introducing herself. I know it must be funny to you, she was saying to the piglet's hard, dusty skull. Here I am Executive Director of this enormous ad agency, used to dealing people in and out like cards. I drive up in my little Honda and steal you away inside. Do you miss your mother already? she asked hurriedly. Can you forgive me? Let me wipe your face. She kept talking as if afraid to hear what she was saying. Sally lifted her own dark, handsome looks and jangling earrings, overcome with the sensation of search that was applying itself to her palm. The pig stood backed against the seat as if waiting for his mother, his flexible snout like a wall of fluid skin ramming itself again and again between her fingers, while she held desperately on, seeing the road signs open and shut. What happened to your smell? he seemed to cry, and his head shoved against her loud with consideration and loneliness. All of a sudden Sally's hand gripped his snout tightly while he squealed brilliantly, his face threading itself out of her fingers. Look at me! Sally shouted, taking her eyes off the road. Do you hear me at all? The feltcovered head collapsed as she let loose. Then they were in the driveway, the pig knew, and while she tried to feel for him again, applying her brakes, he let out a shriek and rolled sideways against the door.

He was still grunting weakly, and Sally looked up for reassurance at her white house with the evergreens pruned into submission, in the shape of cashboxes. The lawn boy had left the mower out, and it stood like a security device or a pet by the driveway, its handle at the level of her eyes. You short little punkin, Sally said looking straight forward, surprising herself with these baby syllables. She heard his complaining and worrying and couldn't stand it anymore. Look, she said, hefting him under the belly straight up into the air. This is the kind of animal Connecticut has, she laughed, parading him gently back and forth so he could see the mower and lowering her face toward him trying to smile, but he thrashed and suffered so high up and his mouth broke open into screams so intense she cried, Then tell me what you want! and turned him abruptly against her shirt, and he rooted there while her own eyes rolled in comparable quantities of despair. Then she opened the door and put her legs out of the car.

The pig glanced around the kitchen as Sally stood drinking a martini. The olive danced and quivered and she thought of the various dances the piglet seemed to do, all the time looking through his thick lashes, his pale eyes, and of her own lap as he stood rocking over his little legs. Confused images of pines, flesh and asphalt came into her head. She saw her own face in the mirror, sticking out her tongue. She shut her eyes. Then she pushed her hand against her silk shirt, remembering something. I have a date tonight! and with Sam! Oh boy! and she put her head against her arm, and grabbed her hair, perplexed. And just when he's been telling me these nice things. Poor joker. She jumped away from the pig, who was sniffling her foot. Stop that, she said, taking a jump. The pig moved blindly forward. I want you to come along with me now, Sally said, desperately clutching her drink. The pig was following her foot everywhere. I want you to come while I take my bath. Come on and you can play with the towels. She looked behind her all the way up the carpeted stairs afraid the pig wouldn't listen. But he came into the bathroom and was scratching a flea when she dropped her robe, and at the sight of her he squealed and ran frantically back and forth over the tiles. It's all right, it's all right, Sally cried, clutching her throat and splashing water every which way, her free hand flying over his back. It's just me, it's just me, I'm just sitting in some water! Used to the sound of her voice by now, the pig gradually ran in smaller circles. He banged into her hand to calm himself and his eye skipped with a separate existence between her fingers, and Sally felt her own flesh rise.

She was soaped and rinsed. She stood up tentatively, grabbing the towel rack. The pig came up. She was clutching the towel to her legs, and he put his snout against her knee, scoured it in slow revolving circles so complete her skin answered and a more general haze than steam rose in front of her, and she saw herself fallen back on the bed and the pig came nearer, grown bigger. Her mouth opened in the fragrant air and soap slid down her nose. Then her eyes focused on the unbelievably fragile fold of creased skin along his neck. She was staring down at the top of a baby's nose. You're a baby! she cried. A baby! And look what you're making me do! And she felt the nose plunge and search for what it could feed on, grant itself a name by, and her arm flogged the air in horror. You're a baby! she screeched, flogging her arm at the ideas that spilled into the air like steam.

She ran across the white carpet and into her bedroom, her bed was shaped like a circle and she fell on top of it. The piglet threw back his head and screeched Me! Me! Me! while he ran round and round in circles and she retracted her feet. Finally she could not stand it any longer and hauled him into her arms while he sucked air and dragged her fingers into his hungry mouth uttering little barks of gratitude. He pushed her and then pulled her with his feet and his gracious, clothlike nose. She fell somewhere a long time and then came back to where she was. She looked down at the hoof marks on her chest. You come here and do this to me, she stared down plaintively, What is all this for? she mourned into his wet hair. The little pig had his eyes closed.

Late that evening Sally got ready to go on her date. She had all kinds of fancy clothes, labels from everywhere. She pulled out a dress from her closet. She locked the bedroom door and found a dish and put milk in it and unlocked the door and left it inside. Between dressing and calling the ad man in question she managed to find some straw in a neighbor's paddock, and filling the Smirnoff's box she'd dragged up from the cellar, took a long look in her mirror then fit his heaving feet inside the carton. She lifted her hand, holding his smell from her dress. His feet swung unbelievingly, back and forth.

Listen, she said, and her heart was folding and tearing. Her pearls swung out in the air. The pig's skull was very narrow and tipped, and a tiny pointed eye glinted from one side. He stood sideways below her, looking off. Sally swayed on her high heels and then fell forward and the pig shoved his dense, sharpened brow quickly against hers, and trembled there. He was drinking his milk, staggering. Listen, Sally began again, panting, I won't be long, it's only an evening. I won't stay there with him. I promise I'll be here tonight. The piglet stumbled and fell forward in the box and Sally caught her lip. She was crying, I'm sorry. Forgive me for forgetting you. Her tears fell on the pig's head. Oh, forgive me, I lead such a difficult life.

Mountains
Patricia O'Donnell

They were in Colorado: huge, empty skies broken by spires of conifers. She had never seen the mountains before. Her first view had been at night, driving in from Iowa. At the end of the long plains, a solitary light on top of a dark spot in the sky. "There they are," the man she was travelling with said. "Oh, you're kidding," she said, "That's just a light in the sky." "No, this is the beginning of the mountains." She had never really believed they would be there, though she had heard about them since early childhood. As the sun came up over them, she felt she was acting out a dream. The man beside her said he had no real awe of the mountains; she was too amazed to respond. As they drove into the city, even the gas stations and quick food stands were romantic, unbelievable, the early light dusting them with a foreign glow. The man beside her had long, slim fingers; unusually pale for a man. They tapped the wheel lightly, alternating, as he drove.

They arrived at the man's friends' house where they would be staying. They were three young men; just waking up, they were bare-chested, tousled, genial. The house was pale pink stucco, with two large pine trees out in front. Throughout the day the sun barely filtered through the thick needles, and the scent filled the house. The young men became boisterous as the day wore on; they worked little, obtaining their sustenance by various, not always discreet or legal, ways. She soon became their friend, a sort of group mascot. By not saying too much, smiling a lot, and occasionally going off into long gales of laughter, she attracted their affection. Any one of three, if given the chance, would gladly have fallen in love, had they not known how she felt about their friend, the man she was travelling with. It was on her face; she rarely laughed when he spoke, even when he spoke lightly, but instead would savor each word, watching as he talked, then would turn her gaze to the wall or table, and be still a moment.

That night they went out on the town. Strains of "Night in the city looks pretty to me" alternating in her mind with the horns, the flashing lights, the attractions of this place. Walking arm-in-arm down the street with one of her new friends and the man she travelled with. Into a bar where a girl in a skimpy fake suede fringe and satin danced on a little stage; it all seemed very funny. A sign volunteered "Go-Go girls needed." "Why don't you apply?"

one of the friends asked. She looked at the fringe on the girl's gyrating body, her smooth, plump thighs, then down at her own blue-jeaned body, "No, I don't think so."

She slept on the couch that night, her friend sleeping downstairs. In the morning she crept down to his small room, entirely filled by a waterbed, and crawled in with him. They talked, rolled in a quilt, exchanging confidences. They toyed with their fears. In mid-morning one of the others brought down a gallon of wine, and for the rest of the day they drank, they laughed. In late afternoon they ventured outside. The air was light and fresh, the day in relaxed, fading mid-stream. She said "I feel as if this is where I should be, here with you." The mountains were clear in the distance, surrounding the perimeters of the city. In the grass the man she came with found a bright green worm, a fat, brilliant thing. Curled around a twig, they held it up to the sun, agreed it was beautiful. Turning it, they suddenly injured the thing, a drop of red blood swelling from its side, becoming almost as large as the worm itself, curling around its wound. Horrified, the man put the stick back on the grass, saying it depressed him, it was awful. They sat silent, arms curled around their knees, the pines casting long, fragrant shadows on the afternoon.

The next day they went up in the mountains to camp. They chose one of the higher foothills, one covered with pine trees all the way up, except for scattered bare patches. Choosing one of these for their campsite, they pitched two tents, a large one for the three men, a small one for the other two. Below them was a small river with fast-running, clear water. The three men showed them how to slide down the hill on the pine needles; getting a good running start from the top of the hill, they slid the rest of the way on their tennis shoes, occasionally lowering themselves to their haunches and finishing that way. The girl and her friend were timid; at last he gave it a try, sitting down most of the way. She walked down. The sky was being covered with patchy, fleecy clouds. They could see it raining in spots on the hills around them. As they were going down, a rainburst caught them in a sudden, violent shower. Alone in the pine trees, she could hear their shouts at the suddenness of the shower, but could not see them. Running, sliding for a large tree, she reached its dry safety and crouched there, the branches too low for her to stand. Breathing deeply, she thought "I could stay here under this tree, no one would ever find me." She sat very still as the shower went on, having no music in her head, no words, no laughter, only the sound of the rain on the needles and the suddenness of one jagged lightning bolt across the sky. The shower passed as suddenly as it had come on; she could see it moving its dark shadow across the hills. Still she sat there, hearing her own breathing, and it wasn't until the sky was blue and sunny again that they came near, shouting for her, and she crawled out of her hiding place.

That night they had tea after supper and sat by the campfire watching the slow sun go down from their vantage point in the clearing. All five were quiet, breathing in the clouds of the tea she had made, sipping its sweet, hot flavor. As darkness came on it grew chilly; they piled wood on the fire and donned sweaters and sweatshirts. Her travelling companion suggested they play a game called "What do you want?" Starting with him, there were to ask until he gave an answer that satisfied them, that they believed. She jumped at the chance.

"What do you want?" "Happiness." "No, what do you *really* want?" "To be an astronaut." "No, what do you *want*!" "The adulation of millions." "Come on, what do you want?" Long silence. "A baseball with Mickey Mantle's autograph on it, and what's more, I have always wanted Mickey Mantle to be my father, and my mother to be Marilyn Monroe. And that's what I really want!" She took his answer lightly until it was her turn, when she was pushed and pushed, and finally all she could think of was: "I want to be a tree. I want to be a tree." And it was true.

That night she lay beside his dark bulk in the tent. Long spell without words, the only sounds the crackling of the remains of the fire and the rustling overhead. She said, "I feel very strange lately. Things that used to be ugly are beautiful — things that have to die, old things. Like an old, decrepit woman on her sickbed with her face full of lines — that seems beautiful to me now. So clear, and sharp; maybe it's the air here." Through the open flap of their tent she could see the shadows moving; the night was alive, strangely light. After a moment she could discern the sound of the stream. She could sense the city they had left behind, in the valley below them, on the other side of the hill. It was full of people, and noisy, and in a bar there was a plump girl in satin and fringe dancing, but up here there was sky, and quiet, and this man beside her in the tent. Because she wanted to stay here always, and never go to sleep, she wasn't aware when she finally did.

The next day she found herself feeling a freedom, a realease. She decided that it was the relaxing and dissipation of a fear, the fear being that whatever she was experiencing now was temporary. As they drove past rocky cliffs, turning off the road to stop at a riverbank for lunch, she was working this over in her mind. These scenes were temporary; the exquisiteness of this spot, for example, that very branch rippling between her gaze and the river, the voices in the background. But she felt something growing in her; perhaps she was becoming another person. That was it, she was sure — she had never felt this way before. It was this abandon to being what she perceived, this giving up of old thoughts and ways of feeling, that gave her this feeling of strength today. Certain things did not matter any more; for what could matter in the face of this trembling beauty? If there was a sin in this existence, she decided, it would be to try and hold experience and feeling, either her own or another person's, and imagine that they would never leave.

That evening they returned to the stucco house behind the pines. After supper she and her travelling companion decided to take a walk; a suggestion was hardly necessary, they were out the door together. The streets were quiet, only an occasional car. They walked through an alley, climbed over a fence, and reached a private, deserted lot. It was a round valley, like a bowl, or one half of a sphere, the other half the sky. The stars were brilliant, amazing; there had been no skies like this where she came from. They saw a falling star, then another; the night was full of falling stars. They were knee-deep in the waving grasses, they smoothed down a spot for themselves to sit on. They were hidden from the world. The stars were their company, the conversation punctuated by their bright dots and dashes. She felt that whatever she said he understood; and what's more, he illuminated those parts of herself of which she was yet unaware. She felt like bursting, a firecracker display across the sky. She would light up the mountains and be their friend, they would at last be aware of her and know her as she knew them. Later when she tried to remember exactly what they had talked about, it seemed trivial, ordinary. She decided she must have forgotten most of it, for that night she felt they uncovered great truths.

Their last night in Colorado she slept in the waterbed downstairs with him, curled close in her red and black flowered nightgown. She had made that nightgown before she left for Colorado; silly thing, her mother had exclaimed at its impracticality. Now the man said that she looked like a flower that blooms at night. He said they could not make love; how take another person, how ever to understand another person? The innocence in her face hurt him like a stone. They lay close all night, rolling in their dreams. She dreamed she was crossing a stream on a swaying bridge. The sun was lighting the leaves all around her. Her friend was across the stream, laughing. There were leaves under the bridge, tickling her feet. When she woke it was late, the man she travelled with was tickling the soles of her feet with a feather.

They stood by the car, bags inside. Every excuse for delaying had been used. Finally her friend said to her, why are we so sad? You'd think we were going to die today, or never see each other again. She laughed, agreed with him, got in the car and slammed the door. They waved to the three young men in the pink stucco house as they drove away. The mountains in the distance glimmered faintly, a glow on them she had never seen before. She held hands with the man she was travelling with until the mountains were out of sight.

Night Game
Pamela Painter

The three of them were driving all night. They were headed back to the Hilton Hotel in Athens. A telegram had been sent with their mail to the Youth Hostel just as she and Jim were leaving Thessalonika for Philippi and Thassos to see the classic plays in the old theatres. It called them back to Athens saying the government couldn't guarantee their safety unless they returned to the city. There, protection and hotels were assured. The 'Government' was not identified. It was an order.

One of the clerks, Niki, who had talked and gestured nonstop two days before when he met them in a taverna, went into the kitchen and packed them a sack of food — two cheese pies, bread, sausage. "Keep driving," he said. He wouldn't answer any questions, pretending not to understand Prin's Greek without the background of music and retsina. He just muttered "governments" and walked them back to the old Buick, turned around and went inside, firmly closing the heavy door. He hadn't looked back.

And now Prin was driving. Her hand hung on the wheel with a heaviness meant to control. From time to time her fingers would go to sleep but then the numbness seared her more. One at a time she shook her hands, flexed her fingers, grew more alert as they tingled, almost hurt, from the return of circulation.

Jim, her husband, was asleep in the back seat using a sleeping pack for a pillow. They had been traveling for most of June and July ever since they had finished classes and sublet the apartment till September. They had flown to Paris, leaving England for the following summer, and traveled slowly south to Italy. Greece had been her idea. They had no time schedules for sightseeing, eating, making love. Just whenever, whatever happened was all right with them. Until now — she could almost feel the change. She could see his hunched shoulders in the rear view mirror. He hadn't moved since he left the wheel, giving her breast a soft pat. The gesture had annoyed her.

Now, Brodie sat beside her playing a small harmonica. Telling her to name another song. Finding chords. He had joined them about five miles out of Thessalonika from behind a sign reading 'Athens'. The news had reached him too. His first words "Christ, you're from the States." made them laugh with

111

relief, homesickness. And now his gear was tied on top of the small sedan; theirs filled most of the trunk, spilled over into the back seat.

The chords moved into "When the Saints" and she sang along for the first few measures, surprised at finding the words, until she ran out of their memory. Where had she dredged up that title anyway? But the music was all there and she could hum along, softly following the song to its close, waiting as he chorded another, recognizing it and again finding enough words for a few lines here and there.

"Name another," he said, still holding the harmonica against his mouth. His lips were full, his mouth wide. The harmonica would be warm, moist.

"Just play," she said.

"Hey," he said. "I'm keeping *you* awake. It has to be something you know."

"I know them all," she said. "I just can't remember names. Go on, play."

He shrugged and drifted into what she thought was "Red River Valley." She came up with a few words to show him her intentions were good. From their he strayed in the same key and picked up "Don't Fence Me In" and she sang along with that for a while too.

They stopped for gas in a small town. Prices had gone up from 7 to 9 drachmae. Six or seven men were sitting outside the station, talking. They all turned to watch the car pull up to the pump. One of them came over to fill their tank and then before giving her change went back with her money to the group of men. Another stood up as though his back hurt him, stood up and peered at them.

"Tell them to keep moving," she pieced together from the sentences he said. "They can't stay here." His tone wasn't hostile. Those were the facts. And we won't, she thought, if the car holds out. It was overheating again. They'd have to rest it a while and then drive slower. The night seemed to stretch before her into an infinite amount of mountain turns and curves.

Jim sat up as they pulled away and then slumped back against the pack once more. Brodie fumbled through a few measures of "Never on Sunday" before returning to the old songs.

Finally the music stopped. "You O.K.?" he asked. She nodded and Brodie too hunched up against the door, leaving her alone with the vast night that stretched away into darkness on either side of the road as if oceans were lapping soundlessly at the pavement's edge. Just as oceans circumscribed most of Greece. She had always hated driving at night: not knowing what lay beyond the brush that caught the soft gleam of headlights. Often she and Jim had camped just barely off from the deserted road in that same ocean she dreaded, only to wake up the next morning to softly rolling hills and hard solid earth. It had been safe in Greece. Now the sunrise was hours away and still the only danger in this hot, slow-moving country seemed to be the trip past the limits of their rest.

The road pulled her along for two hours or more until in desperation she pushed the window vent open to let in a cool stream that wakened her face. She sat up straighter, arching her back.

When she felt her eyes close for the second time she pulled to the side of the road and stopped the car. The silence startled her and she prodded gently at Brodie's shoulder, calling his name. He said, "Yeah, I'm ready to drive," and walked around the car as she slid across into the passenger's seat. Bread-crumbs sanded her legs.

"What time is it?" he asked, rubbing his eyes.

"I don't know. Close to two, I think." She couldn't see her watch. She could tell Brodie was still sleepy. She'd talk to him soon but she needed a short nap first before she could concentrate or care where he was from, where he was going, who he was. They had only about four or five hours to go — if they stayed alive. She bunched Brodie's jacket under her head and leaned back on the seat. His smell would be more familiar to her than any other knowledge she had of him. He started the car and edged up onto the road. Soon they were moving on and she could feel herself driftng off to the drone of the car's engine.

She woke with a start when she realized that the car had slowed almost to a stop, was slowly moving to the center of the road.

"Brodie." she shook his arm and his head jerked up, his eyes went wide with fear.

"You were falling asleep, weren't you?" she accused.

"Christ! Must have been," he said. He rubbed his eyes.

"Want me to drive?" She pushed herself up straight against the back of the seat. His jeans seemed to catch and pull on her cotton skirt.

"I'll be O.K. You must still be dead." He glanced over at her, then back to the road.

Jim mumbled something from the back seat and Prin turned to smooth his jacket up over his exposed back. Then she pulled her canteen out of her pack and splashed some water on her face before drinking. It tasted cool, but no longer fresh. The road stretched in front of them, from time to time silver rocks appeared at the side as if brought to life by the headlights of the car. Brodie held out his hand and she watched as he took a long drink and handed it back to her. His hands hung loosely on the steering wheel.

They rode in silence for a half hour or so and soon her eyes began to close, the pull of lids against the dryness of her corneas, the sealing of the membranes when they met. When the car swerved she instinctively reached for the wheel, her hand closed on Brodie's, his arm against her breast. And then she felt her cheeks go warm and she wasn't sure the car had swerved or if the motion had been her own drifting into sleep. She leaned back, but closer to him. Still scared, but awake now.

"It was a dead animal," he said. "You were falling asleep again. Maybe Jim is ready to drive?"

She turned around and pushed at him. "Jim, Jim? Can you drive now? We're almost there."

"Sleep just a little longer," he said. He didn't open his eyes, didn't say anything more.

She turned around. "Sorry I grabbed the wheel. Christ, I could have wrecked us."

"Forget it," he said patting her leg. She moved under his touch. He left his hand there, warm on her leg as if her skirt didn't exist between the two.

They rode in darkness for a few more miles and she had almost forgotten his hand was there when he began to move it along her leg, moving her skirt higher on her thigh. This time she didn't move, either nearer to him or away and his hand instead went higher until it had found the center of her. But again she didn't move and so he glanced over at her and raised his hand to her blouse, to where the lacings held the front together and then his hand was inside, moving down over her breast, her nipple in between two fingers, back and forth.

She leaned back and closed her eyes. Not sleepy now but knowing he wasn't either. Allowing herself to take her eyes off the road. Leaning back as his fingers made hard rocks of her nipples and wondering if her breasts too gleamed like silver under the clear Greek night.

When his hand moved down again, she moved too, away from him, her back against the door, his jacket fallen somewhere there, her knees up and her legs parted for him. And he had only one hand on the wheel but somehow they were safer now and his other hand tugged at her pants, pulled them toward him and off. He tucked them into a pocket while she waited more awake than she'd been in two days. And then he was with her again, first pressing the flat of his hand down on her stomach to the soft mound of her hair before his fingers outlined her, before his fingers moved in and around, rhythmically, evenly, knowing the direction without ever taking his gaze from the road.

Solo Dance

Jayne Anne Phillips

She hadn't been home in a long time. Her father had a cancer operation, she went home. She went to the hospital every other day, sitting for hours beside his bed. She could see him flickering. He was very thin and the skin on his leg was soft and pure like fine paper. She remembered him saying 'I give up' when he was angry or exasperated. Sometimes he said it as a joke, 'Jesus Christ, I give up.' She kept hearing his voice in the words now even though he wasn't saying them. She read his get-well cards aloud to him. One was from her mother's relatives. Well, he said, I don't think they had anything to do with it. He was speaking of his divorce two years before.

She put lather in a hospital cup and he got up to shave in the mirror. He had to lean on the sink. She combed the back of his head with water and her fingers. His hair was long after six weeks in the hospital, a grey silver full of shadow and smudge. She helped him get slowly into bed and he lay against the pillows breathing heavily. She sat down again. I can't wait till I get some weight on me, he said. So I can knock down that son of a bitch lawyer right in front of the courthouse.

She sat watching her father. His robe was patterned with tiny horses, sorrels in arabesques. When she was very young, she had started ballet lessons. At the first class her teacher raised her leg until her foot was flat against the wall beside her head. He held it there and looked at her. She looked back at him, thinking to herself it didn't hurt and willing her eyes dry.

Her father was twisting his hands. How's your mother? She must be half crazy by now. She wanted to be by herself and brother that's what she got.

115

No More
John L. Phillips

Tom Quinion's wife went mad by degrees, and when she finally had at him with a carving knife he put his money in his pocket, locked the door to the livery stable and left. His oldest son, Bill, who was 27, said he wanted to go along, and Tom said that would be all right.

On foot they moved north and west, through Litchfield County, up past Torrington and Salisbury and into New York near Copake Falls. In Canaan, on a remote outcropping called Dean Hill, just east of the Massachusetts line, they saw and bought the abandoned Kirby place.

The farm's long untended fields had gone to second growth, mainly alder and sumac. With hand tools and with implements drawn by a team of chestnut yearlings, they gradually cleared and reclaimed their 40-odd acres. They began grubbing out a side-hill living — hand-planting corn, stocking Rhode Island Red laying hens, building up a modest herd of scrawny Black Angus — that would carry them for more than 20 years.

The Quinions lived alone. Their weathered farmhouse had no electricity, telephone or plumbing. Half of it was a tool shed that also held their small assemblage of hunting rifles and traps. In the kitchen was a dry sink, a table with two stools, a wood-burning stove and two kerosene lanterns. Off the kitchen was a room with two mattresses on the floor. The walls were hung with coonskins. The house smelled of urine.

As time passed, father and son fell into the rhythms of subsistence farming. They worked until daylight failed and they slept from darkness to dawn. The first one in from the fields did the cooking. They mostly ate vegetables, fried potatoes, corn fritters and flat, heavy bread. When a cow died they chopped it up right away and lived high for a while, but most of the cattle were sold at the Chatham auction, which Bill attended every year.

Every two months Bill hiked or snow-shoed to Canaan, eight miles away, for provisions — flour, raw sugar, lard, kerosene — and the mail, usually a pennysaver and sometimes a Sears Roebuck catalog, which he glanced at and then threw away. He also had an egg route along the Lebanon Valley. He walked it once a week. When the gunnysack of egg boxes was empty he cut cross-country straight back to Dean Hill.

Once a year Bill walked the 15 miles to Pittsfield to pay the farm's taxes and to put the rest of the egg and cattle profits in the bank. The pink deposit slips from Berkshire Bank & Trust were the only pieces of paper in the house.

For all his walking Bill stayed a roundish man with chubby arms and a muffin face. His father, four inches taller at six feet even, was flat and thin and hard. His sharp face was even more angular under his ratty felt hat. Bill was partial to a long-billed railroad cap.

Tom never left the hill. He said he was content where he was. The closest he ever came was when a young candidate for a minor judgeship came up scouring for votes. During the halting conversation the Quinions asked how long his opponent had been in office. The man said 12 years, which brought father and son simultaneously up from their stools; in their experience, political longevity was a guarantee of villainy. Tom said he'd go down to Canaan and register, but on Bill's next trip for staples he convinced the town clerk to let him register for his father. In the fall he cast his own vote and proxied for Tom.

The Quinions were suspicious of the outsiders who from time to time showed up on the hill. Some of them asked about the availability of parts of the property, which to the east commanded a handsome view of the Berkshires. Tom painted and staked up a couple of board signs, one by the house and one near the barn. They read: SNAKE KEEP OUT. The Quinions had the notion that most visitors were sharpers who knew for certain what they themselves only suspected; that there was vast mineral wealth — uranium, probably — all over the hill.

They had learned of the existence and importance of uranium only by chance. In the mid-fifties an NBC executive who owned adjacent property hired them to mow his fields. In payment he gave them two portable radios. The Quinions were fascinated. For months they sat at opposite ends of the supper table, each listening to his own radio. When the batteries went dead, they threw the radios away.

The Quinions trusted, even liked, people they knew. A neighbor who used to slog up through the drifts unannounced around Christmas with a Mason jar of maple syrup once mentioned he was thinking about planting a vegetable garden in the spring. One day the next April, the Quinions appeared on his property with their team and plow. Tom asked the man where he wanted that garden he'd been talking about.

Certain neighbors were allowed to hunt coon on the hill — they were fair game, Tom said, because they got in with the chickens and corn — and periodically a hunter brought them liquor. Confronted by a jug of any size, the Quinions finished it off on the spot, although they disapproved of "drinkers."

Tom Quinion was 84 when he died. He had put in a full day's work, but had eaten little that night and was too weak to get up the next morning. Two days later Bill walked to the firehouse in West Stockbridge and said his father was dead. Before he died, Tom had told Bill how he wanted his funeral to be.

On the following Monday, then, with a heavy mist and a sporadic downpour obscuring the farm's shoulder mowings lower down, Bill went out to the barn and hitched the ancient workhorses to the newly painted flatbed wagon. He headed the team for the house, where he carefully backed them up to the small side door. He eased the dark gray coffin, made from spare barn siding, off its saw-horses and onto the flatbed and then swung a tarpaulin across the wagon's ridgepoles. In the coffin were Tom, his hat and hunting rifle, a few rounds of ammunition, some candy and a tin of tobacco.

Bill had dug the grave beneath a butternut tree sixty yards from the barn. Under the tree huddled 27 people, the largest gathering on the hill in years. Next to the grave was a Mason jar of zinnias.

Bill moved the wagon up. He stayed seated as the local Congregational minister climbed up, stood on the tailboard and, rain dripping from the brim of his hat, read briefly from the Bible. Then Bill got down and moved aside the planks that had been covering the grave. He and the minister and two neighbors in coveralls lowered the coffin. Bill unhitched the horses and led them to the grave; they stood for a time, he quieting them in the rain, and then he gave them each an apple. Bill put the horses back in their traces, climbed into the wagon and clucked softly. Letting the reins trail, he cantered the rig back across the meadow to the barn. The people drifted away.

Tom had been explicit about his grave: It was to be well secured. Within half an hour, a truck from Canaan Cement & Gravel was laboring up Dean Hill. It maneuvered gingerly into place and poured five cubic yards of concrete over the coffin.

Bill had to wait eight months before the right buyer came to him, one who would pay for the farm in cash and would let him keep title to the half-acre with the butternut tree at its center. When the deal was closed and he had the money in his pocket, Bill left without telling anybody where he was going.

Noel
Michael Plemmons

Mrs. Hathaway brought the children downstairs single file and seated them on straight-backed chairs around the reception room, boy-girl-boy-girl, seventeen in all. In the corner stood a robust Christmas tree bedecked with candy canes and tinsel tresses. The air was thick with the scent of pine and furniture polish as a phantom choir sang "Noel" to the strains of a vinyl disc orchestra. Mrs. Hathaway was still fussing over their appearance, fixing the boys' neckties and correcting the girls' posture, when the first couple arrived. In hushed tones they spoke with Mrs. Overton at the front desk. "We were thinking about a girl," said the woman. Mrs. Overton smiled broadly and made a sweeping motion with her hand. "We have a wonderful selection of girls," she said. At this the girls came to attention in their places, each freckle blooming on rosy cheeks. And as Mrs. Hathaway presented them, each one stood and curtsied on cue. "Christa is a lovely child, age eight...Melinda has a beautiful singing voice for carols...Stephanie has an exceptionally sweet temperament..."

The clients turned to Mrs. Overton and quietly indicated their choice. She nodded, poker-faced, and prepared the papers. Money changed hands. The girls eyed each other nervously as Mrs. Overton recited the rental stipulations: "You understand that this is only a 48-hour agreement. The girl must be returned by noon on the day after Christmas or late charges will be assessed at ten dollars per hour and you will forfeit the insurance deposit." When everything was in order she looked over at Mrs. Hathaway and said, "Melinda, please." A little squeak of joy escaped into the room as Melinda jumped up and rushed to join her hosts for the holiday. The other girls watched her go, their hope renewing as another pair of patrons entered the room from the foyer.

Throughout the afternoon they came two by two, childless on Christmas Eve. They were high-rise dwellers and they were pensioners from South Side bungalows. A few were first-timers, uneasy, unable to meet the children's eyes. (The repeat customers, who each year made up a majority of the business, had reserved their "Kristmas Kid" by name, weeks in advance, and had come by in the morning for express pick-up.) Most of those now arriving to browse among the leftovers were last minute shoppers.

The girls were in great demand, especially the youngest candidates in curls.

119

Dimples and bangs, once again, were very popular. And for the boys, missing teeth and cowlicks were favorite features. Considering the irregular inventory, business was good. Of the original lot, only two rather plain-looking lads remained at six o'clock, closing time. Both bore the stigma of a pubescent mustache.

Mrs. Overton finished her filing while Mrs. Hathaway affixed the "Closed" sign on the door, unplugged the Christmas lights, and drew the window shades all around. The boys sat silent, watchful.

Said Mrs. Overton, "I told you about those two preteens, didn't I?"

"Yes, ma'am, you did."

"Then why did you bring them down with the others?"

"Well, I was hoping, I guess." Mrs. Hathaway glanced at her rejected charges. They gazed guiltily into their laps. "It did no harm to give them at least a chance."

Mrs. Overton regarded her for a moment, then answered calmly, "I suppose not." She was pleased with the day's proceeds, too pleased to argue over a minor transgression. Anyway, she did not want to discourage a certain degree of compassion, believing it was one of the qualities that made Mrs. Hathaway an effective matron.

Outside it was beginning to snow. Before leaving, Mrs. Overton wrapped herself in a muffler and donned a woolen cap. "I'll see you day after tomorrow then."

"Goodnight, ma'am," said Mrs. Hathaway, then turning to the boys, "Come along."

As they slowly ascended the stairs, one of the boys emitted a peculiar nasal sound, a congested sentiment perhaps.

"Quiet, child," said Mrs. Hathaway.

The Third Drawer

Doris Read

SATURDAY

Talking makes me very tired and anyway, there is no one I am interested in talking to, they are all so silly and most of them are deaf. I prefer to stay in my room. Actually, I'd like to go to bed but I can't because I don't have a nightgown but she doesn't listen to me.

"Look in the third drawer," she tells me. No matter what I ask for, she says, "Look in the third drawer."

I know there are no nightgowns in the third drawer. I open it and look in but I can't see any. It isn't as though I were asking for a present. I would pay for anything she bought me. I have enough money for a couple of nightgowns. And slips too. Why should they want to deprive me of my underwear? It doesn't make sense. I have to wear the same things day after day because there are no clean ones to change into. When my daughter comes she takes away the dirty things in the laundry bag but when she brings them back clean she hides them from me.

But now I am too tired to think about it any longer. Here in the closet is that green dress I don't like. I will wear it as a nightgown tonight.

SUNDAY

On Sundays we have dinner at lunch time and now it is over. I am sitting here thinking, as usual.

I have two daughters but I keep forgetting which is which so I call them "Daughter." That way they don't know that I get their names mixed up. That is rather a clever solution, I think. One of them lives far away and I think she has forgotten about me, although the one who lives near me keeps saying, "Here is another letter from — from, whichever one it is." But I don't remember the letters.

It is time for my daughter to come. Here she is, but she has not brought me any clothes.

"Where is the clean laundry?" I ask her.

"I don't have any today," she says coolly. Oh, the villainous girl! "Once a week on Wednesdays I take it away and bring it back on Friday. This is Sunday afternoon, Mother," she says.

"But I don't have anything clean to wear," I tell her.

"Come over here, Mother, and let us look in the third drawer. You have lots of things in here."

I go where she directs, although I get dizzy walking across the room. My daughter opens the third drawer and points to things.

"Here are nightgowns. Here are slips. Here are —"

But I can see nothing there and feel faint.

"I must sit down," I tell her.

"If you would wear your new glasses, you would see better," says my daughter. "Then you would be able to find your things."

I don't like the new glasses. They are heavy on my face. I don't look like myself when I wear them. Besides, I have never worn glasses except for reading, and why should I start now? If my friends came to see me, they wouldn't know me with these glasses on. But I can't explain all this to my daughter. I did try, once, looking in the third drawer while wearing the glasses, but I couldn't find anything.

"Perhaps it would be better, Mother, to move these things out of the third drawer and put them someplace else. Perhaps somewhere in the bathroom. Or in the clothes closet."

"No no," I tell her. "There is nothing there. Why can't you buy me just a few things? I don't need much."

"Mother, if you had any more nightgowns, you could open a shop," she says. She is playing games with me.

"If that is the case," I tell her reasonably, "why did I have to wear that green dress to bed last night?"

"You didn't have to," she says.

Now she is looking at her watch.

"I must go," she says. She kisses me goodbye and rushes out.

She never stays long, although often she takes me out for a ride in her car. I pretend to enjoy it but getting in and out of the car makes me very tired. Still, it provides a change of scene. I don't like it because she drives too fast, although when I cry out in alarm she tells me she is doing only twenty-five. She keeps pulling over to the side to let others cars go past, so I suppose she is telling the truth but it seems faster to me. Also, I am always afraid the door will open and I will fall out.

They take care of me here but not well enough. Often when I call them to tell them the lights are out and I can't find the switch to turn them on, they say they will come right away but they don't. I wait and wait but no one comes. I keep calling them in the office to tell them what is wrong but they don't pay attention. Sometimes I lose the office phone number, and then I call my daughter — her number is taped to the phone — and I ask her to call the office, but she is likely to say no, not unless it is really an emergency. She does not understand that it is an emergency to have to sit in the dark because you can't find the lights.

I think today I will get my nightgown ready before it gets dark, in case I can't find the lights again. This afternoon my daughter was going on, as usual, about the third drawer, so I will open it a little bit and look in. I am afraid to pull it open very far because it might fall out, so I pull it just a little and look inside but, of course, there is nothing there.

Mal

Henry H. Roth

Once upon a time, out of nowhere a car appeared and headed straight for Mal Bennett. "Long time, no see," the engine roared, and the clanging muffler agreed. The car embraced Mal, really soul-kissed him, then said "Farewell," tossing him back onto his beloved sacred lawn. Moments before, Mal had been observing a new shift in background scenery. Diagonally across the street there had always been an empty high-weeded litter stop for passing car droppings; it also was a very favorite haunt of loose and walked dogs. Suddenly the lot had been transformed into something not better or more interesting; but merely the stage for a shoddy, rapidly aging, unoccupied two-family dwelling. One positive fact Emily brought up right away — far less litter would be hurled at a living area and the local dogs, too, would lose their prime hangout. However, Mal immediately perceived that now all those damn dogs in their mighty confusion might begin trotting over to his spacious property. And so Mal's surveillance intensified. The new house and its concrete front and back lawn disturbed and mocked him; two or three times a day Mal strolled over to confirm its shoddy exterior and attempt to guess the gloomy future of its occupants. It was on one of those daily excursions that a noisy car with Jersey plates saw Mal and fell hopelessly in love with him and went right over to say hello.

Mal Bennett had always guarded his lawn from trespass and was always on the lookout for wily bugs, idle kids, nasty dogs, and bully weeds. A great new fool had recently moved into Ripley — a young stoned hippie who walked with his dog but never used a leash; therefore, the huge gross animal was free as a wild beast to chase squirrels, harass cats, attack other male dogs and running children, and — most important — foul all the lawns in the county. Twice the dog had been clipped by passing cars as its dumb owner railed against the innocent drivers and his innocent beast. All the great fool had to do was leash his property! But soon it was Mal's turn to be struck down. The astonished drunk/punk driver froze at the wheel, spying this old man run right up the car's hood and tear and claw at the windshield wipers before the fool could be flung back to his own property.

Long long ago for a Father's Day assignment in the third grade, Mal's daughter Paula had written: "My father is pretty great. He loves my Mommy.

And he loves me too, of course. We have plenty to eat but we aren't rich. We have no pets. My father is a very hard worker in his store and at home. He works very hard on his lawn. My father never gets mad at any of us. I think he loves the lawn best. He watches it grow and always plays with it every day." Paula had been a most troublesome child — very bright and relentless in receiving poor grades, barely graduating high school. She had two abortions before her senior year. In time she married; in time she also divorced. No one was really surprised about her divorce, though it was the first such split in the Bennett family archives. When the car hit him, for a long articulate moment Mal wheezed, "Damn! It's Paula driving. I just know it has to be." But it was some drunken kid from New Jersey whom the police were never able to trace. The lawn was beaming under lovely spring sun as Mal landed back down on his perfect lawn, soft as a cottontail.

Mal knew and accepted that his life was not done, but surely not undone; that is, in many important aspects it was all over. On the final Thursday of each spring and summer month there was a village pickup for unwieldy possessions. For the longest time, there had been no carting away at the Bennett residence since Mal perceived correctly there were no more wasted possessions to be ever picked up — no more wrong or obsolete choices. Also, Emily would no longer tolerate lovemaking. Told him right out. As a token of past times she would toss his organ if he insisted, but *he* and *it* were no longer to have any entry to her body. No smooching or touching, either. Her eerie voice had filled out the empty moon-soaked room. He tried to understand, then did understand and he didn't bother Emily ever again for any damn thing. The lawn, too, seemed to be on its own. Fungus, crabgrass, dandelions, and stray weeds never loitered; still Mal carefully balanced and fed the soil proper vitamin dosages and checked and rechecked — for a lawn was still like an incredibly healthy robust child that could be mortally felled by the common cold.

Mal was not a friendly man — consistently, coldly polite to his children, grandchildren, neighbors, and strangers. When he first landed face down on the lawn, passersby didn't even notice anything awry right away. As one wise guy kid put it to a peer companion: "Lookit! Mr. Bennett's humpin' his lawn!"

Emily's mother had noted Mal's obsession right away.

"Oh, he loves that lawn, dear."

"It's not another woman, Mother."

"You can tire of another woman, you know."

"Silly."

"Mal has a cruel side."

"Stuff and nonsense."

"He's cutting down all your beautiful trees."

"Mal explained. He said eventually they will have to go; they'll topple during storms and clutter up the yard and possibly damage the house. Dead branches will always be underfoot. He's explained it all, Mother."

"Dear, we all have to go one day, but we don't run around assassinating each other in our youths!"

"Oh, Mother! Mal works hard at the store and at home. He's just a very hard worker."

"Emily, I do hope so."

Mal was slumped on the far corner of the lawn, staining that edge pretty bad. For months afterward, the boy from Jersey returned with his hit-and-run Buick and circled and recircled the block, waiting to see if the old man would dare begin another quixotic assault.

By the end of the year, Paula decided to move in with her mother. Emily loved having grandchildren underfoot. There was more than enough money (the store income, Mal's life insurance, etc.) but Paula got a job anyway and donated her salary to thorough lawn upkeep. A gifted semi-retired gardener consistently pleased the pampered lawn's demands with consumate ease and loving instinct. But no one could solve the dilemma at the far corner of the property. The spot where Mal had landed, bled, and expired became grayer and blacker each month until it was a bare and sterile ugly hole. Predictable gossip was Mal would have just hated that cruel sore. Sharp-eyed Paula knew better, had seen better, and therefore cautioned the gardener to leave that area alone. More than once Paula had seen dogs, cats, and children venture toward the lawn only to be violently jarred away. The children, knowing better than to cry out, just fled; the dogs escaped stiff-legged on their fright and flight pattern.

The hippie still walked his dog without a leash, but he now carried a shovel to scoop away his ward's debris. Paula got a raise and threw that, too, back into the lawn's absolute perfection. Emily was never happier — cooking for noisy children again and not ever being troubled by Mal.

No one had moved into the house across the street. It was like a stupid toy no one would claim. It just rotted there and even seemed to be sinking. Paula's kids grew like healthy flowers. The kid from Jersey sold his killer car and purchased a domesticated Chevy and stopped coming around. The hole never got much bigger after the first year and people, being people, accepted it as a peculiar beauty mark and historical spot and that was that.

The Whole Story

Naomi Rothberg

Vivie's mother never slept at night. It was a torment. It was destroying her face, breaking down all the pretty parts like used furniture. But she would sooner that, it seemed, than be one of those who did manage to "get their beauty rest"; "asleep as soon as their heads hit the pillow"; "Nothing troubles them"; their nervous systems fashioned out of something dumb and unresponsive as rope.

She had only to look in the direction of any of her children to be troubled past all possibility of rest. Everything they did. . . And how to help them? How to guide them when they resisted all advice? Practically held their hands over their ears. Deaf to her sure knowledge of all the disasters they were heaping up for their futures. They fled the truth.

Everyone fled the truth. She had also had, most of her life, a husband.

Once the worry stops the grief begins. Who are the merry widows? If one has no more anxiety than from reading *The Times* each day, how even then does one find sleep? No pill could hold her under more than three hours.

Which made things difficult in the morning. In the light which was cruelest to her face. Often she would still be in the first layer of her underwear when Vivie arrived at the foot of the bed on her way to nine o'clock class high school, to nine o'clock class college, to her job, home for the weekend (with her own little daughter to be tucked in the extra bed). The girdle her mother intended to compress around herself for a neater (unindentable) appearance flopped still over the back of a chair. She would have made the bed (that too should yield no evidence of soft parts) and then, just for a minute, lain back down. Never expecting it, but it was always then that sleep overtook her, dropping over her lightly as it would on a cat in an alley. But sleep nonetheless.

Her mouth would have fallen open. The white arm she had thrown over her eyes for just that *instant's* relief would melt closer to them. The hand resting on her belly relax.

All of her curves milk and white bread; the breasts sliding like cream from the stiffness of the brassiere, the delicately browning skin of her abdomen where it sloped over her ribs.

The looseness of her nylon bloomers which she chose for sensible service disloyally calling out the luxury of her lap.

127

No one but Vivie knew. She carried this body so well hidden below the ruined face. Years of this body each morning lying unknown to anyone, the thighs at ease against each other, little damaged, only the tiny blue lines and small places where the flesh wadded down (so many years of marching).

Her daughter guessed a chilliness in her thighs. Guessed her mother dreaming of someone who threw a light blanket over her. Covering as well the gleaming calves and big clean feet.

Too big and too flat for any vanity. Serviceable, well-kept, trimmed according to the "cut straight across" method earnestly received in Hygiene class in 1921 and re-dictated as earnestly to the ignorant parents (with their splintered pleasant toenails), to the just discernibly grateful husband and then to the children, so totally, inexplicably, heart-breakingly resistant, one after the other.

It was the feet Vivie yearned most to take into her hands. To knead and stroke and work with her fingers between the powdered toes.

She would never dare do it. Other considerations aside, her mother did sleep like a cat and the terror she would cause the woman to jolt her awake by the sensation of being touched, only to catch this most bewildering of her daughters standing at the bottom of the bed, *caressing* one of her big clean feet . . .

The Subject of the Conversation
Walter Sanders

Start here. At lunch, I am told, the women in the office talk either about their children or their husbands. From reports, the children have childhood ailments and childhood problems, typical, predictable. A cold, a sore throat, a quarrel with a sibling, a matter of disobedience, a bout with the flu — the whole family will probably be down with it before long, of course. Concern for the child's condition elicits further complaints about all the trouble they cause. Sam began kindergarten and at the end of the first day reported that his jeans would not do. He would not return, could not return to school the next day in such pants. His had bell-bottoms, how could his mother have made such a mistake? No one in Sam's class had worn bell-bottoms to school that day. Solution: Sam got straight-leg jeans that evening and now no one, five years or older, can tell, should they look at the area between his knees and the tops of his shoes, that his jeans are any different from those of the rest of his classmates. Of course children do not like to look different from others. But what, I ask myself, is going on here? Are the pressures on the parents or the children greater? I regarded the story as containing some humor. Sam's year went well after the change. His alphabet and reading and art work are much like those of other five-year olds. Or. Harold broke his wrist in a fall from a place he had been warned not to climb to. He got a cast. His cast is five weeks old and Harold is seven. Harold spent the day at the office with his mother and the other women who work in the office. Harold sorted papers according to their color for the women until the doctor could see Harold and his cast that afternoon. His cast was removed by four. The women didn't get much work of their own done that day because they spent most of the six hours that Harold was placed with them finding things for Harold to do that Harold enjoyed and would do. It is not known to me whether Harold reads books, but it is assumed that he can. He is seven and should. Emily and Stevie can't get together in any sort of agreement about what TV programs they shall watch. Maybe each child, a woman suggests, should have a personal TV. That's what happened in her house. Now each child goes to his room and watches whatever he wants. Peace about TV. But then, this other mother wonders, if she and her husband get another TV set what will they do when they want to watch a program and all the sets are being watched by the children? Occam's Razor: unheard, because unspoken there, my wife informs me, cut out TV viewing until the children learn to share or compromise. I am privy, through my wife in the office, to all. Sticky, consuming problems that make me groan.

Worse. Husbands, yes husbands, are the source of much of the lunch discussion and complaints during breaks which occur as the occasions demand. They can do no right. They are stupid. They are insensitive. Something is wrong, I think, when I hear report of this public display. Where is the emotional support? the intimacy? This talk is different from that about the children. Bill forgot an anniversary and Susan knew he would for she began talking about the possibility two weeks at least before the day slipped by without a card. All the women in the office heard, over and over, almost each day of those two weeks, the prophecy that Bill, this year, finally, would forget the day. Sue's prophecy was fulfilled, she announced, triumphantly it seemed to my wife, the day after the event. And what did Sue do the night of the anniversary? Solution: she triumphantly reminded Bill that he had forgotten. What happens in their homes? What do these women want? What are they so angry about? When I go to pick up my wife at the office I am civil, cordial, pleasant, gracious at times and the other women, I have come to suspect, detest my wife but not me for what I do. But my presence does not stop them in their attacks, their bragging, really, of whose husband has been most brutish, most recently. My wife complains to me that she has nothing to talk to these women about. Awards should be given for the woman in the office who has suffered the greatest indecency the day or night before. Oh, the problems I hear.

Kathy's birthday came and went. She had drawn up a list of birthday presents George was supposed to get her this year. It was a long list which she read to all the office. "He'd better get me everything on that list," she said, "or he'll never hear the end of it." My wife took a cake, which I had baked, to the office the day of Kathy's birthday. The cake was eaten, I heard, in a fury, for George had failed to get Kathy all the items on her list. Who do I sympathize with? I get lost in emotions.

Again. I hear Helen's husband is reported to have done something really stupid, just what Helen expected him to do. "Clark is so stupid all the time," Helen said. "I can't rely on him. I don't know what to do with him. I told him to pick up the cleaning on his way home from work last night and he didn't do it. And I told him that because of his stupidity I had nothing to wear this morning. He always forgets to pick up the coffee or the milk or whatever. I don't know where his mind is. Sometimes I wonder if he even thinks. He's so stupid." The other women in the office, my wife tells me, nod their husbands into the same condition, compare notes about their husbands' stupidities and agree that, indeed, men are out to make the lives of their wives as miserable as possible.

I have come upon these women toward the end of day, when work has ceased, when their husbands and children will be meeting and joining in their secret lives together. I wonder what these women will say when they rejoin their husbands and begin again living with them. Lately, as I have entered the office, I have heard the sound of the other women in my wife's voice as she greets me with, "So there you are, finally, I thought you were never coming or that you had forgotten me." It's no reunion. I am not late. I look at the clock on the wall hoping my wife will follow my eyes. I recall the eagerness, of a moment earlier, of my thoughts of seeing her again. I am coming to realize more and more that she is doing what they all do, only more tentatively since I am there. I wonder what has been said during the day, and my thoughts begin to dwell on the possibilities among my latest blunders. I believe that my wife has begun to imitate the others. Maybe that's how it starts. But I notice that the other women are aware of the tone of the greeting, these days, and that they smile, slightly, not at my appearance in the office, but, I think, at the fact that finally my wife has begun to become one of them. When I mention the effect of a comment to her, I am told that she had not been aware. Privately I consider that worse than a conscious effort. I wonder if tomorrow my wife will join in wholeheartedly with a particularly juicy tale of some lapse of mine. I think whether I have forgotten to do anything I had agreed to for this day.

I can see it coming. My worry is a personal worry. I do not know how to escape the delight that they take in seeing one of us fail. It will not be long now before, I fear, I will become like George or any other or all of them. And it will not matter what I have done or left undone. I will have ceased being myself and will have become one of the husbands who irritates more than he pleases. The disaffection will not mean that I have changed so much as it will mean that the women in my wife's office have a new recruit. Somehow they could not bear her not joining in. I will stand guilty in collusion with the other men. What will I do with my civility and my charity? Which husband will I outdo in my cowardliness?

The Honeymoon
Kathleen Spivack

When they got to Paris he lay down and went to bed for two weeks. Eunice was stunned. Was this how she was going to see Paris: from a hotel bedroom? "Oh no!" she cried in dismay, but "You go," he offered. "I've had enough of cities."

"But this isn't a city; this is Paris!" she retorted illogically. Still, he would not be budged. So Eunice went out alone and walked through the streets of Paris that were like pictures of the streets of Paris. She walked, selfconscious, with a quick tight fear. She worried about being alone, and her French was not good.

Still, "Bonjour, Madame," the owner of the little cafe across from the hotel greeted her each morning. He smiled and pulled out her chair: one chair. "And how is Monsieur?" Monsieur was back at the hotel, lying on a bed, reading. He had had enough of dragging his body around Europe. "I'm happy here," he assured Eunice. "Go out. Enjoy yourself." For it was she who had been most adamant about this European trip. And Paris! Paris was to have been the culmination. "The Piece de Resistance," she said to herself. But she couldn't very well force him to come out if he didn't want to, could she?

But though Paris looked exactly like a stage set of Paris, as Venice does a set for an opera about Venice, still, the actors were all wrong. They took up too much space, they walked with a long and lanky stride, they talked too loudly, in flat tones, and all carried baggage. Knapsacks, bedrolls, and suitcases: they were, in fact, Americans.

Everywhere Eunice looked she could see Americans. Americans at the Cafe Flore, Americans at the Deux Magots, in the museums, in the parks and gardens, Americans sitting on curbs. She tripped over their long and outstretched legs. "Hey, Kansas City," one boy called to her as she picked her way through the crowd, "got any spare change?" while "Want some grass?" muttered another in her ear. Eunice craned her neck and hoped she might see Sartre.

When she came home in the afternoons, Nick seemed genuinely pleased. "Tell me about it," he called from the bathtub. He was soaking in scented hot water; the steam rose around him. "Did you have fun? What did you do today?" "Oh, I went to a few museums." Eunice did not say that she had gone, expecting to be awed, and hadn't been. "My feet hurt." She had stood there, in front of masterpieces she might never see again, and tried to build up her emotions, hoping to conjure tears.

But truth was, she had stood, even before the Mona Lisa, and had been totally unmoved. "I wish you had been there," she called to him. Why? He would have been even more impatient: insisting they move on. "I've decided I've had enough of museums," he called back over the steam. He splashed cheerfully. "This whole city is a museum!" she cried reproachfully. "I know," he said, "but I'm ready to go home."

"We can't go home yet, " she said, alarmed. "Our flight doesn't leave for another six days." She felt guilty; it was she who had planned the trip. "And we can't give up our charter tickets." "No," he agreed, not seeming too bothered. "I can wait. Just don't expect anything very much from me these next few days."

Eunice was disturbed. She didn't understand him. His insistence on staying behind was like a weight, dragging on her. She could not shake off her inertia, her feeling that she should be staying with him. But once in Paris, she was determined to see all of it. She cast one longing look at Nick on the bed, the pile of bright books lying around him, and went out again. "Ah." He settled happily into a book: free for a few hours.

On the way back to the hotel one midday, Eunice stopped to buy some bread, and then she bought some cheese. She took it into bed with Nick, and it was the best bread both had ever eaten. The next day she bought some wild strawberries, in a little basket of leaves. They lay on the bed, eating strawberries, and looked out at the sky.

"Why don't you call your friend Cynthia?" Nick suggested. Their time in Paris was running out. Eunice was disturbed: she had deliberately chosen not to look up her college roommate, now living in Paris. Eunice wanted to preserve Nick, her discovery, for herself. But, at Nick's suggestion, she phoned Cynthia anyway.

The two women had not seen each other since college, where they had a mysterious and unspoken falling out, a drawing away, mutually, from each other. They had been French majors, both, and Cynthia had actually come to Paris, right after graduation. Eunice could not explain the lightness she felt, when Cynthia left the country. But now she was delighted to see her old friend. "Eunice!" Cynthia squealed in delight, and even her American voice sounded French. Cynthia's conversation was now accented, with little shrugs and moues. "After all," as she explained to the couple, all in the hotel room, huddled on the bed. "Paris is impossible, yes?" "And I should know," she added, and for a moment her voice was pure Missouri.

Cynthia worked, as a bi-lingual secretary, for rich American firms that had branches in Paris. She went from one to another. "It's amusing," she said, "and it lets me live." Cynthia had come to Paris, Eunice remembered, on some vague romantic errand. "A friend," Cynthia had said, understating. "I must stay in Paris." "Male or female?" Nick quipped. Cynthia silenced him with a look.

In truth, Cynthia had a number of "friends," but in Paris everything is possible. Although she was charming, attractive, and "with it," not one of the friends who professed such interest in her had ever invited her to their homes, she told the couple. Some were married, some lived with their parents still, some had houses in the country. But to not one of these homes had Cynthia ever been. "The French are very closed," was all she would say. "They are conservative."

Of her latest friend she said, "We are living together." But still, he did not take her home to meet his parents: they would never approve. "Have lunch with me," she said to Eunice and Nick, "I know a place." And Nick got up and got ready; they went out.

Afterwards Nick went back to the hotel. Eunice and Cynthia stayed on together. They strolled through the streets, stopping here and there. Eunice felt totally relaxed, now that someone was with her. She was breathless with happiness, seeing her former friend: somehow Cynthia now represented, in a paradoxical and absurd way, the essence of Paris to her. They rode up the Seine. "Oh, it's so much fun to do something touristy!" cried Cynthia. She had been too busy in Paris. "If only you had called me before."

It was Eunice's last day in Paris. That evening, Nick comfortably ensconced in his room, Cynthia took Eunice to a restaurant along with some French friends. Eunice let Cynthia order for her. She basked happily in a language she only half understood.

Before they left the restaurant, the two women went to the ladies' room. Cynthia's friends waited for them outside. Cynthia went in first, and came out saying nothing. When Eunice went in, she found the bathroom lined with mirrors: on the floor under the toilet and bidet; the whole of the walls, and the ceiling. Eunice watched herself peeing, her hairy mouth. She did not know what to make of it. "Did you see?" Cynthia asked her when she came out. Eunice nodded, embarrassed.

Then Cynthia took her hand and led Eunice into the ladies' room again. She motioned to Eunice to undress, and slipped out of her clothes herself: she held Eunice's hand throughout. The two women took off their panties and spread their legs, solemnly regarding their sex, reflected in the floor that was a mirror. Cynthia gently clasped the sex of Eunice and, as they both watched in the mirror below, inserted one finger. Cynthia gazed steadily into Eunice's eyes: Eunice's eyes glazed over.

As they walked back together late at night to the hotel, and Nick, the noises of the Americans seemed especially loud. Eunice walked, conscious of moisture between her legs. She held her friend's hand: she was in Paris. Soon, the voices of the Americans stopped.

"Well, did you have a good time?" Nick asked, when she got back to the room. He had been waiting up for her. Eunice stood by the window, drowsy and intoxicated. "Yes," she could hardly answer. "I can't wait to leave Paris," he said. He put his arm around her and led her to the bed. "I'll be glad to get home tomorrow," he said, stroking her. "Won't you?"

Beyond Their Reach

Deborah Stewart

I am so afraid it's going to come crashing down around me. One morning the bank will call to say my money is not enough. My mother will call to say my father has died and my brother will stop by for tea and explain once again how I ruined his life with my grades and good manners. My father-in-law will invite me to Sunday dinner so he can quiz my husband about the last investment of thousands that did not pan out despite the desperate efforts of my husband, and my sister-in-law will telephone to say she has bought grandmother an $84 suit for her birthday and would I help pay for it?

Then the washing machine will break in mid-cycle and the electric garage door will spring a chain. The dog will throw up on the living room rug and I will notice for the first time how suddenly threadbare the living room couch is. My son will grouse about breakfast before I give in to his request for a Pudding Pop at seven in the morning.

Next, I will call the public school system to inquire about observing and the secretary will behave as if I have insulted her. When I arrive, the woman who points me in the right direction will look at me through half-closed eyes, suspicious of God knows what. Then I will be touched by the janitor who escorts me to room 150 where the children sit quietly in rows watching in the dark a television film about light, refractory and reflective light. I will gaze at their faces in the still light of the shaded room and wonder about their sweetness, their innocence.

The child nearest me will have crutches leaning against his legs. I will become aware of his gaze on me. With my eyes I will trace his child's hands, the dirty fingernails, the small scratches. When I touch his shoulders in my mind I will see they are firm and developed beyond his age from bearing so much weight so soon. As he prepares to leave the room to return to the handicapped class next door I will want to reach a hand to touch his head. He will wait until the others have gone. Clearing a space for himself, he will position his metal crutches and hoist his weight. He will walk, side-saddle, from the room.

The halls outside the classroom will remind me of my days in elementary school and a panic will swell up but I will fight it back down. I'm weary of such desperation but I know it's there. I can't change that. I will remember so vividly Harvey Diamond's mother coming to our sixth grade class and standing near him in the hall. We were lined up against one wall, leaning against the mass of concrete block painted pale yellow. Harvey's mother was dying. She had cancer. I don't remember why she came that day. I just remember the look on her face as she gazed at Harvey. She reached out and touched his hair. His hair was deep black, glowing black like hers.

I will leave the building knowing I can't send my children there. It's too much my past, too much what I struggle daily against. I can't allow them the same deadening.

My doctor will say of my well-educated sister-in-law, "She went to the best schools. Does she show any signs of education?"

He knows I can't abide my sister-in-law. She is selfish beyond belief. She is mean too. I stopped by her house to pick up clothes for charity. She offered me a small bag and looked in my back seat.

"Looks like you have a load. That's a nice coat." She eyes the coat I had set aside for the mother of the family our Sunday School class was helping.

Grandmother, who will be 89, will call to check on my wallpapering and painting. I am not wallpapering or painting but she will have it in her mind that this is how I spend my time.

I am frightened of creditors. Before brushing my teeth in the morning I will look in the mirror and say, "They can't get me if I am dead. I can always die if it gets too bad. I can always put myself beyond their reach."

Then my doctor will look at me.

"Why should it matter?" I will ask him.

"Why shouldn't it?" he will shrug.

"Because there's nothing I can do about it."

"Are you sure?" he will ask.

"What do you think?" I will reply.

"I think you don't want to deal with it," he will say.

"Can't you understand I get tired sometimes?"

"This has nothing to do with fatigue," he will reply.

"How can you say that?" I will feel my voice catch.

"Because it's true," he will say.

"Well, what do you suggest I do?"

"I suggest you deal with it," he will respond.

"How?" I will fit the word around my whole body.

"What do you think?" he will ask me.

"You want me to stop trying to control the situation."

He will sit silently.

"You want me to relax and stop beating myself over the head with it," I will whisper.

He will be like a stone.

"You want me to consider my own pain for a change, deal with how I've been punished." I will sink back against the chair.

He will remain silent.

"You want me to show myself some love." I will close my eyes to stop the tears.

"I want," he will say softly. "I want you to deal with it."

Patterning
David Surface

At first we were going to their house once every week but that changed and we went every two weeks. The room we came into was bright and smelled like the sheets folded on the table and his arm was already bare and warm when you took it.

What would that be like, to live in a body with no future, with none of the complexities and deceptions that come with having a future and a body, to have everything you'll ever be gathered together in one place so close that anyone could cover the whole thing from end to end with two hands?

She makes us wash our hands before we begin. We have to be very careful not to get any dirt near his eyes or mouth because he's never played on the floor and picked up any of the regular immunities.

We are ready to begin.

This arm is so white in my hands, when I hold it my fingers look heavy and gray like things made of cement. She puts on music, a record of string quartets. Short reliable rhythms like an animal's pulse. The music helps. We begin.

The theory of patterning therapy for brain damaged infants is this — the child's arms, legs and head are manipulated to stimulate the rhythmic movements of crawling. In this way the electrical signals buried in the brain can find their way back out into those empty places and the body remembers what it never learned.

We stand around a small table, one of us at each corner and one more at the end to hold his head. It is very bright in this room and no one speaks except for her. She has made coffee for whoever wants it. This is her house and everything here belongs to her.

Take his arm in both hands, one at the wrist and one below the elbow. Bring it forward until the hand is level with his head. Move in circles. Then pull it back in toward his body. Like this. Watch the person across from you and keep in time with each other.

Now the only sounds in the room are the cellos pulsing from the record player and the soft sliding noise of his arms and legs going back and forth across the plastic cushion.

Kevin's father is not with us. He is at the college on the hill teaching the theater students how to build sets and light up a stage. He is leaning on the edge of his desk smoking a cigarette while the whole class watches. He is telling them about the great David Belasco and his cigarette makes patterns back and forth in the air. After we leave he will come home and tell more things to Kevin. He will tell them all walking with Kevin across his shoulder, pressing their two heads close as one head and whoever watches them watches terrible confidences passing between them and is frightened. That will all be later. Now he is telling the class about David Belasco who brought trees and grass and live cows into theaters to make the most lifelike sets on the American stage. Of course that was all very long ago and today we know how few materials it takes to bring a stage to life.

Now she is talking to him, turning his head from side to side between her hands, making a conversation for the two of them out of any object that is close enough. A ball of sunlight on the table. The way his hair keeps falling into his eyes.

Hair that is white and almost weightless. Two eyelids, soft and big as moth wings. A face.

I've been moving his arm around in circles for ten minutes and already the room has grown warmer. He doesn't resist us or help us. He lets us do what we want with him. He is being patient with us. We have so much farther to go but he is all here in one place. He is complete and we are not.

We are finished for today. They want me to get into the car with them and drive away but there is too much of me scattered all over. There are trees behind the houses and the trees are taller and simpler than the houses. I've grown up wrong. Now I have to go back and begin all over.

After Kevin died the four of us were never all in her kitchen at the same time again. They had another child, a girl. She grew bigger and wore dresses and laughed at people.

I talked with a student who was taking a class in lighting-design from Kevin's father while the boy was still alive.

"One day he had the room dark when we came in. After everybody got into their seats he flipped a switch and all these spotlights started coming on over our heads, not all at the same time but one after another, you know, like dominoes. He'd make all the patterns with them in the ceiling, great big spirals and figure-eights. He must have been there all night rigging those up. When the last one came on everybody went crazy and he just smiled and leaned back on his desk and said, 'Let there be light.'"

Alice's Snazzy Pajamas

S. G. Tyler

Alice bought her pajamas in the lingerie department. They were a pale grey silk, with square-cut short sleeves and long pants. A little line of white piping edged the cuffs and ran the length of the shirt front, the buttons had the lustre of pearl. New they'd cost two-hundred and twenty dollars.

Alice got them at Goodwill for three bucks. She'd been desperate for a flannel nightgown, but when she'd gone through the ratty, worn pile of night clothes in the back corner of the store, she'd stopped short when she'd come across the pajamas. The seam under one arm was gaping open and they were wrinkled beyond belief, a dead giveaway of their authenticity. At first she couldn't believe it.

When she got them home, she took out Ivory Snow and washed them. She hung them on the back porch where she had her clothesline, putting pieces of Saran Wrap between the material and the pins. When they were dry she brought them inside and mended the arm, and then set up her ironing board. She had been waiting for this moment. Like magic the silk smoothed out and the garments became slinky and soft. She draped them carefully on a hanger in the doorway and stood looking at them for a long time. Then she spread them out on her bed and fingered the material. Never in her life had she owned anything like these. Never had she expected to. She was spellbound just looking at them.

Every night when she got off work, she'd start thinking about her pajamas. The winter streets were dark and slippery and the buses out of the city were packed, but Alice would fight her way to a seat, or stand patiently holding a strap, wrapped in a lot more than her thin cloth coat. She felt like someone special.

The pajamas got her through four and a half months. She would wear them for an hour or so every night after her shower and before going to bed. Sometimes she would arrange herself on the pillows on the sofa and read movie magazines. Other nights she'd prop herself up in bed and watch TV. It depended on her mood.

Then in March her sister came over. She'd left her husband, the bastard, and arrived on Alice's doorstep at nine o'clock one night with her two-year-old and the new baby. Alice had just been reading about the Academy Awards.

139

They put the baby to sleep in the laundry basket fixed up for a bed, and Alice gave her nephew something to drink and a paper and pencil to draw with while she tried to comfort her sister and get the whole story. The upshot of the evening was that the grape juice got knocked over and spread across the tablecloth. It also stained the pajamas. There was nothing to be done. Through her tears her sister decided to move in until she could get a place of her own.

It was crowded. There were only two rooms. But they worked it out for six weeks until her sister returned to the bastard to try again. They both knew she'd be back before long, but for now at least it seemed okay.

Alice never mentioned the pajamas. She tried washing them out, but nothing would remove the grape juice that wouldn't bleach out the color of the fabric as well. So after a couple of tries, she ironed them smooth, folded them in tissue paper, and put them away in the bottom drawer of her dresser with a lavender sachet. Every now and then she'd lay them out on her bed and admire them, folding the stained edge of the top back and covering the spots on the pant leg by turning them under. But she never put them on again. It wasn't the same.

Alice continued to visit Goodwill every week to look through the merchandise as usual. She always looked for nice things. She picked up a wool blazer for only seven dollars, and one time came across an almost new leather purse. Though she never found anything much in the lingerie corner, Alice kept looking. Knowing those snazzy pajamas were at home in her drawer was enough. She knew anything was possible.

The Cat That Had
The Power of Speech
Marian Ury

A cat came to the home of a couple in Piedmont, California, and said, "I want." It was a pretty cat, with round bright eyes and orange fur, a bushy tail, a snub nose, and the short legs and sturdy frame that when the body was properly fleshed out, would entitle it to be described as "cobby," an aristocratic term. It was raining; the cat was shivering, and even if it had been an ugly cat the couple, who were kind-hearted, would surely have brought out something for it to eat. As it was they let it in and conducted it to the kitchen, the husband preceding and the wife following behind with a towel to wipe the muddy paw-prints from the floor. "I want," said the cat. "Nice kitty," said the wife, pouring a saucer of milk. "Do you suppose it's all right?" said the husband. He was a lawyer and by this utterance was referring simultaneously to the health of the cat considered from the cat's point-of-view, the inconvenience to themselves in the likelihood that it should die — for its meager belly was quaking violently — and the Law of Found Property. It had occurred to him that the cat might be claimed as his if no other owner came forward — but suppose someone did? He felt uneasy. "I want," repeated the cat, which had polished off the milk and now shook droplets from its whiskers onto the kitchen wall. "Nice kitty," said the woman and opened a can of tuna. "Let me," said her husband, spooning it onto a plate. The cat polished that off too, said "I want"— or perhaps it said "I love you" (which is the same thing) — wiped its face, pillowed its head on a paw and suddenly fell asleep.

Husband and wife both had always longed for a cat, though neither had ever spoken of it, and now that they had one that was handsome, that despite the husband's fears was in no immediate danger of death, and that moreover had the power of speech, they were thrilled. The next afternoon the husband felt himself growing vague while instructing a client on a delicate point of law. Pleading a sore throat he hurried home and found the cat curled up, nose to tail in what is known as the "contented cat position," on a cushion. True, it was that of his favorite chair. "It said, 'I want,'" said his wife apologetically. "Nice kitty," said the husband. Already the cat looked fatter,

141

its fur glossier, its whiskers longer and whiter. It seemed, in fact, likely to become quite a proper cat. Husband and wife watched with pride as it slept, its paw-tips twitching.

The woman, childless despite many years of marriage, thought the cat would be company as she did her chores, and she set herself to train it to follow her around the house. "Now kitty," she would say, "I'm going to dust the sofa legs and give the cushions a good shaking," or "Now kitty, I'm going to sort the silver and stack the napkins." The cat was not attentive, preferring to eat and sleep at its leisure, stalk birds in the garden, investigate closets, the undersides of chairs, and the tops of tables. But perhaps the reason was that her tasks were not that interesting. Still she tried. Once, too vigorous, she grazed its tail with the vacuum cleaner. "Ouch," it cried, "it hurts, it hurts!" and turned and sank a fang into her knee. "I'm sorry, kitty," she said, trembling. "I want," said the cat. She fed it, and after a while it went to sleep.

Despite this failure the woman thought she should train the cat. If only it could be made to expand its vocabulary: then it could expeditiously be told the difference between a bench — meant to be sat on — and a table-top — forbidden. She tried to show it her reasons. "Now kitty," she would say, "it's all right to sharpen your claws on the doormat, but the rug you absolutely mustn't." Or, "Now kitty, you may bite on the knitting yarn, but the lamp cord — no!" But the cat did not seem to understand and only repeated "I want" until it was fed more tuna, or let out of doors, or allowed to jump onto her husband's favorite chair. The man, too, tried to instruct it; he came home early these days, often feeling unwell. In his office his thoughts turned to the furry creature at home and he grew vague; once he found himself mumbling nonsense to an important client. "I want," said the cat, ensconced at that moment on their bed; extending a paw it snagged a corner of the bedspread. "No kitty, nice kitty," the man said. He was feeling unwell indeed, with a headache and a scratchy throat. "I want, I want," screamed the cat, seized the fringe and began to gnaw. "Kitty, mustn't!" said the woman. "I want, I want," it shouted, ripping a swathe from the fringe, wrapping it around its hind legs and hurling itself convulsively onto the rug. Husband and wife looked at each other. "It's been awfully bad-tempered lately," she said timidly. "Do you suppose it's all right?" he asked, and they rushed it to the vet.

The vet had a bristling beard and a manly manner. He poked and prodded the cat, squeezed its belly, took its temperature, gave it for good measure a rabies shot and one against feline enteritis. The cat said nothing but squirmed and whimpered. "There's nothing wrong with it," said the vet. "It's a perfectly normal cat." "I really don't care about the bedspread," said the wife, though she did. "Nor do I," said her husband patting her hand, though he did. The effort of comforting each other, greater than they had made in years, exhausted them, and they drove home without further speech.

The woman fed the cat kidney, to apologize for the insult. The man fed it tuna, because it had whimpered. It took some bites of each, leaped on the table, attacked the rug, chewed the lamp-cord, and leaped onto the favorite chair, where it went to sleep. The husband stayed home the next day; he lay in bed with a high fever. The cat ate and slept at its leisure, stalked and caught a bird, disarranged a closet, clawed the underside of the sofa, gnawed the curtains, and left paw-prints on the dining-room table. Only once did the wife venture to reproach it. It had just leaped onto her husband's favorite chair and was sharpening its claws on the back before settling down to sleep. "Oh kitty," she said, "sometimes I think you're just not trying to communicate." "Are you out of your mind?" cried the cat in a loud, clear, and remarkably ungracious voice. It never spoke again.

Let Us Know
Diane Vreuls

My son bought a kite, a Waybe Highspy, the kind the wrapper says sailed up six miles over Utah and collided with a jet. He went out with his grandfather Thursday. They took ten rolls of twine and a Number 200 Highspy Twine Winder, with the cord tied to the grommet in the keel. We bring them sandwiches in relays, and bolsters to prop them on the field. Every few hours they add on a ball of twine and pay it out slow through the winder. The kite's got too high to see. If you cross our quadrant and meet it, let them know.

I knew a man named Larvey who made wooden nickels. Made them twice lifesize, of pine. He liked carving the buffalo, though the reason he gave was different: had to do with a Mr. Felix Schlag and his face of Thomas Jefferson reading In God We Trust. Schlag's design had won a contest to replace the old five-center. Just a matter of time, said Larvey, and the buffalo would be gone, gone from our pockets, purses, piggybanks, gone from the linings of jackets, the cuffs of old trousers, gone, and taking the Indian with it. "Schlag," he said, "Schlag!" and sat carving; each coin took more than six weeks. Well, that was back on Ninth street, back when they made them of nickel. But nickel growing scarce, they changed to copper, copper growing thin they tried lead. Then zinc, aluminum, chromium, plastic, tin. Now it says in the paper they're thinking of going to wood. Let him know.

Eino Eskola was drafted in 1942 and sent to one of the few remaining troops of the cavalry. He hated horses. A simple farmboy from Wakefield, he deserted. Rode the train up to Ironwood, took the bus towards home, then hid in the woods near Wico. He made his way to Anvil Location and camped in the company buildings near the old mine. In summer he bathed in the pits, in winter shot deer and rabbits. Once we found a sauna built of birches. Once a clothesline strung in a clearing and, nearby, a small plot of greens. A few years ago we approached him to tell him he was safe: the statute of limitations had finally expired. But he ran from us, as he always did, this time towards the border. We were frightened of the forest and didn't follow. If you go North, let him know.

Rula went to her eighth grade reunion. It was a high school class of '50, but the things they recalled happened sooner and the men looked less than eighteen. "I love those people," she said to me later, "I loved walking into that room of children who appear row by row in my dreams." She interviewed them intensely. They answered, releasing secrets kept under wraps for twenty years. She liked best talking to those who started so poorly but had come mid-age into their own. But the thing she wasn't prepared for was the way they questioned her back. Hadn't she really got famous? What of their plans for her? Oh no, she reassured them, she was married with four nice children and spent her days weeding the farm.

"I thought they'd be pleased we'd grown closer. I thought now they'll finally forgive me for winning all the awards."

But they were troubled. "Surely there's more?"

"Oh no," she said, "I'm quite happy." She never once mentioned her work.

Her work. "Do you think I should have told them, they seemed to believe in me so?"

Yes, I think she could have told them. If you see them, let them know.

Because our name is a town in their country, the two Dutch exchange research chemists called for my sister each morning to skate across the lake. They were insistent and prompt; as a compatriot she had to go.

Wisconsin is cold at five in the morning and that winter was very long. Lake Mendota froze in November and still supported cars in late March. They had to dodge those cars, driven mid-lake by fishermen who huddled over ice holes and were startled by their flashlights when they skated past before dawn.

She never made it across. They started flanked, then my sister dropped from the center and half-way was two blocks behind, lingered at fishing holes, tried to warm up at the stoves, talk to the men in grunted exchanges that broke their attention on their lines. By December she headed straight for the cars and asked to wait inside, where she dozed with her blades braced on dashboards or, breathing a hole in the window frost, watched for the Dutchmen's return. She could just make them out: two black figures in flapping coats, bent like grackles, growing larger against the far shore. They'd collect her and see her home and say she'd do better the next day.

One morning she stopped. It was after a night of study, she had an exam, a cold, swollen ankles, and didn't answer the bell. Their knocking roused the housemother, who pulled her by her robe to the door. She couldn't face them, only yelled through the mailslot, I CAN'T, I FORGOT TO TELL YOU: I'M HALF SERB. They skated alone till thaw. Soon after, they went back home.

Aging, she wakes early. It's just as cold. Stops only for coffee. Laces up, heads across the lake. She makes it in twenty minutes, less when the wind shifts. She'd like them to know.

But that's not the point; it's the examples. You saw that at once; I didn't, was thinking instead of what happened to Meg.

Meg wouldn't go with me. She was supposed to meet Mark in the Highlands but bogged in the moors. Her boots cracked, her pack split, bus drivers passed in the rain. She made it to Whitby in high season, took hours to find a hotel. Residential, you paid by the week. She moved in to dry.

She wove the scaling rope window to doorknob and hung up her clothes. Dressed only in felt bootliners and her rag of a raincoat, she stumbled out to the abbey, down for food. There was no one to talk to. The English read paperbacks in wet deckchairs or crowded the upstair tearooms, ordering sweets. They wore tweeds they had purchased in pink the previous Easter and draped macs on every free chair. She tried to phone Mark. His landlady answered and said he had gone to France. Or was it an operation? This was a long time ago.

On the fourth day she grew melancholy. That evening in two pairs of sweatsocks she struck out towards the High. The cinema was sold out, the newsstands and pharmacies closed. Back in her room between washlines, she grew desperate and did it: fell back on her Inner Resources, the ones she'd been saving for years. Saving for the plane crash, the floating month on the raft, for the eighteen-hour surgery when the laughing gas tank ran dry. Poetry learned in the seventh grade. Commercials, songs from Kukla, Fran and Ollie. The periodic table, the Succession of Norman Kings. Fifteen minutes, she ran out. A measly fifteen minutes. After seventeen years of schooling, she needed something to read.

She read the framed door portrait, the one with the list of rules. The Managers are not Responsible, "Naturally. No one's responsible: not Mark," she said, "least of all me. I have never believed in the Highlands, the low road is faster every time." That's what the song says. She sang it. Her accent was bogus, she sneezed on each refrain. She read the doily on the dresser, looped almost into script. Squint, you can catch the moral. She looked for a Bible instead.

The lampstand, however, seemed empty, the cardboard wardrobe bare. Someone had left a box of prophylactics behind the seashell figurines. She did drawers. Attacking the highboy, she found her hopes answered in print. A magazine was unstapled, its pages spread to keep underwear from snagging, to cover old stains. They lined the drawers in consecutive order, starting with the Contributors' Notes. She worked her way through Letters, Bovril ads and four sides of the Queen. In the third drawer she found it: a story called "Wings." He is in the RAF. She's the wife who waits. It's the early 1940s, but the agony endures. He is off on dangerous missions, but the sacrifice is hers. Drawer four seems sympathetic to the woman's side of the case, but pull out the bottom one, she's gone bad — spoiled, unpatriotic, undermining esprit de corps. The story continued in the lampstand and onto the wardrobe shelf, where she seems to be mulling divorce, or at least an affair with someone named Ned. Then nothing. The room ran out of drawers.

It was eleven o'clock on a week night. Still, there were noises through the wall. A radio, sounds of furniture being bumped. She went into the hall and listened, rapped at the next door down.

The woman who answered was drunk and understanding, after the third repeat of the plot. Hastily unpacked her bureau, down to the Whitby *Mail*. The lampstand was lined with blotters, the desk drawer newly shellacked. But there on the shelves of the wardrobe underneath her pairs of shoes they discovered the continuation, intact. They read it aloud. After several close calls, the wife remains faithful and welcomes her husband on leave. She tells him they are pregnant, at which the drunk lady wept. In the cabinet under the window lurked the penultimate scene: he must face a deadly airlift, it is certain he won't return. They checked the umbrella stand, the mattress, the wall patches under the sink. They raced to the hall, no drawers, none in the W.C. The man in the next room was sleeping; the room next to his was locked. They returned to the lady's quarters and sweeping stacks of clothes off the bedspread, sat down and had a long drink. There were two ways it could end, only two. They reread the shelves from the beginning but couldn't tell which it would be.

Look for thin wartime paper. Ask for room 305. Whitby. The Sea Shingle, on Warder Street.

Finally this.

We counted on lasting the century and promised to meet. At the Water Tower, north side, at midnight. Or was it the clock at Marshall Field's? No, that was V-J Day. It was the Water Tower. Or else a lion in front of the Art Institute. The north lion? No, we would have said *left,* the left one. You distinctly said north. And I remember talking of cows, or kicking the bucket. I'm not sure now.

You were wearing — what were you wearing? Sometimes I see a necktie — or is it a scarf? — with yellow roosters. It startles me. Is that because it's unlike you? Sometimes the roosters are tiny boats. Either way, it's a clue. A person who keeps appointments. Resolute. I see us raising glasses of warm champagne, but that was back in the fifties and must have been papercup wine. "To Two Thousand," was that the toast? It doesn't ring any bells. Paper bells. Hats and streamers. Was it that kind of New Year's Eve?

Only once I heard bells on New Year's. I was living in Zurich with people who went to bed. Babies. My husband. They went to bed early, no matter what. It mattered to me, to wait until twelve, knowing all the while it was false, a local celebration in the wrong time zone for me. I wound open the window on Klosbachstrasse, leaned out and heard the bells. It was snowing, and bells. I watched it snow. Before my New Year's came, I fell asleep.

Will it be snowing on Michigan Avenue? Snow on the clocks, the old Water Tower in the year two thousand A.D.? Whoever you are, will you wait?

An Instance of Spring in Oregon

Stephen Weiser

Look! it is today.

The Oregon spring sun has bloomed: morning, almost ten o'clock and warm. Never mind the brown stain hanging over the trees, it belongs to the city — Eugene, Oregon, 97400. Beyond, look at the real sky arching over the vast verdant scope of the Willamette valley, over the pineblue mountains, the waterfalls, the pools. It calls you to the ocean. Hey! I said it's spring: things to bloom as I wave my hand. Trees to pop their buds as I blink. The world is to explode. And everyone to be told — I riding through the downtown streets in a station wagon with loudspeakers bolted to it, waving, shouting, entreating: Lay down your pencils, close up your tills, come out with your brown paper bags and eat a ten o'clock lunch on the roofs of cars, march naked to the Willamette and float like pale porpoises to the sea, calling to your kind until the towns are swept away before the flood.

He turned from the porch to his bathroom. it was today even in the peeling gloom. "You're old," he told his reflection, baring his teeth. They looked yellow, surrounded by the virginal white of shaving lather. "You're twenty-eight, man, and you have a wife and child. That's pretty goddamned old!"

In the mirror his wife's face appeared at his shoulder, still dumb with sleep. "Did you say something?"

"I am an old fucker," he nodded.

"Yeah," she smiled.

"Still a graduate student."

"A teaching fellow."

"You are forced to labor because my contributions are small stipends."

"Not today," she said. "Today is Wednesday, and I have Wednesdays off."

"So it is." He bent to her breast and left a touch of meringue. "And as soon as I finish shaving," he said as she rubbed the meringue into his back, "we are going to get into the car and drive to the mountains."

"Why not the ocean?"

"Everyone goes to the beach when the sun shines. The mountains are Diana — virgin and undisturbed."

"But you have classes?"

"But you have the day off."

148

"I have the washing to do."

"But you're not going to do it."

"It needs to be done."

"Then we'll take it along. You can spend the afternoon beating clothes on a rock at the bank of the stream."

"No," she said. "You'll have to choose: me or the wash."

"For some men," he said, "that might be a thorny dilemma."

He called the department secretary and explained that he was wracked with a violent ague, congenital blindness, and paralysis of the heart, which would make it impossible for him to meet his classes today.

"It's really beautiful out," she agreed.

It was still chilly in the mountains, but the dogwood knew it was today. Snow clung to the shadows of cuts and cliffs. About an hour east of the University of Oregon, Eugene, Oregon, 97403, they stopped at Sahalie Falls and took possession of the empty parking lot. They went first to the promontory below the falls and lost themselves in the sprayladen roar of eighty feet of writhing wool drawn into an astoundingly blue pool and recollecting itself around mossy rocks and boulders. Hours later the child moved restlessly in its mother's arms. Their faces were cold.

Hand in hand they walked back toward the parking lot, then shuffled down a frosty incline which began the trail looping up to the head of the falls. It was a short, easy climb. He slipped off his rucksack with its soft bundles of food and the wine, and pitched pine cones into the water, leaning out over the bank to watch them disappear in the tangled wool. It was not natural wool, but bleached, brilliant white tinged with blue. Perhaps it was even cotton. Their laughter came in clouds.

About fifty yards upstream was a smaller fall, about five or six feet. The water curled over the top of itself like the translucent fracture edge of obsidian. He helped her up the rise stairstepped with tree roots. Behind the fall was a pool, dark and glassy in the forest light, and beside it he spread groundcloth and blankets. They had been here before, and the rush of water was like the distant songs your mother used to sing sitting at the piano. He unscrewed the cap from the wine and she sliced the bread and sharp Tillamook cheddar. The flavor of earth and turpentine rose around them, the calm transpiration of the forest and the flavor of the wind drifted through the uncountable needles of uncountable pine. The cold crept into their inactivity, and they wrapped themselves in a blanket, sharing the bottle. The child drowsed, sharing their laps.

It is today, and the world is to explode.

They rise, shuck their clothes, and run laughing to the pool. Their teeth chatter and the child cries, but the pantonal swell of Sahalie Falls soothes coldness and fear. They glide through the clear heady water of the pool. The current draws them over the obsidian wall, and they splash in the eddies like hard trout. At the head of the falls they hesitate, then plunge into the soft rush of wool, down into the astoundingly blue pool, down the rapids, down the McKenzie into the Willamette below Eugene, down past Corvallis, Albany, through Salem, Oregon City, laughing into the Columbia under Portland's busy bridges, following powerful currents into the deep and silent ocean.

Allison's Hair
Monica Wood

Being pregnant ruined Allison's hair. It used to be very blonde, naturally wavy, and full of highlights. Now it is limp and the color of shredded wheat. She stares at it in the mirror, trying to perk it up with some combs her mother bought at the hairdresser. Nothing works. She looks at her face, the unlovely hair, the blotchiness of her complexion. She looks down at her body, naked and white, flabby in the middle, and says aloud: "I am twenty."

Jonathan is a slow child. He was slow to roll over, slow to crawl, and even now is unsteady on his feet. He totters into her mirror view, carrying the yellow truck and Kermit the Frog that he is rarely without. His nose is runny, his mouth and cheeks smudged with jam. She turns her back to the mirror to really see him.

"Mummy hot," he says. Jonathan is four, and these are his only words, learned when he was two, when eighteen-year-old Allison refused to hold him all summer. "Mummy hot," she told him, "go play in your pool!" He had obediently retreated to the blow-up wading pool, saying "Mummy hot" to the yellow truck and Kermit. Allison had not told anyone about his first words.

Jonathan looks like a homely little girl. His face is flat and pale, his mouth thin and red. He is towheaded; Allison has never cut his hair. It falls in fine curls over the sides of his face, over the soft indentations left by forceps. He is dressed in a striped shirt with matching shorts, and slippers with cats on them. When Jonathan stares at her nakedness, Allison gets up to put on a robe. "Hi, Jonathan," she says, touches his head, and leaves the room. Jonathan toddles over to her bureau and uncorks her perfume bottle. He pours it over his shirt and leaves the stopper on the floor.

In the kitchen Allison pours her own coffee. "I'm not helpless," she says to her mother.

"There's my baby," Allison's mother says, seeing Jonathan at the door. His eyes are small and close-set, red-rimmed. He has many allergies. "Whew! What have you been into?"

Allison knows that Jonahthan has taken her perfume and dumped it on himself. She knows her mother knows. They have both stood at the door in silence, watching him, many times. Allison's mother thinks this ritual means something.

Allison gets up from the table and takes Jonathan by the shoulders. There is no expression in her eyes. "Stay out of my perfume, Jonathan," she says, quietly. "Do you hear me this time?"

Allison's mother says nothing. She loads the dishwasher and moves toward the basement door. "Do you have enough clean uniforms, honey?" she asks. "I'll need one for tomorrow," Allison says. Allison's mother and Jonathan descend the steps together.

Allison works at Henry's diner, three T-stops from home. She enjoys the clatter, the smell of grease, the old fixtures, the talk. It was Henry who convinced her to finish high school at night. She is a good waitress: quick, friendly to customers, neat and clean. At Henry's Allison acts the way she did before she got pregnant.

Henry's is not popular with young people, but yesterday two of Allison's friends from high school came in for coffee. They were on a break from classes at Northeastern.

"Your mother saw my mother at Jordan Marsh and said you'd been here two years. I couldn't believe it was that long since I'd seen you," Holly said.

"I heard you got your diploma," Jean said.

"Night school," Allison answered, rubbing the counter with a wet cloth. She could have attended school right through the pregnancy — lots of girls did. She hadn't wanted anyone to see her fat belly. She spent the entire eight months and one week in her mother's house.

"How's Jonathan?"

"Fine."

They ordered two muffins and left a five dollar tip. Allison was angry.

"They think I'm some kind of welfare mother," she said to Henry in the kitchen.

"They don't know nothing," Henry told her.

Allison stays at Henry's because it makes her feel as if her life is on hold, waiting for something to happen. Restaurant work is temporary. It is what artists and actors do in New York, between shows. It is something college kids do when they are full of plans. She is working at Henry's "for now," she has told her mother repeatedly during the past year.

Allison regrets that Henry gave her the day off for her birthday. She thinks she has outgrown birthdays. She is an adult who pays room and board to her mother, who is at this moment suggesting ways to get Allison out of the house so she can bake a cake in secret. "Take him for a walk, Allison. You see him so seldom."

It is hot in the park, and Allison feels sticky and irritable. Seeing Holly and Jean yesterday made her ugly, and she has been thinking of them ever since. Jonathan sits on the bench next to her, watching her with his rheumy eyes. Goldenrod. Or smog. Or milk. "Here," she says, unpleasantly, taking his ball from his hands and throwing it a short distance. He goes after it silently, a little skip to his step, and falls over when he nears it. She sighs heavily, trudges over to him. "You're all right," she says, and returns to the bench, Jonathan trailing behind.

Jonathan does not cry. Allison thinks he was born without emotions. She thinks they both went into a coma at the moment of his birth and have never recovered. She thinks her mother is waiting for a cure.

If Allison had not gotten pregnant, she would be at the university now, rooming with Holly or Jean, studying philosophy, going to concerts, bringing her laundry home every other weekend. She hates Jonathan for ruining her life.

Sometimes she thinks if Jonathan had been a girl, she would have been all right. At the end of the pregnancy she had begun to imagine a baby girl, putting her in hair ribbons and pink dresses. She began to think of being a mother as fun. Then Jonathan came, the homely boy.

Jonathan's father lives in Colorado now. Sometimes he sends money. He is younger than Allison, and when he offered to marry her it was with such a pained expression she told him to leave her life, which he did. She is not sorry about that part of it. She expects nothing from him, having never loved him. The pain and complications of Jonathan's birth she remembers as punishment for all her bad choices.

Jonathan climbs into Allison's lap, digging his small shoes into her calves for leverage. "Stop that," she says, and lifts him to her. He will not get down. She carries him home, his face deep in her hair.

Allison's mother is decorating the cake, a spice cake with peanut butter frosting. The decorations are the same every year: pink candle holders with pink and white striped candles. The cake decorating chatter is also the same, except now she addresses Jonathan instead of Allison's father, long dead, or Allison herself. "On the day your Mummy was born," she tells him, "the mercury hit one hundred. The hospital had no air conditioning and I thought I'd pass out." Allison smiles out of pure habit. Jonathan sees her and shows his narrow teeth.

"Do you want to come with Grammy?" Allison's mother asks Jonathan. "Grammy has to get Mummy a present."

"Don't," Allison says.

Allison's mother looks angry for the first time in years.

"Life goes on," she says, and takes Jonathan's hand.

Allison is on the couch drinking a Tab when they return. "Grammy and Jonathan have a surprise for Mummy," Allison's mother says from the door, and something in the voice makes Allison turn around. Her mother stands behind Jonathan, whose curls are gone. He looks like a little boy with a man's hairstyle. Allison has seen pictures of first haircuts, and this is what they look like. His hair is parted severely on the side, closely cropped around the ears. The haircut magnifies the shape of his head; he looks like a slow child.

Allison stands up and opens her mouth. Jonathan's own mouth turns from a tentative smile into a wavy line, and his tiny eyes become moist and shiny. Allison stares at him, begins to walk toward him. Her body feels pliant and stringy, she feels blood swirling in her head. As she drops to her knees in front of him, something breaks in her body. "My hair! My hair!" she cries, her hands in fists at her sides. "My hair," Jonathan says, pressing himself to her breast.

152

Vinyl Repair

Allen Woodman

Noble was absently sprinkling salt over half a ripe tomato when he saw something black lying in the sand next to the shoreline. He had been re-coloring the vinyl seats in the High Tide Motel lobby from blue to red, and was now taking a few minutes for lunch. It was off-season and no one was in a hurry.

The black spot turned out to be an abandoned bikini top. Noble examined it. It had a label that read, "Cole of California. Size 36B." It pleased Noble to look at it. He hadn't expected such an item.

Noble thought about the act of a woman in white-hot summer pulling her top off and smoothing her skin with smears of cream or lotion. It was easy for him to love the things of people he didn't know.

Once he had a job repairing the mayor's chairs. Some kids had broken into his office and burned holes on the arms of his desk chair with cigarettes. The chair was only brown naugahyde, but it had once belonged to the mayor's father. Noble fixed the arms and reconditioned the whole chair so well that when the mayor sat down in it and rubbed his hands across the places where the damage had been he started to cry. Noble followed suit in a friendly, unreasoned way. It was like he had loved that old chair, too. Neither of the men was known for easy tears.

Noble held each cup of the top in his palms and imagined the breasts that once filled them. Then he replaced it on the sand where he had found it.

Noble walked back to the lobby and started recoloring the seats. Colleen came out from behind the front desk to watch. He was going to tell her about the bikini top, but he didn't. He thought it'd be like telling a secret someone had made him promise not to tell.

"That red color's good. It's what the lobby needed," Colleen said.

Noble placed his brush into the Perma-Bond Color Coat can. "This'll color anything," he said, and pointed to his white shoes. "Guess how old my shoes are?"

"They look brand new," she said.

"Three years old. I coated them myself a week ago."

Colleen brought out a pair of white shoes from her kitchenette in the back, "Can you make these new again?" she asked.

"Wherever I see vinyl, I can do business," he said, and traced his fingers along the shoes' outline.

"They were my wedding shoes," Colleen said. "My Warren loved me so much that he tried to kill me with them. He threw me around this very lobby one night. I kept banging into those chair legs. Then he pulled the shoes off my feet and started hitting me on the head with them. He kept shouting parts of the wedding vows, 'To have and to hold. Till death do you part.'"

"What happened?"

"Since then, I've never been to another wedding. I can't even stand to watch one on TV."

"No, I mean about your husband?"

"He shot himself in room seventeen. A guest heard the shot and told me. When I opened the door, I didn't even recognize him. I thought he was some tourist."

Noble waited to speak. He could feel she had more words to get out.

"If the Tastee-Freez hadn't been closed he would still be alive. Everytime we had a fight he'd go next door and have a chocolate malted. Sometime he'd bring back a cup of soft-serve. But this time the Tastee-Freez closed early. There was a closed sign on the door. The boy inside cleaning up remembered my husband coming by and banging on the glass."

Noble didn't know what to say. They were just standing there looking at each other, and looking at the shoes.

"I'll restore these free for you. But tell your friends I charged you three dollars," Noble said.

She offered him a cup of coffee. She had just made a fresh pot.

Noble sat down on the sofa in Colleen's room. The sofa was perfect. No holes or cracks in the vinyl. Colleen gave him some coffee and sat down beside him.

"Doesn't sound much like love," Noble said.

"It was love."

"The way he beat you with your wedding shoes?"

"It was true," Colleen insisted.

Noble lifted his coffee mug in salute. The mug had an illustration of a card from a Monopoly game. It was Boardwalk. Monopoly was Noble's favorite board game as a child. He wondered if his childhood edition was still around, stored in an attic someplace. It was nice to think about that game for a few seconds. He remembered giving it up about the same time he stopped reading Sunday comics. "Then love is knowing what to overlook," he finally said.

Then he did something. He didn't know what else to do. He picked up her hand. He felt the hard bones under her skin. What good bones, he thought.

Afterwards they sat on the sofa. Their knees bumped. "Now say something so I don't feel like a whore," Colleen said.

Noble took her hand again and raised it to his lips. He was thinking about the tan lines that made cuts where her torso had been separated from the sun. She looked like some sort of board for a game that had not been created yet. The sections of unsunned flesh seemed luminous.

"We're lucky," he said.

Biographies

Henry Berry is the editor/publisher of *The Small Press Book Review,* in Southport, Connecticut.

T. Coraghessan Boyle is the author of five books of fiction: *Descent of Man, Water Music, Budding Prospects, Greasy Lake,* and *World's End,* which is forthcoming from Viking in the fall of 1987.

Raymond Carver lives and writes in Port Angeles, Washington. His most recent work includes two books of poems, *Ultramarine* and *Where Water Comes Together with Other Water* (Random House), the story collection *Cathedral* (Knopf), and *Fires: Stories, Poems, Essays* (Vintage).

Mark E. Clemens lives on the West Coast and holds an MFA from Montana.

Valerie Cohen "spends winters in Cedar City, Utah, and summers in Jackson, Wyoming."

Nicole Cooley is a junior at Brown University, majoring in Comparative Literature/Literary Translation. She has studied with John Hawkes, Robert Coover and Philip Levine, and was a finalist in the *Mademoiselle* fiction contest.

Janet Desaulniers teaches fiction writing at Northwestern University. Her fiction has appeared in the *New Yorker, Ploughshares, TriQuarterly* and elsewhere.

Stephen Dixon teaches in the Writing Seminars of the Johns Hopkins University. He has published some 250 stories, five story collections, and three novels. His most recent novel is *Fall and Rise* (North Point), and his most recent story collection is *Time to Go* (Hopkins).

David James Duncan lives in Oregon. He notes that he has sometimes been known as "the Lawn Ranger."

Stuart Dybek teaches at Western Michigan University. He was winner of the Nelson Algren Prize in 1985. His new story collection is *Childhood and Other Neighborhoods* (Ecco).

Thomas Farber has published several story collections, including *Who Wrote the Book of Love?*, and the novel *Curves of Pursuit.* He has held both Guggenheim and NEA fellowships. He is a native of Boston.

Patrick Foy continues to write short stories. He was born in Pasadena, California, grew up in Miami Beach, and graduated in 1970 from Columbia University. He spends two months of every year "traveling in Europe, meeting interesting people and going to museums."

Pat Therese Francis has published fiction in *Prairie Schooner* and *The Massachusetts Review.*

Thaisa Frank lives in California. Her fiction collection, *Desire,* is published by The Kelsey Street Press and was listed as one of the Best Small Press Books of 1983. Recent work of hers has appeared in *Mississippi Review.*

C. P. Fullington lives and writes in Albuquerque.

John Gerlach is a professor of English at Cleveland State University. His publications include *Toward the End: Closure and Structure in the American Short Story,* published by University of Alabama Press.

Ruth Goldsmith is from Florida and has contributed to such diverse magazines as *The Atlantic* and *Fantasy and Science Fiction.*

Peter Gordon is a native of Framingham, Massachusetts. He studied at Yale with John Hersey, and has had work in *The New Yorker* and the *Antioch Review.* He has held a fiction scholarship from Breadloaf.

Mark Halliday grew up in Raleigh, North Carolina, and Westport, Connecticut. He is a founding member of the Rhode Island Feminist Theater, and holds a Brown University B.A. and a Brandeis Ph.D. His poetry collection, *Little Star,* is forthcoming from Morrow.

Carolyn Hardesty is the editor of *Iowa Woman* magazine, and is in the American Studies Ph.D. program at the University of Iowa. Other work of hers has appeared in the *Montana Review* and she is completing a story collection tentatively entitled *Loving Married Men.*

Shulamith Hareven lives in Israel, where she has been an activist since she was a teen-aged medic in the haganah underground during the siege of Jerusalem. Presently she is a member of Peace Now and is an essayist on cultural and political issues. She is the only female member of the Academy of the Hebrew Language; her nine published books includes poems, essays, stories and a novel, *City of Many Days,* published in the U.S. by Doubleday.

Edward Hirsch has held the Amy Lowell Traveling Fellowship and a series of first prize awards from the American Academy of Poets. His books of poetry are *For the Sleepwalkers* and *Wild Gratitude*, both from Knopf.

A. C. Hoffmann teaches film and fiction at Rhode Island College in Providence, and lives in Newport. His work has appeared in *Quarterly Review of Literature, Epoch, Ascent,* and *Webster Review.*

Eric Johnson is a writer, musician, and photographer. He lives with his wife, Geri, near Santa Cruz, California.

Alice Jurow is a San Franciscan whose ambition is "to retire to Kashmire and Ladakh."

Ken Kalfus is a writer and freelance critic living in Philadelphia. His stories have appeared in the *Sonora Review* and *Pulpsmith,* his book reviews in the New York *Times* and the *Nation,* and he is a frequent contributor to the Cleveland *Plain Dealer.*

Pat Kaluza is a typist and bookbinder from the Twin Cities.

Eduardo Gudiño Kieffer is the author of three novels and three story collections, all published in Buenos Aires. *Carta abierta a Buenos Aires violento (Open Letter to Violent Buenos Aires),* from which his story here is taken, was placed under censure in 1977 by the city's Secretary of Culture. *John G. Copeland,* Keiffer's translator, teaches at the University of Colorado.

W. P. Kinsella lives in the state of Washington. His best-known novel is *Shoeless Joe* (Houghton Mifflin), and his most recent story collection is *The Alligator Report* (Coffee House Press).

Sandra Kolankiewicz holds the master's from Johns Hopkins and the doctorate from Ohio University. Her work has appeared in *Mississippi Review, Chicago Review* and *Revista InterAmerica.* In 1986-87 she is teaching in Asia; she makes her permanent home on Isla Mujeres, Mexico.

Barry Lopez is the author of *Winter Count* (Scribner's) and other story collections.

Lissa McLaughlin was born and raised in upstate New York, attended Oberlin College, and was in the graduate writing program at Brown University. She has published film reviews, children's books, and, with Burning Deck Press, two short fiction collections.

Patricia O'Donnell teaches at Southern Connecticut State University. An Iowa native, she holds the M.A. from Northern Iowa and the M.F.A. from the University of Massachusetts. She has published other fiction in *The New Yorker.*

Pamela Painter lives in Boston and teaches creative writing at the Harvard Extension School. Her first collection of stories, *Getting to Know the Weather,* won the GLCA New Writers Award in 1986. She was a founding editor of *Story Quarterly* and a recipient of a 1985 Massachusetts Artists Foundation Fellowship.

Jayne Anne Phillips is the author of a story collection, *Black Tickets,* and the novel *Machine Dreams,* both published by Delacorte.

John Phillips is an editor of the International *Herald Tribune* in Paris. He is a New Englander, has been a journalist for 25 years, and notes that he is also a "chronic re-reader of stuff I know to be good; cat-lover, dog-abider; parachutist."

Michael Plemmons is a former newspaper reporter, now the creative director of a small advertising agency in Chicago. His stories have appeared in *Pulpsmith, Touchstone, Image,* and other small press periodicals.

Doris Read lives in Santa Barbara. Her stories have also appeared in *Kansas Quarterly, Mid-American Review, Wind,* and *Crosscurrents,* and she has won writing prizes from the National Writers' Club and *Writer's Digest.*

Henry R. Roth is a lecturer in English at City College of CUNY. He has published more than a hundred stories in such magazines as *Ploughshares, New American Review, Story Quarterly,* and *South Carolina Review,* and two collections, *In Empty Rooms* and *Jackdaw.*

Naomi Rothberg is a New Jersey resident and a law school graduate.

Walter Sanders chairs the English Department at Mansfield University and is a member of the literature panel of the Pennsylvania Council on the Arts. Other stories of his have appeared in *Fiction International* and *West Branch.*

Kathleen Spivack lives in Massachusetts and writes both poetry and fiction. Her short story collection, *The Honeymoon,* was published in 1986 by Graywolf Press.

Deborah Stewart is a native of Kentucky and a graduate of the University of Louisville. She lives in Louisville with her husband and two children. Other stories of hers have appeared in *The Louisville Review* and *The River City Review.*

David Surface is a Kentucky native who played in rock and roll bands in the South for ten years before moving to New York City to write. He has twice held fellowships at the MacDowell Colony. He is Coordinator of the Readings/Workshops Program for Poets & Writers.

S. G. Tyler teaches English and writing at West Springfield (Massachusetts) High School "when not on the road seeking adventure, intrigue, answers, and sometimes questions."

Marian Ury is on the Comparative Literature faculty of the University of California, Davis, specializing in Japanese literature and culture. She has authored a biography of translator and dance critic Beryl de Zoete, and is working on an essay on 1930s musical life in Chicago and Berkeley centered on piano pedagogue Alexander Raab and his circle.

Diane Vreuls has published a book of poems, a novel, and a children's book, as well as short stories. "Let Us Know" is the title story from a collection published by Viking (1986). She teaches in the Creative Writing Program at Oberlin College.

Stephen Weiser has lived in the Netherlands as well as in the American northwest.

Monica Wood lives in Portland, Maine, with her husband, Daniel Abbott. She studied at Georgetown University and the University of Southern Maine. When she is not writing, she is a high school guidance counselor and a singer/songwriter who performs in the Portland area.

Allen Woodman teaches in the Creative Writing Program at Northern Arizona University. His short story collection, *The Shoebox of Desire and Other Tales,* was published in the U.S. by Swallow's Tale Press.